ALICE

ALSO BY SHANI STRUTHERS

ALICE

A CHRISTMAS GHOST STORY

SHANI STRUTHERS

Old age should burn and rave at close of day.'
Dylan Thomas

Acknowledgements and Foreword

Christmas comes but once a year. Thankfully, though, help with my books comes more often, in the shape of beta readers, editors, formatters and designers. A huge thank you to Lesley Hughes, Sarah Savery, and Kate Jane Jones for stepping in as beta readers during this busiest time of the year, and also to Rumer Haven for editing, and Gina Dickerson for design and formatting. As some of you may know, I try to produce three books a year, the last one being a Christmas Ghost Story. To that end, *Alice* joins the ranks of *Blakemort*, *Eve*, *Carfax House*, *The Damned Season* and *Wildacre*. Why this fascination with ghosts *and* Christmas, though? Is Dickens to blame, and my enduring love of *A Christmas Carol,* or do I simply agree with English writer and humourist Jerome K Jerome who once stated, "*It is always Christmas Eve, in a ghost story.*" Who knows, but it's a tradition I love, right back from childhood, when always our family looked for something spooky to entertain us on the eve of Christmas, enjoying the delicious thrills it would impart, somehow preparing us for the festive season, acknowledging the darker side as well as the frivolities. And perhaps therein lies the reason, that this *is* the darkest time of year, when one chapter closes and another begins, the past and the future colliding with the present, and suddenly anything seems possible…even ghosts. Always, I pour a lot of my own experiences into my work, and *Alice* is no different. There are many family anecdotes included within (including the 'slithering snake' story!), a family, who, like Alice's, once lived in India, but had to leave due to the fall of the Raj, and come to the country of their heritage, but which they'd never visited before. England. What happens when Alice reaches these shores is then tied up with a popular urban legend, one that still endures today. It's creepy in places, it's dark, but also, as with all my ghost stories, it's very human. Wishing the world peace and love for 2024.

Prologue

December 2023

It was wild outside. The wind blowing and the rain slashing down. *Freezing* rain, threatening to become snow. She had to get home, though, find a way. Today, of all days.

Bloody weather! And bloody National Rail for cancelling train after train, cutting any hope of people reaching loved ones, *ruining* Christmas.

It was the morning of Christmas Eve, a peak time to travel. The station was full of people, some complaining bitterly, some angrily, others crying or silent, simply standing there mortified. Of those who were vocal, 'It's Christmas!' was their rallying cry. 'You can't leave us stranded at Christmas.' As frustrated as she was too, Lottie felt sorry for staff members having to deal with them, especially those who'd begun to hurl insults, as if anyone in uniform was personally responsible for such a catastrophe. She raised her eyes to whoever resided in the heavens above, gazing down – God, whom she always had trouble believing in. If she was wrong, though, if he existed well enough, he was the one responsible, technically. *You won't stop me. I'll get back to London, to her, Alice.*

No matter how hard some people protested, the trains were *not* running south, east, west, or further north, the weather too hazardous and they in the epicentre. At this rate, she'd be stuck in Sunderland, not just unable to see Alice but any of her family, her mother and brother. Alice, though, was priority. What Lottie'd found out…would it bring her solace? She had a feeling it might, that at the very least Alice would die knowing someone believed her, that she wasn't mad, as she'd been told all her life, deluded.

"Fucking ridiculous, isn't it?" someone said beside her. When Lottie ignored whoever it was, too preoccupied with her own predicament, the person repeated himself, louder, more pointedly, clearly wanting a response. Sighing, she gazed his way.

He was older than her, around thirty, whereas she was nineteen, and he was dressed in jogging bottoms and a black bomber jacket, his black hair cropped. Not just swearing, he was snarling right at her, desperate to vent, to be validated. Rather than take offence, she offered a sympathetic smile. Validation right now was what she was all about.

"Yeah, it is," she said, "but if it's dangerous to travel—"

"It's not fucking dangerous!" he retorted, refusing to let her speak further. "A bloody leaf on the line and this lot down tools. I've got to get home for Christmas. I've got a kid."

"Where is it you're going?" she asked, still trying to look interested.

"Fucking Carlisle," he spat.

"Oh. Further north, then."

"And you?" he said, a few seconds after she'd pointed out the obvious.

"London."

The thing was, there was no snow forecast for London, so if she could just get a bit further down the country, to the

Midlands at least, the trains should run okay.

She checked her watch: 10.00 a.m. The journey from here to there would take around three and a half hours. If she'd caught the 9.02 like she was supposed to, she'd have been back at the care home by lunchtime – around the time carols would be blasting from the radio in the dayroom, no magician this time like last year, no funds in the kitty, apparently, but what staff there were, more and more bank staff, encouraging the residents to sing along. Some would comply, sitting there in those high-backed chairs that squeaked when you moved, with paper hats on their heads, clapping even. Others would remain steadfastly asleep, ignoring any festive cajoling. *Bobby* would have ignored it; she'd have been seething, hating how the elderly were treated, blatantly patronised. As for Alice, what would she be doing? Mute for most of the year, on Christmas Eve it was a different story. At least that had been the case last Christmas Eve, when Lottie had only recently started at Silver Birches. She couldn't believe how someone so quiet, who sat propped in a chair all day by the window, staring at nothing, could change so much and so violently. That was the point, though, when she'd become more interested in Alice, more *aware*.

The man standing beside Lottie in the bomber jacket and joggers fired off a few more expletives, then he was off, thankfully, stalking through crowds of the discontent, maybe trying to find alternative means of reaching Carlisle from Sunderland. *Good luck*, she thought, staring after him for a few seconds, at others who'd begun stalking off too.

She approached a member of staff, a short dark-haired woman who looked as bereft as those denied travel. Her eyes were glassy, clearly holding back tears.

On spotting Lottie, she held her hands up. "Before you start, I'm sorry, okay, but seriously, I mean it. I can't take any more bullets."

Lottie frowned. "Sorry? What do you mean, bullets?"

"From you lot!" the woman nearly wailed. "That's what I mean! Who keep insisting on shooting the messenger. The trains are cancelled, okay? For now. They may start running again later, once we get a handle on the storm, but for now they're cancelled. And I can't change it, as much as I'd like to, can't wave a wand and make it all right again. I don't make the rules; I just work here. There's a storm coming, a *snowstorm*."

Lottie had to say it. "There's no snow forecast for London. That's where I'm heading."

The woman shook her head, dark tendrils of hair falling out of the bun in which she'd sought to restrain them. "Good for bloody London," she muttered.

"Coaches," Lottie said, pushing her own hair – blue, freshly dyed. "Do you think—"

"This is the train station, not the coach station! I'm not the Oracle!"

"Where is it?" Lottie asked. "The coach station."

"Out of here and turn right. It's about ten minutes away, okay?" the woman said as another customer approached her, bracing herself yet again.

Lottie headed towards the exit. The coach station was worth a shot.

Twenty minutes later, her own eyes teary, she found her efforts had been in vain.

"Fuck's sake," she breathed. "What now?"

A return to Peg's B and B, perhaps, although Peg had warned her *many* beat a path to her establishment on

Christmas Eve, those who were alone for Christmas yet couldn't bear to be. If there was no room at the inn, she'd have to find another hotel somewhere, anywhere, or sleep on the floor of the station, and likely wouldn't be the only one.

Snow forecast. Many in the north who'd already battened down the hatches and were safely ensconced in warm, cosy homes would be excited at the prospect, not particularly caring whether or not a storm accompanied it. There was just something so magical about snow, particularly on today of all days, Christmas Eve. Lottie was in no mood, however, to feel even remotely happy for them; all she could do was bemoan her own situation. Christ, it was horrid out there, nothing charmed about it at all. Sleet rather than the promised snow stung her face, and the wind whipped round her like something hysterical. To think she used to love a storm, the drama of it.

When she'd first arrived in Sunderland two days ago, on a mission, she'd thought it a nice enough place; certainly, the people were friendly. The weather had been okay then, or okay-*ish*, grey-skied and rainy, but not overly cold. She'd taken it at face value, simply hadn't thought to check the long-range forecast. Her bad. If she had, she could have returned home the previous night and avoided this chaos. Then again, it was swings and roundabouts, because if she *had* erred on the side of caution, she'd have gone home ignorant, for it was only last night that more pieces of the jigsaw had fallen into place.

I'm sorry for what happened to you, Alice. For all you endured.

For so many years Alice had been in institutions, and not just care homes but *asylums*, for decades and decades. She was ninety-two, so old, so frail, a world inside her that had been forcibly shut down. For telling the truth. For insisting on it.

No one had believed her. And very possibly no one had cared either if she was lying. She was simply a problem to be dealt with. An *issue*. Sedated if too much trouble. Worse than that. Needles coming at her, countless times. A burden on society, and yet she'd hung on and on. Evidence that a spark of defiance continued to burn in her? That someone, somewhere, might eventually take notice and listen.

That's what Lottie had done: listened, in that way her mother always warned her about.

'Why d'you want to encourage that kind of thing?' she'd once said. 'Where's it going to get you? Nowhere. It's qualifications you should focus on, work experience, *practical* things. Oh, Lottie,' she'd sighed, 'it's not even real, this…this…ability of yours. You simply *imagine* things, that's all, build everything into something it's not. It could also be—' and here she'd swallowed, seemed to contradict everything she'd just said '—dangerous being like that, intuitive. It's got a reputation. They used to burn women in the old days for it, you know, or hang them or drown them or whatever. They'd be shunned by society, outcasts. Like I said, focus on what matters, the real stuff. Everything else…leave well alone.'

Intuition. Is that what it really was? Or was there another term for it, a *psychic* ability? Because that's how she'd learnt about Alice, psychically, not via words from her mouth. She also had to face something else: that, after not-so-great GCSE results and just a Customer Service Diploma because she'd been in no mood for A levels either, maybe it was her *only* talent, and if so, then perhaps she should hone it.

Despite what her mother had said, it wasn't something useless, not really, or dangerous, not in modern times. No one was punished for that kind of thing nowadays, the world far more enlightened. If she could help people by making use of it, if they could gain some closure or comfort, then it *was* a talent. Bobby had thought so at the care home, that feisty eighty-six-year-old who'd called herself an inmate rather than a resident, 'a fucking prisoner', in fact. She'd thought what Lottie could do was brilliant, encouraged it, as intrigued by Alice's story as Lottie was when Lottie had confided in her what she'd found out.

That spark of defiance in Alice that she suspected – Lottie had to dig deep right now and find it in herself. Soon this sleet would become snow, and it would trap her, just as Alice had been trapped for most of her life, since she was Lottie's age. How the hell could they have done that to her? The powers that be. The authorities. Whoever was in charge. The ones supposed to protect you, *help* you. The bastards!

Still at the coach station, she stared out the window into such bleakness. Felt it creep into her bones and threaten to lodge there. She'd get home. One way or another. But she needed wheels. A taxi. A taxi that would cost a bloody fortune, money she didn't have, but what the hell? Time was running out for Alice. She could deteriorate, and suddenly. In the year Lottie had known her, she'd gone a little downhill, but today was the day she might become lucid again, might start thrashing and yelling, 'Wish! Wish! Wish! Wish!' like she had last year. Back then, Lottie, like the rest of the care home staff, hadn't had a clue what she'd meant. It was simply the rantings of a lunatic, or so Patsy, the care home manager, had implied, and it'd been easy enough to believe her. Now, though, it was different. Lottie knew what Alice had been referring to. If she was lucid, then Lottie could get through to her, make her listen, really listen. Christmas Eve was the anniversary of when life had changed for Alice, so she'd be more receptive as well as more animated. Surely?

That was the theory, anyway. *So hold on for me, Alice! Wait. Please.*

Lottie rushed back to the counter which she'd only just come from, where she'd enquired about coaches for London and almost been laughed out the building.

The same woman she'd spoken to looked up again, steeling herself like the rail worker.

"Taxis," Lottie said, much to the woman's surprise. "I'll take a taxi instead. Can you give me some local numbers, please?"

"A taxi? All the way to London? Are you serious? That'll cost a—"

"Bomb, yes, I know it will. But I don't care. I have to get back. The snow's imminent, but it's not here yet. Roads are still passable, the bloody rail tracks are, but hey-ho, and there's no snow further south. *Someone*'ll take me."

The woman simply shrugged. "Maybe. Maybe not," she said before relenting. "Okay, all right, ten out of ten for persistence, I suppose. Here you go." She scribbled some numbers down on a sheet of paper, then handed it over, adding, "Good luck with it. Really."

"Thanks," said Lottie, trying not to grab at the paper and failing.

"But I really don't think—"

"Happy Christmas." Lottie forced the words out, forced some meaning behind it too.

The woman again looked surprised, as if she'd forgotten it was the festive season. "Ah, yeah, right. Have a good one, won't you? Whether or not you get home."

Once more by the window, Lottie dug her phone from her pocket and started dialling from the sheet, a prayer in the back of her mind all the while. *Please, please, please.* It was still sleety outside rather than snowy, and the clouds above were so dark you'd be forgiven for thinking it was late in the evening, not first thing in the morning.

"Sorry, love," was the mantra from the cab companies. "We can't go anywhere in this."

Some were *really* sorry, sweeter than anyone at the rail or coach station had been.

"Oh, pet, I sympathise, I do. Hope you can get something sorted out."

By the time she reached the last number, she was crying – not sobbing out loud, making a show of herself, but fat tears rolled down her cheeks, and she was sniffing hard.

A gruff voice answered the phone, a man's. The Tony of Tony's Taxis?

"You what, hin? You want to go to London? From Sunderland? In this?"

The incredulity in his voice said it all, Lottie nearly ending the call and, not only that, but hurling the mobile from her, all the way back to the counter, where the woman she'd spoken to was laughing with a colleague, their heads together conspiratorially.

Immediately, she berated herself. *Calm down! Don't act like Mr Jogger Pants!*

"Hin? Hinny, are you there?"

Hinny…a term of endearment, but it only infuriated her more.

"Hin?" he said again.

"Oh, for God's sake, I'm not your 'hin', okay? What I am is pissed off. Frustrated. *Upset.* I have to get home. Not for my sake. If it was, I wouldn't be trying this hard. I'd cut my losses and get a hotel, FaceTime my mum tomorrow, and my brother – enjoy the respite, if I'm honest, from all that crap on TV I'd otherwise be forced to watch. I'd treat myself to a bottle of vodka instead, a litre, get smashed whilst staring at the snow, should it ever bother to fall, that is. I'd be fine about it. Absolutely fine. Have myself a right old ball—"

"Look, hin, it just isn't safe—"

"I've told you, I'm not your hin, or hinny or whatever! Plus, the roads will be fine, surely, if we leave now, like…*right* now. We can, I don't know, try to outrun the storm or something, leave it way behind us. Be brave enough to try, at least, rather than giving up at the first hurdle. As I've told you, this isn't about me; it's about her. Alice."

"Alice? Who the heck is—"

"Oh, I know you don't know Alice! But she's been wronged. Badly, *badly* wronged. She was shut away for something she didn't do. Called a liar. Sedated. *Operated* on. Kept silent for years and years, for most of her life. She's like, ninety-two now, and it's not fair. Her life was stolen from her! And today's the anniversary of when it happened. Right here in Sunderland. She was taken away on Christmas Eve, a time of despair for her, when you should only feel joy in your heart, and excitement. I just want her to know, today – not tomorrow, not the next day, but today – that *I* believe her, that I know she was telling the truth, that…that…I think she's a warrior. That I'm sorry too. I think it might mean something to her, might help her to rest easier. Be at peace. Finally."

Oh God, she really was crying now, making a right show of herself, the two at the desk no longer laughing with each other but staring at her – along, no doubt, with whoever else was in the coach station, shadow figures that she daren't look at.

Shit! It was a wonder Tony remained on the line.

But as he was, she continued. "I don't know how much longer she's going to last."

"Alice?" he said again.

"Yes, Alice! She's ninety-frigging-two! The sand in the hourglass is nearly all at the bottom. I work at the care home she's at, and…and I don't know how else to explain this sense of urgency to you. I *have* to get back there today. I'm not being dramatic or making any of this up, lying for the sake of it. And I know I'm probably not making much sense either, that you don't have a clue who I'm talking about—"

"Then tell me more about her."

"I'm *trying*! But it's a long story. A strange story. I wouldn't even know where to start."

"Where are you?"

"What?"

"I said, where are you?"

"I'm at the coach station. It's on…erm…erm…"

"Bess Street," the woman at the counter shouted. "You're at the Bess Street office."

"Bess Street," Lottie duly repeated, wiping at her nose with the back of her hand.

"Okay. All right. And you said it's a long story?" the gruff voice checked.

"Long *and* strange."

A slight pause before the man spoke again. "Is it…you

know…a ghost story, like?"

"A ghost story?" Lottie choked back a sob. "Well…kind of…I suppose."

"I *love* a ghost story." The man sounded happy now, almost like a kid.

"Do you?" was all Lottie could think to reply.

"Of course! 'Specially on Christmas Eve. Christmas Eve was made for it!"

"Oh. Right. Well—"

"You said you didn't know where to start in the telling of it."

Not only had Lottie stifled her sobs, she was frowning. "Um…yeah…my head—"

"Usually, you start at the beginning."

Lottie glared at her phone. Was he being facetious, this man who may or may not be Tony from Tony's Taxis? If so, she bloody well *would* hurl her phone, for she was in no mood for it. There had to be other cab firms she could try, someone she could speak to who wasn't such a smart-arse. About to cut the call, the man spoke again.

"The name's Tony," he said, which cleared that mystery up. "And your name is?"

"Lottie," she replied.

"Hello, Lottie."

"Look, I haven't got time—"

"Can you see me?"

"Huh?"

"Can you see me waving?"

"Waving?"

"Aye! I'm outside the coach station on Bess Street. I was only around the corner when you phoned, was going to try and make my way home. Don't think that's an option now."

Hope flared. "You'll do it? Take me to London? In this weather? On Christmas Eve?"

"I'll certainly give it a go," he said. "Go on, look up. I'm here."

She did, saw what looked like a bald man in a white Ford who was not just waving but grinning, *Tony's Taxis* emblazed in bold black letters on the side panel.

"Tony's Taxis at your service," he continued, "Sunderland's finest," adding, "and bravest. Or stupidest, or whatever. We'll have to be careful, agreed?"

"Agreed," Lottie whispered.

"It'll be slow going getting out of Sunderland, but maybe, just maybe, the more miles we put under our belts, the easier it'll get."

"Yes," she said, then louder, "yes!"

"Come on, then, slow coach." Tony chuckled as if he'd made some particularly clever joke, and perhaps it was considering where she was, Lottie realising she was smiling too. "It's a long journey, as I say, but that's not such a bad thing."

"It isn't?"

"No. Want to know why?"

Lottie could only nod.

"'Cause I want to hear every single detail of Alice's story, that's why. So, as I've said, start at the beginning, *right* at the beginning. Leave nothing out, certainly no gory details. On Christmas Eve, the stranger the ghost story, the better."

Chapter One

December 2022

"It's wild out there!"

Patsy Cork was right. Not only was it lashing with rain, the winds were at gale force. Standing in front of Lottie, she looked amazed she'd made it in at all, the new recruit.

"Now you're here," she continued, "let's get you started. There's plenty to learn."

About-turning, the woman, who was taller than Lottie, around five foot eight, her tight-fitting clothes bulging in several places, led her deeper into the building. Silver Birches was the name of it. A care home for the elderly, single storey, built in the sixties or seventies. *Purpose-built*, for the dying. There was a smell in the air, one that only deepened Lottie's grimace. It reminded her of the canteen at school, stale and unappetising, reeking of stew or boiled cabbage, those particular delights slopped onto plates in big, messy ladlefuls for the students to then ignore. Her heart sank, all the way into her Doc Martens. She didn't want this job. Had told her mum, Jenny, who'd secured it for her, there wasn't a cat's chance in hell she'd spend her days wiping drool from people's mouths or worse. But Jenny had played her trump card. 'You *will* work there,' she'd said, 'because I need a contribution towards rent now you've turned eighteen. If not…well, if not, I'll have to let your room to someone who isn't so workshy. And don't look at me like that, like I don't mean what I'm saying. I do.'

She didn't. Lottie was certain. She'd chuck her out to go where? The streets? Then again…there was something in the way Jenny had said it, her expression nothing less than glacial, that had made Lottie refrain from arguing further. She'd do a couple of months at the care home, she'd decided. With some work experience under her belt, she'd stand a better chance of getting a job in a shop or a bar or nightclub. Anywhere but there.

"So, this is the staff room, and this is your locker. Lottie? Lottie, are you listening?"

"What? Oh, yeah, yeah. That's my locker."

"And here's the key for it. Don't lose it or you can pay for the replacement."

Taking the key, Lottie glanced around. The room was tiny, with five lockers, a table, and two chairs shoved in the corner, plus a small countertop with a kettle, some tubs of sugar, tea, and coffee on it. Piled in a tiny plastic sink were several mugs stained with dark liquid. Not just grimacing, she flinched, resolving to bring her own mug in and keep it separate. This whole place…it seemed contaminated somehow. As if simply by being here, you could catch old age. She bet the washing-up would be her task, pure drudgery.

"Your hair," Patsy began, and Lottie had to conceal a sigh. She'd wondered whether it would be a problem. "Do you intend to keep it that colour?"

It was blue. *Mercury Blue*. Why should she change it? Most of the residents here were likely too blind to see it anyway. And if not, then it'd add a splash of colour to their lives, because this place, with its scuffed magnolia walls, cabbage smell, and utilitarian grey cord carpet, was drab.

"Well?" Patsy said.

Lottie had to think quickly. "The thing is, it's really damaged right now, really brittle, so I can't do anything to it yet. I've been advised not to. You know, by my hairdresser. She said it'd literally fall out if I try. So yeah, I'll change it, soon, but I can't right away."

Patsy's nostrils flared, and she lifted one hand to fluff at her own hair, also dyed to within an inch of its life but an acceptable colour, in Patsy's eyes, at least – platinum blonde. Lottie's mum knew Patsy; that was how she'd got the job, *as a favour*, and Patsy was around the same age as Jenny too, fortyish, but trying to look younger, *desperately* trying. Her lips were pumped, and you could drag a fingernail through the makeup she wore, it was so thickly applied. Plus, no way her breasts were God-given.

After a few seconds tantamount to a standoff, Patsy rolled her eyes. "Just make sure you keep it tied back meanwhile."

"Will do," Lottie assured her, suppressing not a grimace this time but a smirk. From feeling so helpless, she'd scored a triumph.

"Put your bag away, and there on the chair is your uniform. You'll need to get changed. I'll close the door to give you some privacy. Soon as you're ready, come out."

A *polyester* uniform, trousers and a tunic top, burgundy. Her mum had never mentioned she'd have to wear a uniform! This was getting worse and worse, the injustice of it causing her eyes to water. Storming over to her locker, she inserted the key and yanked it open. There was dust in there! A thick layer on the bottom. Clearly, getting staff was a problem.

"Shit, shit, and double shit," she muttered, stuffing in her bag and her mobile phone, which she'd already been told she mustn't carry around with her. How would she survive without it for, what – eight hours? No Insta reels or TikTok for some light relief.

The uniform, as she'd suspected, felt scratchy against her skin. It might be cold and stormy outside, but there, in this tiny room, with the strip lights glaring above her, she felt hot and clammy, wanting to rip the tunic and trousers back off and let her skin breathe.

She sniffed hard, remembering Patsy was waiting outside to show her around, *to meet the residents*. What a thought! She was eighteen, and this was how she'd spend her days, with those in their eighties and nineties. It wasn't right, and it wasn't fair. And she'd be getting paid a pittance to do it, barely knocking on the door of minimum wage.

"Lottie? Are you ready? Time's getting on!"

God, this woman was worse than her mother! A real nag.

Two months she'd said she'd endure it for. Two weeks, more like – two days, even.

Plus…she was worried. Well…anxious, really. It was just…being with old people, it sometimes made her think things, *feel* things, other than the current distaste or boredom. It was like…she could sense stuff about them, their emotions, even *see* things, memories that weren't hers, that didn't belong in her mind, just snatches of them, vague, but there nonetheless. She could with younger people too sometimes, but not as often, only those…only those… A tear fell, which she wiped at with the back of her hand. Only those who were close to death, she supposed, despite their age. People like Matt, who wasn't just *people* but her friend, her best friend. Who'd died when they were sixteen.

Leukaemia. It was a word she couldn't even spell when she'd first heard it. Acute leukaemia, which had developed suddenly and snatched him away. Until then, they'd shared everything, their lives, for so long, meeting on the first day of primary. Soul mates, but the best kind, no romance to mess it up. She could read his mind sometimes, and he could read hers. Not because of anything weird, but because they were so close. Often, they'd finish each other's sentences. After he'd fallen ill, though, she could read so much more.

Throughout his illness, she'd sit by his side in his bedroom, lay by his side too for hours, just holding him, listening to his breathing, his soft crying sometimes, his despair that for him it would all be over soon, way too soon, when he had so much to give.

"It'll be all right," she'd whisper. "Honestly, Matty, it'll be okay. It'll be…different, that's all, on the other side. It might even be fun!"

A stupid, stupid thing to say! But it had made him smile. Briefly. After the smile had faded, he'd slept, Lottie still holding him, and that's when she'd sensed what lay beneath.

It was deep and dark and black, a well full of poison, which kept erupting. Hatred for the disease but for something else besides: Lottie.

Why d'you get to live and I don't? Fucking bitch! You're not even the clever one; I am. I could have gone to uni, become a lawyer, an engineer, anything. The world was mine. It should be you in this bed, dying. In pain and in torment. I wish it was! I'd sell my soul for it to be you. Then I'd do what you're doing now, pretend to cry, pretend to care, when really all I'd want is for it to be over, for you to die so I could start living again.

Awful, awful words that had made her heart race, but

then came the visions to accompany them. He was killing her – *sacrificing* her life for his, strangling, bludgeoning, and mutilating, all the while yelling, *Please, please, please, not me! Don't let it be me!*

She'd had to break the connection and get away from him. Climb off the bed and rush to the corner of the room, shake the visions and the words from her head, expunge them.

That was *not* Matt! Matt was funny, he was kind, the coolest dude ever. And clever, he was certainly that; often, his mother would boast about it, her son who was 'destined for Cambridge'. Of the duo, he was indeed the one marked for greatness, something Lottie would also point out. When she did, he'd turn the compliment straight back around. 'You have your talents too,' he'd say. 'You know you do. You're amazing. You're a wonder.'

Because she'd told him what she could do. Only he and her mother knew, and unlike her mother, he hadn't been horrified. She remembered how his mouth had opened and his eyes had widened. How he'd grinned, pushing his floppy blond hair away from his face. She'd told him she could read people, graphically. *Certain* people. Before each of her grandparents had died, holding their hands, connecting with them, she'd seen when they were younger, livelier, the stuff that photographs hadn't captured, how they'd embarked on life together, married, and had children, the wonder of it all. Sweet memories harboured deep inside, experiences that were as much a part of them as anything physical. After her grandparents, she'd tried it again, almost as an experiment, with an aunt, taken her hand and *seen*, that aunt having died a few months later too. But never had she seen stuff like she had with Matt, as dark and as potent.

As *horrifying*.

"It's not you, Matt. It's not you. Not you. Not you."

Still in the corner of his room, staring at him, she'd repeated those words like a prayer. Made herself believe them. Cursed herself too for thinking it *could* be him. But…no way she could've imagined what she'd seen and felt either.

Which meant it had been him.

Maybe, just maybe, there was darkness in everyone. If you felt you'd been wronged. And Matt *had* been. What had happened to him was a travesty.

Matt, who'd died just a few days later.

Her Matt.

Who at the end had hated her because, between them, only she got to live.

Sad. So fucking sad.

A sob escaped her, a proper sob, one that would evolve into a howl if she didn't work to suppress it. "Sorry, Matty. I'm so sorry," she whispered. "I wish it had been me. Honestly, I do. Given the chance, I would have taken your place."

He'd be at uni right now, studying for his bright future, and there she was, working as a drudge in a care home, someone who'd flunked school because she just couldn't focus, not when he'd been ill and not afterwards when he'd gone. Couldn't…*forget*.

But she had to try, because by the same token, it was simply too painful to keep remembering. Maybe her mum was right; whatever ability she had was dangerous.

Despite this, she couldn't help but wonder: What did the people here harbour? Those just beyond the staff room walls, who sat in chairs all day or lay in their beds, not cared for by family but a bunch of strangers who only did so because they were paid.

How resentful were they?

"LOTTIE!"

Patsy's voice cut through her musings, sharp as a bread knife, but rather than it irking her further, Lottie was grateful for it – for the strip light above her head, no matter how garish, and for the world around her, the *real* world, as banal as it was bland.

Sometimes bland was best.

"Coming," she shouted back, yanking at yet another door.

Chapter Two

"This is Joan, and this is Dot."

"Joan and Dot," Lottie repeated. "Hello there!"

How brightly she tried to greet them, making a bit of an effort as she was now there, as this was her job, but her words seemed to fall – literally – on deaf ears.

Joan smiled back at her, but Lottie got the distinct impression the woman, who looked ancient, what skin she could see on her face and hands like that of a Shar-Pei dog, entirely wrinkled, had no idea what she was smiling at. Certainly, there was very little comprehension in her eyes. As for Dot, her eyes were closed, and whether or not she was sleeping, she didn't open them for the sake of a new recruit.

There were others in the dayroom – the rain beating against the windows there, harder and harder as if angry too – including a couple of members of staff, both women and around Patsy's age, no one young as far as Lottie could tell, she the only one.

The staff members were Diane and Mandy, adding to the litany of names being thrown at her. They wore name badges, though, as she would soon, *Lottie* being on order, just a shame the residents didn't. How was she supposed to remember them all?

There were twenty residents in the care home, or 'clientele', as Patsy kept referring to them. It wasn't a nursing home where ill patients were put, tended to by trained nurses – she'd Googled the difference. They'd simply reached an age where they now found it difficult to live independently. All of them had put in 'a good innings', as she'd heard people describe longevity, and so she couldn't feel sorry for them, no matter how helpless some seemed. She wouldn't. Not after Matt.

Stop thinking about him!

Had to stop thinking too about why she had no other friends anymore, not just because they'd moved on or gone to uni but because they couldn't cope with the way Lottie was after he'd died – the grief she'd felt, followed by something worse, perhaps: apathy. How easy it was to be in the world but not engage with it. To just go through the motions. People had expected her to get over his death. And quickly. To dust herself down and start all over again. Even her mother had expected it. The only person who'd shown any glimmer of understanding – strangely, because they'd never been that close – was her brother, Jack. He'd remained sympathetic the longest, sitting with her, as she used to sit with Matt, in her bedroom whilst she'd lain in the dark despite it being a bright summer's day, just…being there. Not saying a word, even. He'd seemed to realise words wouldn't cut it. Perhaps if Jack *had* stuck around, he'd have started speaking, whispered wise words of brotherly guidance, but he'd gone to Liverpool, to uni too, and was now far too busy having fun.

"Lottie? Daydream on your own time, not mine."

Lottie felt the blood rush to her cheeks as Patsy admonished her. She wanted to protest, say it wasn't daydreaming, that it was more akin to obsessing. But the manager of Silver Birches had a point: there was no time for it, either during work or free time. She had to concentrate more fully, live in the moment, *her* moment, no one else's. Possible, perfectly possible, as long as she didn't have to touch anyone. If she got more involved in personal care, she'd do so swiftly, perfunctorily, keep it to the bare minimum.

Aside from Joan and Dot, there was Gerald, James, Tom, and Nelly in the dayroom. Nelly and Tom sat side by side, his hand enclosing hers, the pair of them looking happy enough, blissful, in fact. Both returned Lottie's greeting with almost kittenish enthusiasm. There was also Grace, Silver Birches' oldest resident.

"Ninety-four?" Lottie said when Patsy told her how old she was. "That's…incredible."

"Think so, do you?" Grace said. "I suppose, love. I suppose."

"I'd never have guessed. You look…great."

"Ha! Don't go telling tales! But thank you. Thank you. I've seen a bit of life, that's for sure. When you can, come sit with me. I'll tell you all about it."

Before Lottie could answer, Patsy interrupted. "This way," she said, her tone curt.

They left the room and returned to the corridor, Patsy muttering as she turned left.

"Sorry, what was that?" Lottie asked, having to hurry to catch her.

Patsy replied without turning. "I said some can drone on, often repeating the same things over and over. Grace certainly does. Don't get drawn in."

"Drawn in?" Lottie repeated.

"Uh-huh," Patsy said. "It's not worth it. They'll commandeer you if they can, think that's what you're

24

employed for, to just sit and listen, that you're not needed elsewhere. Right here we are, Dan's room. Those you've already met tend to like a bit of company in the dayroom, but there's also those who can't or won't leave their room. Refuse to."

"Oh, right," Lottie said, following her into Dan's room.

Dan was in there sitting on a chair, leaning over a desk.

"Hi," Lottie said. "Oh, is that a jigsaw you're doing?"

Dan – another as old as Methuselah, strands of white hair covering an otherwise bald head – looked up and gave a shrug.

"Who are you?" he said.

"I'm Lottie. The new girl."

"Oh. Right. Wonder who'll get to leave here first, you or me?"

"Thank you, Dan," Patsy interjected, her nostrils flaring. For a woman who owned and ran a care home, who'd *chosen* this profession, she seemed to lack the most important qualification of all: care. This was clearly business for her, through and through.

More residents were housed in rooms practically identical to each other, each containing a bed, sink, chair, table, chest of drawers, and personal items in various quantities, including vases and ornaments and photographs of loved ones, family members who were off elsewhere, busy with the business of life. Finally, there were generic pictures on the wall of flowers or meadows, but nothing particularly pleasant about them; they were bland too. This entire experience was. God's waiting room. That was another saying she'd heard regarding these types of places. Or, if you were agnostic, simply a waiting room, a bridge between one state of being and another. A stepping stone. And hallelujah!

She got to spend day in, day out there. Could she do it, she wondered as, like a lost lamb, she once again trotted behind Patsy to more rooms, Patsy explaining on the way what was expected of her, her duties – to clean and fetch and carry, but not to sit and talk and 'idle working hours away'. Oh, she was tempted to turn tail, run back down the corridor to the staff room, tear this uniform off and put her jeans and jumper back on, rush out of there through the pouring rain, back to her room, to pull the curtains shut and lie on the bed. She'd do it, she would, but for her mother's wrath.

A clap of thunder resounded, entering the building, shaking it to its very core.

If it startled her, it startled Patsy more so.

"Bloody hell," she yelped, practically leapfrogging into the air. "It's turned into a full-on storm out there! And I *hate* storms."

Lottie didn't. She loved them. The drama. But there came a keening sound, low at first, making her wonder what it was, the wind soughing through the eaves of the building? It sounded almost…ethereal. Then it built, and built, became so ear-piercing it made you squint. Patsy turned around, facing Lottie, but looked beyond her.

"And that's *why* I hate them. That's Eve, that is. Storms set her off." She then began yelling. "Diane! Mandy! You there? One of you come and help. Evie's at it again."

Diane bustled down the hallway from the dayroom, red-faced from the effort. "Coming," she said, looking as fed up as Patsy, as burdened. "Should I call the duty nurse?" she continued. "Get her sedated. This storm doesn't look like it's going to ease anytime soon."

"*Definitely* call her," Patsy said. "I've a lot on my plate today, like settling this one."

This one. Patsy was referring to Lottie as dismissively as she referred to the residents.

The pair left her standing in the corridor. Just standing there. Twiddling her thumbs. Whoever Eve was, she didn't know, hadn't been introduced to her yet. They'd entered her room and closed the door behind them, but Lottie could hear their voices in there as well as more keening – a racket, she had to admit, Diane and Patsy urging Eve to calm down, insisting on it, this woman who was terrified of storms. Maybe, just maybe, if one of them sat with her whilst it raged, put an arm around her and comforted her, she'd calm down without the need for sedation. Who knew? Who cared? Right now, it was her own discomfort that concerned Lottie, her skin still itching in the uniform and dismay only increasing. She hadn't met Eve, nor the residents behind two other closed doors. Should she wander along and introduce herself? Get it over and done with?

Other than Eve's room, rooms nineteen and twenty were all that was left. They might be empty, of course, the occupants those she'd met in the dayroom already, but she'd been counting. She'd met eighteen so far, so, if the care home was fully occupied, there *were* two more residents to go. Then she'd be done, all introductions dispensed with.

Rooms nineteen and twenty... It was as though she were being drawn to them, room twenty in particular – the last room. Who was behind that door? What aged man or woman? She became aware of something other than Eve's keening. Tingles, running up and down her spine. Nerves getting the better of her. Overwhelming her, actually. There was another clap of thunder, but not as loud as the last, not quite ripping through the building, or her, though still enough to make you shudder. Wild, wild weather. *December* weather. Christmas in three weeks. Yet it was all so unfestive.

Room twenty – she was close to it now, her hand reaching out towards the handle.

Breathing. *Hard* breathing. Her own? Similar to how she'd breathed in the corner of Matt's room, a sound more deafening than thunder or keening could ever be.

Darkness. There was more of that too. It seemed to *leak* from the room, beyond which, unlike in Eve's room, was only silence. A silence so persistent it finally drowned out the sound of her breathing, encapsulated her completely.

Her hand was pressing down on the handle; soon there'd be a click, and the door would open. Then what? She'd be sucked into the darkness? Into a tunnel of further despair, further horror, and something bigger than all of it that she recognised all too well: grief?

She'd *fall* into it.

And keep falling.

A click. She didn't hear it, not in the all-prevailing silence, but it occurred nonetheless, the door opening, *slowly* opening. *Come in. Come in. If you dare.* Those were her own thoughts, caught between tempting and taunting her, and then a retaliation: *What happened to you, and why you're like this, is none of my business. I* don't *dare.*

Other than on a work basis, there was no need to get involved. Entwined. *Ensnared.*

Not when she was still reeling from Matt, so afflicted. When she was still…frightened by it. What a terrible thing curiosity was, though. It went against the grain of everything. *What's your story? We all have one. And unlike Matt's, it goes on and on.*

"Hello? Hello?"

Was endless.

"You deaf as well as stupid? I said hello. Can't do me the common courtesy of replying? Kids today. No, forget that. *People* today. Everyone's as bad as each other. HELLO!"

Lottie jolted. Although she'd not set foot inside room twenty, not yet, it was as though she were spat back into the care home from another time, another age.

Someone was shouting at her? Saying hello? Was…grumbling?

She spun round to face whoever it was. A woman with white hair, kept short, cropped almost, who was short too and stout. Who was full of fire, her bright eyes mischievous.

On the threshold of room nineteen, the woman stood there, staring at Lottie as much as Lottie was staring at her, the pair of them getting the measure of each other.

"You new here?"

"Yeah, I—"

"Must be if you're wearing that uniform. Poor sod! It's no place for you."

"For me?"

"Yeah, to be stuck with us. Haven't you got somewhere better to be?"

"My mum—"

"Your mum what?"

Lottie sighed with frustration. If the woman didn't keep interrupting her, she'd be able to tell her! "My mum got me the job. I'm just out of school, you see. I need the experience."

"She needs a good kicking, then, your mum, for landing you with this gig."

Lottie's mouth fell open.

"Oh shit," the woman continued, averting her gaze now,

focusing on someone else who was rushing along the corridor, the sound of keening once again erupting as thunder crashed. "Look who's here! Bloody Nurse Ratched, ready to shut you down if you step out of line, to squash you like they'd squash a fly, and with as much compassion. Come on, come inside. No way you want to meet her, not yet, not on your first day. She's an acquired taste. Well, come on! Don't just stand there gawping! Step into my boudoir. Or my hellhole, as I like to call it. Certainly, my last port of call before I shuffle off this mortal coil. Soon. Please, God, let it be soon. Not sure I can stand much more."

A hand reached out, the woman's, grabbed Lottie by the shoulder and practically dragged her inside room nineteen.

"I'm doing you a favour, believe me. Nurse Ratched and her across the corridor from me, the catatonic one, you've got to build yourself up for people like them."

"Catatonic?"

"That's right," the woman said, closing the door behind them. "So here we are. Take a good look around. This is what I've been reduced to, all I've got left in the world." Her shoulders slumped. "Oh, how the mighty can take a tumble." Almost immediately she straightened back up, adopting a smile instead, as wide as it was dazzling, Lottie only able to continue staring, marvelling, in fact. "My name's Roberta, by the way, but call me Bobby." And then with a knowing wink, she added, "All my friends do."

30

Chapter Three

Bobby was a hoot! The only thing that made this 'gig', as she'd called it, bearable. She'd hauled Lottie into her room on her first day, and Lottie had stayed there far longer than she should have. Even when Patsy had emerged from Eve's room and called out for her, she'd stayed, the pair of them giggling at the rising annoyance in the boss woman's voice.

Eventually, she'd had to emerge, returning to the corridor, which Patsy was stomping about in, mystified. Bobby was hot on her heels, though.

"Sorry, I was just—"

"She was seeing to me," Bobby said, once more interrupting Lottie. "Turns out I don't much like storms either. Evie okay now, is she?"

"Evie's fine," Patsy said, those pumped lips of hers no doubt thinning if they could. "Are *you* all right? The storm's passing, I think."

"I'm fine," Bobby told her. "So don't go trying to stick any needles into me."

"It's only ever as a last resort," Patsy retorted, a tired retort, though, as if she'd said it a thousand times before, been forced to. "Now, if you'll excuse us. Lottie, come with me—"

"Not going into room twenty?"

Patsy had turned away, was heading back down the

corridor, having beckoned Lottie to follow her, but Bobby's words stopped her in her tracks. She didn't immediately reply, though, causing Bobby to raise her voice and repeat herself.

"I said, you not taking Lottie into room twenty?"

"No," Patsy eventually answered over her shoulder. "No need. She has the lunches to prepare."

"What muck is it you're serving today, then?"

Now Patsy turned back to her, her nostrils flaring and twin spots of colour burning brighter than the blusher on her cheeks. It was barely past ten, and, clearly, she'd had enough.

"If you don't like it at Silver Birches, Bobby—"

Bobby squared up. Despite her age – she'd told Lottie she was eighty-six – she looked formidable. Lottie went one step further in her musings – she looked *magnificent*, all five feet of her, as broad as she was tall.

"Then what?" she said, interrupting Patsy. "I can pack my bags and leave, is that it? 'Cause I've still got a brain and I can use it? Because I call you out, tell you how it is? The food *is* muck in here. You buy the cheapest cuts of meat you can find, stuff I wouldn't give to my dear old dog had I ever had one, that I doubt you'd feed to your animals either. *Everything* is cheap. *All* corners are cut. There's barely enough staff sometimes either. Oh no, I'm not going anywhere. My money's as good as anyone's. I'll stay, continue to keep an eye on you. And meanwhile, thank fuck for Deliveroo on speed dial."

If Lottie was at a loss for words, Patsy was too. She simply stood there, continuing to glare at Bobby. If she thought her eyes could convey as much fire as the older woman's, however, she was wrong. Patsy was no match for her, and she knew it. Cutting her losses, she turned away, muttering something to herself, which could well have been 'I hope you choke on your Deliveroo,' although perhaps Lottie imagined that, every bit as much as what had happened at the door to room twenty. *Hoped* so, anyway, on both counts.

She followed Patsy into a large industrial kitchen, where another member of staff was, Maja, who was prepping lunch. Lottie was to help her, chopping and cutting, stirring and dividing portions onto plates – a stew of some kind, big chunks of grey-looking meat floating about in it and, lo and behold, boiled cabbage as an accompaniment.

"You have some too," Maja said once cooking was well underway. Her voice was accented, and Lottie wondered where she was from, some part of Europe. "For lunch."

"Not hungry," she lied, envying Bobby her food delivery. She'd have to bring sandwiches in from now on; no way she'd eat the meals there either.

It was a first week that passed in something of a blur, Lottie confined mainly to the kitchen and the dayroom, tending to the residents there, no time to really get to know anyone or even try, as she was kept so busy. No personal duties, not yet, but plenty of cleaning and cooking and assisting with feeding. Bobby hardly ventured down to the communal area, keeping mainly to her room, as did the jigsaw-loving Dan, even though there were jigsaws in the dayroom too, which were half completed and gathering dust. Lottie wasn't on room duty yet, as mainly Diane and Mandy helped with those more bedbound. She'd be trained to assist soon, though; she'd been assured of that.

Apart from the incessant chatter of a TV, it was always so quiet in the dayroom. A lot of the residents didn't speak, not much; they simply sat there, either gazing into space or sleeping. The duty nurse was always on call, but Lottie hadn't spotted her since that episode with Eve. Plenty of pills were administered, though, sometimes several times a day by Patsy, Diane, and Mandy. Likely that's what kept most of the residents dazed, so when she'd try to speak to them, when she was helping to spoon food into their mouths, then wiping what collected in the corners of their lips gently away, she didn't get much in return, not even from Grace. And so, she contemplated it, laying a hand on theirs, just for a short while. Perhaps she'd see sweet memories and thoughts as she had with her own grandparents and aunt, *normal*, which would help to flesh them out a bit. History was present in every one of them, but it was also hidden, had sunk beneath flesh and bone, the good, the bad, happiness, suffering, and regrets. So much of everything.

They reminded her of empty shells, the residents. *Most* of them. Nelly and Tom were different; they stuck to each other like glue, always sitting side by side, with Nelly often giggling, and Tom too. They only had eyes for each other, and Lottie wondered, were they imagining themselves young again and elsewhere, which is why they didn't engage much with others? If so, she didn't blame them. They were squeezing extra happiness from life. And so she longed to see Bobby again, wondering when she could head back along the corridor to her room, knock on the door, and ask to come in.

Room twenty, though…the room that housed someone supposedly *catatonic*… She'd Googled the phrase – a 'condition', apparently, someone who reacted either very little or not at all to their surroundings but who, by the same token, might also behave in ways that were unusual, unexpected, or even unsafe to themselves or others. It was actually not a million miles away from the condition of some others at the care home. Even so, once in the corridor, would her hand enclose the door handle again? Would she open it? And if she did, if she was *brave* enough, would the same thing happen as before?

It was in the kitchen, chopping more limp vegetables alongside Maja, an ever-replenished supply of carrots, swede, and turnips to go in more greasy soups and stews – good hearty winter fare, as Maja called it, a woman from Poland, she'd since learnt, who was friendly enough but brisk too, very no-nonsense – that Lottie had an idea.

The radio was on, and Christmas jingles were blaring out – the usual culprits by Mariah Carey, Shakin' Stevens, and Slade, et al. Lottie loved Christmas, or at least she had until a couple of years ago. Remembered too her favourite Christmas song, her's *and* Matt's, 'Fairytale of New York' by the Pogues, how they'd sing it at the tops of their voices, hurling the insults it contained at each other with increasing drama before falling about laughing. They'd be doing that now, probably, this Christmas if he were still here. It was the little things that amused them, the stupidest things, hours spent in each other's company chatting rubbish but laughing, always laughing. And yet, such darkness in him…

"Ouch!" Lottie sliced into her finger, a deep cut, blood pouring from the wound onto the vegetables. Such a familiar pain, one that was…distracting.

"Oh dear, dear," Maja fussed, immediately noticing. She hurried over with some kitchen towels, grabbed Lottie's hand and wrapped the paper around it. "Be more careful when dealing with sharp knives! Now go, go. Rinse the blood off. I will get you a plaster."

"Sorry," Lottie mumbled, obeying her instructions.

"It is an accident. Nothing more. Rinse your hand, then let's continue."

George Michael was crooning 'Last Christmas' by that point, tears filling Lottie's eyes as she stood at the sink with the cold water running. Hurriedly, she blinked them back. No time for that, not here, a meltdown; she could do it later, in the privacy of her own bedroom, try to release the pain. Somehow. George continued, however, somewhat mercilessly, the sadness of the song permeating her heart further. For some people in the care home, this *would* be their last Christmas. Patsy had warned her of that. 'Don't get too attached,' she'd said. 'It's not worth it. People *die* here. Develop a thick skin.' In Lottie's opinion, Patsy certainly had, like that of a rhinoceros. To say it wasn't worth it, though, was callous. Had she always been as heartless, Patsy? Or was she absolutely right, a woman of experience who knew what she was talking about, who'd been softer once, perhaps, when younger, filled with good intent to help, but when people you cared for died, and not just one but one after the other, did it…harden you? If so, it was all the more reason to move on as quickly as possible. But whilst there, couldn't she make it a little more pleasant? Not only for others but for herself.

"Maja," she said, having applied the plaster to her finger. "Can you excuse me for a minute? I need to speak to Patsy."

"We're busy," Maja replied, chucking vegetables into a pan. "Lunch service is in less than an hour."

"I won't be long, I promise," Lottie assured her, removing her apron and skedaddling before Maja could protest further.

Patsy was hands-on, Lottie had to give her that, but when

not on the 'shop floor', as Lottie had heard her describe it to Diane, she could be found in her office, just beyond reception – a largely empty reception, for Lottie hadn't seen hordes of relatives coming and going, and those who did didn't tend to linger.

Having reached her office, Lottie knocked on the door, Patsy calling out to come in after a few moments, banging shut a drawer on her desk as Lottie entered. She looked flustered, actually, by the unexpected interruption. Nonetheless, Lottie continued to pitch the idea she'd had – to hang Christmas decorations, lots of them, not just in communal areas but in rooms too, and get some entertainment organised for Christmas Eve.

"We *do* decorate," Patsy told her, somewhat defensively.

"When?" Lottie replied, trying to sound pleasantly benign rather than pushy.

"A week before Christmas. And there's a nice dinner on Christmas Day too, roast beef or turkey on offer and all the trimmings. The clientele look forward to it."

Lottie tried not to grimace at the thought of *boiled* beef and *dry* turkey. Maja, she was learning, was no great cook. Luckily, she herself wouldn't be subjected to it, as she had Christmas Day off. What a thought that was, spending it here!

"It's just…can I start sooner with the decorations? Like…now?"

Patsy looked stunned. "You're too busy for that!"

"But what if I stayed after my shift and did it? And a cousin of mine's a magician. What if I booked him for Christmas Eve? He'd give you mates' rates, I'm sure."

"There isn't the budget—"

"Better than mates' rates, then! He'll be cheap, really

37

cheap. When I say he's a magician, he's practising to be one. So this'll benefit him as well as the residents. Give him a bit of experience. He can come in for an hour or so, liven up the atmosphere."

Patsy was quiet for a moment, as if contemplating. "Okay, as long as he *is* cheap, mind. We really don't have any spare cash for this, so if it comes in above budget, you'll have to subsidise. Oh, and the decorations are in the loft area, above the staff room."

"Okay. Great. Is there a tree?"

Patsy nodded, another curt gesture, no smile on her face at all, no enthusiasm. This was her business, her *chosen* business, so why look so pained to be there?

"I'll check it out, then. *After* shift. It'll be exciting."

Patsy's laugh was derisive. "You realise most of them hate Christmas around here, don't you? That they've had enough of it."

"They're still lucky."

"Lucky?" Oh, if only the woman could frown; she was certainly trying to.

Lottie shrugged. "I meant they're still lucky they've, like, seen so many of them, that they get the chance to decide, eventually, whether it's their thing or not."

Patsy just stared at her. She was her mum's friend, but exactly how friendly were they? It wasn't as if Lottie had heard Jenny talk about a 'Patsy' before. If they were close friends, then she would know what Lottie was referring to; she'd know about Matt's death, a *child's* death. Instead, she looked completely baffled. She was an acquaintance, more likely, a friend of a friend or something, which brought relief. Being friends with this woman didn't exactly paint you as the best judge of character.

"Look, I'm busy—" Patsy said, rising, a movement so abrupt it caused a whoosh in the air, a piece of paper subsequently flying off her desk to land at Lottie's feet.

Lottie bent to retrieve it even though Patsy protested.

It was a receipt. For a huge sum of money, eye-watering, in fact. A hotel stay, it seemed, one of the posh central-London ones, and a meal included that had to consist of caviar, lobster, and champagne for that amount. The care home might be short of a bob or two, but Patsy certainly wasn't, not if she could afford that.

Patsy, who was standing in front of her with her hand out.

"That's private," she said, and there was steel in her eyes, defiance. "Give it to me."

This close up, Lottie could smell her perfume – nice, actually. Subtle. *Expensive.*

"Give it to me and go."

Lottie nodded. "Sure. I'll head back to the kitchen," she said, turning, but slowly turning, in her own way, just as defiant. Only just stopping herself from adding, *to serve up slop.*

Chapter Four

"Bobby? Hi! Are you okay? I haven't seen you since my first day, and…well, I thought I'd come and check on you. Not just check on you – actually, I've got some Christmas decorations. You know, some tinsel and paper chains to hang about the place, and a little Christmas tree too. It's cute. It's all sprayed with that snowy stuff."

How different the woman was to when Lottie had last seen her! Then, she'd been full of vim and vigour, a force to be reckoned with, not afraid of the big boss woman, putting her firmly back in her place. Lottie had witnessed the exchange between them with nothing but admiration for the older woman, how she'd stuck up for herself, for the entire care home, really, refusing to be intimidated. But now…well, now she looked so frail!

After dumping the decorations she'd brought for room nineteen on the ground, Lottie hurried over. Decorations she'd paid for out of her own funds, not Patsy's, because when she'd checked what was in the box in the attic there, she'd found it pitiful. Bobby hadn't been wrong when she'd accused Patsy of cutting corners, which was a joke being as Lottie's mum, Jenny, had told her how much residents typically paid to be kept in such exclusive splendour. And so she'd gone home, pilfered what she could from their own supplies, then spent what money she had on adding to them.

The dayroom had been transformed. What a difference a bit of glitter could make! There was tinsel galore in bright, cheerful colours – red, green, and gold – hanging or wrapped around just about everything, and the home's own tree, although rangy, was so weighted with frosted baubles it looked really quite merry. As for the residents, some had been open to a bit of decoration in their own rooms, but others, as Patsy had warned, firmly eschewed it.

Jigsaw-loving Dan was one of the latter. "Never saw the point of Christmas," he'd grumbled, although Lottie had noticed it was a festive-themed jigsaw he was currently working on, having completed one of a ship sailing on stormy seas.

"That's pretty festive," she'd said, pointing to the snowy country scene.

"Coincidence," he'd insisted. "The only one of mine I haven't done yet."

Hilda had also refused. "It just makes me sad," she'd said, "thinking about Christmas."

"Why, Hilda?" Lottie had gently asked.

"Because of how it used to be," she'd replied. "When my family were young, when I was needed. When my George was still alive, when he used to dress up as Santa, ring bells at midnight that the kids listened out for. They should've been asleep, but they'd wait, always they'd wait for the bells, for that 'ho, ho, ho'. That's when Christmas began, you see." She'd stopped at that, likely couldn't continue reliving the past. Instead, she'd clutched at a handkerchief she held in her hand, brought it up to her eyes and dabbed at them.

"We've got a magician coming on Christmas Eve," Lottie had said, soldiering on. "It's my cousin Phil. He's a practising magician, to be honest with you, but very enthusiastic."

Hilda had simply sighed. "The magic's all gone," she'd said, then turned away.

After that exchange particularly, Lottie was looking forward to seeing Bobby again, and so it'd been a shock when she'd finally got there to find Bobby a pale imitation of herself.

She sat beside her. "No one mentioned you were ill!"

"Ill, love?" Bobby said, a croak in that once strident voice.

Lottie nodded vehemently. "Yeah. No one said."

"I'm not."

"Oh—"

"I'm old, is all."

"Oh. Right. I see. Of course." As soon as she said it, she cursed herself. *Of course.* What the hell did that mean? As with Matt, at the end, could she not say something more meaningful? Mortified, she quickly apologised.

Turned out, though, it *had* been the right thing to say, because it got a laugh from Bobby.

"You've nothing to be sorry for, girl!" she said, also shifting herself from a lying position to half sitting up, Lottie trying to help her. "We *all* get old. If we're lucky." Lottie didn't know what her own expression conveyed when Bobby said that, but clearly it was enough to prompt the woman to press home that point. "It *is* luck if you can survive for as long as we have. Weather all that life throws at you. Don't you agree, then?"

"No! I mean…yes! Of course I do. I want to get old," she said, trying to disguise the catch in her throat. "To…live. Make the most of it. Do all the things I've dreamt of."

The years dropped from Bobby when she smiled. "What

do you dream of, then?"

Lottie shrugged. "The usual. Travelling to far-flung places, backpacking, you know, in Thailand and Cambodia, places like that, seeing the wonders of the world, I suppose. Eventually, I'd like to meet someone, fall in love, and have kids. Get a decent job too. A proper career." Again, she winced. "Not that this isn't a decent job. I didn't mean—"

More laughter. "You don't have to explain yourself to me! I've said, this place is no place to end up in, let alone work in. But...needs must when the devil drives; it's all that's left for some. Funny that, you know. How big lives can become so small. Everything reduced to one room. *This* room. Which someone else will occupy after me. Everyone just waiting to take a turn." The smile faded from her face, but as she adjusted her gaze to the bag on the floor, it returned. "You've brought some decorations, you say? That's nice."

"It *is* Christmas," Lottie said. "Nearly."

"Yes. Yes, it is."

"We can't *not* acknowledge it."

"'Course we can't!" Bobby enthused, or at least made a good show of it.

"Plus, we've got a magician coming on Christmas Eve to entertain us. My cousin Phil. You'll come, won't you?"

"To the dayroom?"

"Yeah."

"To rub shoulders with them lot, the elderly?"

It was Lottie who laughed this time. What a strange thing to say when Bobby was older than some of them! Bobby grinned too and leant forward conspiratorially.

"I'm not like them," she told Lottie. "Inside...well, inside I'm nineteen."

43

There was a framed photo on the chest of drawers that Lottie had noticed before. Of a slight woman, actually, slighter than she'd thought Bobby would be, her hair long and dark. A pretty woman, a touch of sadness in her eyes, though, in her smile…a longing.

She was still looking at it when she asked Bobby, "What were you like back then? What was *life* like?"

Bobby had followed her gaze but then quickly averted it, focused again on Lottie.

"It was better. In some ways. And it was worse. In some ways. Just like life is now. There are highs and there are lows, and no way to avoid either."

What an intriguing answer! What a character she was, so interesting. "Tell me, then," Lottie urged. "Or tell me something, at least."

"You sure you got the time? What if Attila catches you?"

"Attila?"

"Attila the Hun. Patsy," Bobby clarified. "That's just one of my pet names for her. I call her Helga too. Part of the bloody gestapo. All that hair, those tight clothes, and heaving bosom. And don't get me started on her lips. Mutton Dressed as Lamb's another favourite."

"I see," said Lottie, giggling.

Bobby pointed to Lottie's hair. "I like the colour."

"Patsy wants me to change it. Back to something normal as soon as possible."

"Does she, now? Don't."

"I won't, don't worry. I like it being blue…being a bit different."

"Different is good. I've come to realise that. It's the best way."

Not just sitting up, Bobby was pushing the covers away

now and urging thickset, mottled legs over the side of the bed, her shoulders hunched but gradually straightening.

"We need more of your sort in these places," she said. "It'd be a whole new ball game if that were so. Okay, I'll tell you about me, a little something, at least. But I'd like to hear about your life as well. Because I can tell, you know."

Lottie was mystified. "Tell what?"

"That you've been through stuff. And by that, I mean painful stuff. There's no disguising it. Not when it comes to the eyes. So let's do a trade. Whilst you hang up the decs, I'll tell you about me, and you tell me about you. I'll tell you about this place too, Silver Bitches."

"Silver Bitches?" Lottie questioned. "Oh no, it's called Silver—"

Another hearty chuckle. "I know what it's called! I'm just kidding. I'm not senile yet; don't make that mistake. It's just another of my preferred names."

"Silver Bitches," Lottie mused. "It has a certain…ring to it."

"Makes us sound like warriors, rather than fit for the knacker's yard."

"You're not—"

"Don't."

Again, Lottie was perplexed. "Don't what?"

"Don't patronise me, girl, okay? That's all anybody ever does when you get to a grand old age, start treating you like you're a kid again, not even a kid, a baby. And granted, some do become as helpless, but not all, not me. My *body's* fit for the knacker's yard, but up here"—she tapped at her skull—"is something *wonderful*. Something that's brimmed with life, with experiences unique to me but which somehow add to the great big melting pot of experiences that everyone has, enhances it, *informs* it. So if we're going to be friends, never patronise me. What you should have is the utmost respect, because if we're living and breathing still, then we're exactly that: warriors."

"I do have respect," Lottie breathed, astounded, really, by the words she'd just heard, the sentiment. From this woman who was not just a warrior but a rebel, a veritable Jedi in a floral nightdress. "I really do." Or rather, she did *now*.

"So…those decs going to put themselves up, then?"

"Oh…no, no. I'll crack on."

She returned to the carrier bag and began pulling out what she'd brought – one of the mini Christmas trees in particular, with its snowy branches, a nice one from M&S. She'd spared no expense, just for a few of them, for Hilda, Dan, Bobby, and—

"You been in there yet?"

Having placed the tree on the chest of drawers beside the framed photo, Lottie spun around, pushing some strands of hair out of her eyes. "Been where?" she asked.

"Over the road," Bobby returned. "To room twenty."

Lottie shook her head. "Not yet. I plan to, though, after yours. Her name's Alice, right? Alice Danes?"

"So I've heard. Do me a favour?"

"Yeah," Lottie replied. "Anything."

"Tell me what you think after you've been in there. Because…there's a feeling I get."

The things this woman kept saying! "A feeling?"

"That's right. Only seen her the once, when she was first wheeled down the corridor, haven't done so again. Never comes out of that room, see? A bit like me in that respect, but for different reasons, I think. *Wholly* different reasons.

Tell me the feeling you get when you first meet her, and, again, let's compare notes." She then breathed out as if with relief, the dark look she'd temporarily adopted, the…troubled look when mentioning the occupant of room twenty, easing. "My, oh my, oh my," she continued. "I'm so glad you're here, someone…*with* it. Me and you, I can see we're going to have *lots* to talk about."

Chapter Five

December 2023

"Hold up, hinny. I've just got to focus for a bit. Pick up the story again in a minute, okay?"

Riding shotgun, Lottie did as Tony instructed and quieted, actually every bit as nervous as he suddenly was. They'd done it, escaped the centre of Sunderland, heading out on the A1018 south to Yorkshire to meet the A1 and then take the M1 into the waiting arms of London. Outrunning the storm. Turned out, though, that the storm was pretty fast-moving too, spreading its wings far and wide, the snow remaining behind them for now but threatening to get closer and closer. The wind too was fierce, kept doing its utmost to knock them sideways, Tony's hands clutching at the wheel, keeping them on track.

Wild outside, but in the cab, now she'd stopped speaking, it was quiet. *Eerily* quiet. They were putting all their faith in this Ford, a trusty metal steed, battling valiantly away.

As insistent as she'd been, she now felt bad, wanted to apologise for making him do this journey alongside her, risking life and limb, because no doubt about it, they *were* at risk. A worst-case scenario could unfold too terrible to comprehend.

It was Christmas Eve, only midmorning, yet the skies

still so dark. She looked over her shoulder again at snow that had settled on the hills in the distance. A tantalising sight. Ordinarily. Especially at Christmas. But only really from the comfort of your living room, where flames danced in the fireplace and the smell of pine from a freshly cut Christmas tree filled the air. Not that Lottie had ever experienced a white Christmas, but she'd seen how they were portrayed in the movies and read about it in books, the idyll that was portrayed. Right now, though, it was nothing but a bloody nuisance, and she wished it gone, for the skies ahead to continue clearing so Tony could put his foot down.

No other traffic on the road, or rather very little, only people like them, like *her*, the desperate, willing to take chances because of the time of year and its supposed specialness.

Perhaps…perhaps she could phone the news through. Call Patsy's mobile and ask her to take it along to Alice and hold it to her ear. *I know the truth. I know who you are. What they did to you.* It was an option – a last-ditch option – because despite her fears, they *were* still moving, still inching their way south. Telling Alice to her face was the goal because…she deserved that much. Plus, Lottie wanted to see it…recognition in her eyes, an acknowledgement, wanted to know she'd got through to her, not have Patsy snatch the phone back after she'd said what she had to, assuring her that 'Yes, she heard it; it's sunk in,' lying blatantly, which she would because it was easier, because all Patsy ever did, as Bobby had first pointed out, was cut corners to suit herself.

"Oh, oh, oh." Not just being shunted by the wind, they were sliding, actually sliding, Tony gripping the wheel harder as he exclaimed, although, again, finally righting it.

49

Lottie's nerve gave out first. "If this is too dangerous—"

"We're all right, pet. We're safe. Just got to take it slowly on this stretch, that's all. There's some black ice. Don't want to go into a tailspin now, do we? End up in a hedge."

"Tony, your family…I don't want to ruin things for you."

"My family?"

"Yeah." She shrugged. "Your wife, kids. This is so kind what you're doing, and I really appreciate it, but once you've dropped me off, *if* you drop me off, you've got to turn around and face the storm again. Head back into the heart of it. You'll be stranded for sure."

"Don't worry your head about that." Tony chuckled. "And guess what?"

"What?"

"Who says I haven't got family in London? That I'm not planning on staying over?"

Lottie's shoulders slumped with relief. If he was, that was good to know. She didn't feel as bad. What a kind man, like the dad she wished she had. Of course, she had a dad, but he wasn't particularly kind, nor interested either in the fruit of his loins, her and Jack. In fact, she'd barely seen him in the last ten years. Never had he listened to her like this man was, engrossed in the story she told, wondering where it was leading, the reason why she was so desperate to get back to Alice. She'd mentioned Matt, losing him, and he'd agreed – it was cruel and unfair what had happened to him, 'a waste of a good 'un'. What she *hadn't* gone into such detail about was what she'd sensed deep within Matt just days before he'd taken his last breath, not because it made her look weird, or rather weird*er*, but because she didn't want his memory sullied. She'd bear the burden alone. It tormented her, though, was always on her mind. Had he taken that dark stuff over to the other side with him? When he should only be at peace.

"So," he continued, clearly feeling it was okay to talk again, to listen, "before we get to Alice and room twenty, tell me more about Bobby. She sounds grand."

"She was an amazing woman. My best friend there," Lottie enthused. Her best friend anywhere, actually. After Matt, her *only* friend. "She used to ride a motorbike, smoke, and knock back whisky like it was going out of fashion. She once owned a hotel too."

"A hotel?" Tony was clearly impressed. "Where?"

"Down on the coast in Brighton. A small hotel, a house, really, that had been converted. Four stories, though, so big enough to sleep a decent number of people. She'd hold soirées in the bar. Had a lot of repeat bookings. Said they used to have a whale of a time."

"A grand woman indeed," Tony murmured, leaning forward slightly to peer through the windshield. "My imagination, pet, or in the distance there the sky doesn't look as black, does it? The clouds aren't as threatening. By the time we hit the A1, we might well be okay. Fingers crossed, anyway. Was she married? Bobby?"

Lottie swallowed as she shook her head. "No, never married. Never had kids. There was someone, though, but I'll get to that as the story goes on." Best not to jump the gun.

"All right, fair enough. What I want to know is, though, if she owned a hotel…"

"Why'd she end up in a care home?"

"Aye."

"She was getting older, it was getting harder to manage,

and so she sold it. Plus, other options were opening up for travellers – Travel Lodges, Premier Inns – that were more up-to-date, cheaper, so places like hers fell out of fashion. She didn't get as much as she thought for the building; it was quite run-down by that time, apparently. By her own admission she, like, hadn't been great at maintaining it. There was a property boom, especially in Brighton, but she sold just before it. She managed to buy a decent enough flat with the proceeds, though, two bedrooms. Thing is, it was in a high-rise, and the lift was dodgy. As time went on, and more often than not, she found herself trapped there."

"So it was destination care home," Tony said.

"Destination Silver Birches, that's right. Owned by her, by Patsy."

Tony turned his head. "A vulture, by the sounds of it. That true?"

Despite what Bobby had thought, Lottie stumbled over answering. Because she still wasn't sure if Patsy had been *born* a vulture or whether she'd gone into the care home business, once upon a time, for the right reasons. Shit had happened to her too. Over the year Lottie had worked there, she'd seen a variety of men come and go in her boss's life. All younger and all on the take, Bobby'd thought, after nothing more than a lobster dinner and hotel stay in Mayfair. 'What goes around, comes around,' Bobby had said. 'And it's nothing more than she deserves. She creams off us, then they cream off her, and so the cycle continues, a rotten wheel that keeps on spinning.' But what Lottie saw – what was so obvious, no need to take hold of a hand to see it – was Patsy's loneliness. Her anxiety too, etched on her face, every time she waited for one of her younger companions to pick her up from Silver Birches – wondering, always wondering, *would* they turn up, even though she was paying for everything.

'Soft girl,' Bobby had called Lottie when she'd pointed this out. 'Don't be feeling sorry for the likes of her. She's lonely, I agree. She stinks of desperation, is clearly on a highway to nowhere with those paramours of hers, they're users, but the likes of us shouldn't be funding that desperation. That's my point here. It shouldn't be coming out of our pockets.'

Feeling sorry for Alice, however? She'd encouraged that.

Lottie leant forward too. "Those clouds *do* look better."

"Aye, hin."

"We'll get there?"

"To London? We're doing our best."

"Still so stormy, though."

"Storms pass. You hungry?"

"A little."

"We can stop if you like, get something to eat?"

"I just…I'd rather we kept going."

Tony chuckled. "Thought you might say that. Open the glove box. You'll find my private stash in there. Chuck us over a Snickers bar and help yourself to whatever you like."

She chose a Snickers as well, grateful for some sustenance, a bit of sugar to enliven her. As they both tucked in, another gust of wind hit the side of the car.

"Shit!" exclaimed Lottie, before rapidly apologising for swearing.

"Tornado Alley, this stretch is called. You can feel even the slightest gust."

"Which this isn't."

Tony glanced sideways at her. "No, which this isn't. But like I said, storms pass."

"Not for some, they don't."

"Sorry, hin. Speak up. What was that?"

Lottie turned to him. "I said not for some, they don't."

"Ah, right," Tony replied, taking another bite of his Snickers. "By the way, a quick aside, did you know these used to be called Marathon bars back in the day?"

She shook her head. They'd always been Snickers to her.

"Used to be a hell of a lot more peanuts in them too."

"Oh, right."

"Hey, don't sound so down! We're moving, aren't we?"

Immediately, Lottie forced a smile. "Oh, I know. Sorry, I—"

"But you were thinking about her again? Alice."

"Yeah. Yeah, I was. My heart breaks, you know, for what happened to her."

"Which I still don't know about."

"Not yet, no. But for her, the storm raged on for so long. In fact, it's still going."

Tony scrunched up the chocolate bar wrapper and tossed it over his shoulder. "I'll grab that later, don't worry, bung it in the bin. So where were we, then? You'd gone in to see Bobby to hang up some decorations, and she'd asked you if you'd met Alice yet."

"Which I hadn't."

"But you were going to?"

"That's right. After Bobby's, I was going into Alice Danes' room."

"And Bobby said she got a feeling about her, that she was troubled by her. That right?"

"Uh-huh," Lottie answered.

"So this is the part where it gets spooky?"

"This is where it gets very strange indeed."

Chapter Six

December 2022

"Hello? Hello, Alice? Can I come in, please?"

Lottie was pushing open the door of room twenty. Behind her, in the doorway of her own room, Bobby stood watching. It was just a room ahead of her, with just a person in it, an old lady by the name of Alice Danes, who'd been there a little under a year, had arrived soon after Christmas last December. Wheeled down the corridor from somewhere else. Another care home, perhaps? It had to be. A woman whom Bobby had described as catatonic. Perhaps that was on her notes too, the ones Patsy kept in a tall filing cabinet behind her desk. If so, if it was an official diagnosis, Patsy hadn't mentioned it.

Just a room. Just a person. Absolutely nothing to be worried about. What she'd experienced before, though, what she *thought* she had, a room where the darkness choked you, is that what she'd feel again? And if so, why? There'd been darkness in Matt at the end, a *justified* darkness – the young wanted to live, not be felled like that just when life was truly beginning – but Alice *wasn't* at the beginning. She *wasn't* young; she was one of the oldest residents at Silver Birches. Was there no light left in her at all?

Before going any further, Lottie looked back at Bobby,

who nodded, urging her onwards, as curious as she was, the door almost fully open now.

She braced herself.

The darkness didn't come rushing at her. Nothing did. There was silence, only that.

She stepped into that silence, noting the curtains were open despite the fading day and the electric light above as stark as in the staff room. Alice was there, in a chair by the window, with her back to Lottie. All she could see was a plume of white hair against the red high-backed leatherette and the corner of a floral cushion peeking out from the side.

Before venturing deeper, she took in more of her surrounds. There was the basic regulation furniture: a bed, a table with two chairs in the corner, a chest of drawers, and a picture of irises on one wall, a mountain stream on another. Other than that, there was precious little else. No framed photographs, favourite books, or, in Dan's case, favourite jigsaws, no special ornament loaded with sentiment to prompt a smile. The spoils of a life long-lived, no longer counted in quantity but quality. In Alice's room, however, there was *nothing* of a personal nature, even though Lottie scanned and scanned again, almost willing something to appear, just materialise out of thin air. Alice had been moved into this room in all its generic glory, and generic it had remained.

No need to be afraid. Saddened, maybe, but not afraid. Her breath, however, was slightly ragged as she drew closer, all too aware that the door behind her – on a closer – had shut, entombing her alongside its occupant. *Buried alive.*

"Alice, hi," she said, trying to keep her voice steady. "My name's Lottie." Still staring at the back of the woman, she continued, "I'm new here. I started about a week ago, and

I'm…well…I'm putting up some decorations for Christmas."

If — as catatonic people allegedly could — Alice could suddenly burst into life, be a danger to herself or others, why had no one voiced any concerns? If not Patsy, then Diane or Mandy? Perhaps because she was so old, it was impossible to be dangerous; she was simply far too frail. Even so…Alice appeared to be of no concern to anyone.

Despite the fact Alice likely couldn't acknowledge her, Lottie would introduce herself properly before hanging what tinsel and paper chains she had left, then placing the last mini tree from M&S somewhere Alice's gaze might fall upon it when in bed.

Stepping round the chair, Lottie at last came face-to-face with her. She'd expected wizened, a face lined with wrinkles and the skin loose. White hair thinning, that too, and for her to be tiny, occupying a body so old it was literally collapsing in on itself. And that was what she got, all those boxes ticked. But what she *hadn't* expected was the rush of emotion on first sight, the sympathy that raced through her veins like a freight train and filled her, vessel-like, from head to toe. An *aching* sympathy that stabbed at her heart, and her eyes too, making them water, blurring the image in front, mercifully, allowing a few moments' respite whilst she took another deep breath and knelt.

Knelt, but not touched. Not yet. She was overwhelmed enough already.

"Hi," she said again; she *breathed* the word.

Nothing in return. Not even a blink. The woman continued staring outwards, causing Lottie to turn her head too. There was *nothing* to stare at, not this side of the building. Bobby had it better opposite, as she overlooked a patch of garden, a few tables and chairs scattered around that'd be utilised in summer, no doubt. All there was here was an expanse of fading sky and, below it, buildings every bit as unimaginative as this one.

It was, she was to later find, where Alice sat every day. Not at her own behest, not if the woman couldn't talk, or wouldn't, but Diane and Mandy, after feeding and washing her, would lift her from her bed into the chair and wheel her into position. Then, at night, they'd do the reverse. Alice Danes was ninety-one, nearly ninety-two, and that was all that was left for her. A tedium Lottie didn't blame her for trying to escape from.

She rose to her feet, stifling a sigh. Christmas was coming, and, at Silver Birches, she was trying to make something of it, to varied reactions. When the tree had gone up in the dayroom, then festooned so extravagantly, Nelly and Tom had come over – Nelly had hobbled, actually, her hip playing her up, but they'd oohed and aahed over it with delight.

James too, who was a veritable youngster by Silver Birch standards, only seventy-seven, although he suffered memory issues. 'That's lovely, duck,' he'd said. 'Really eye-catching.' With others, though, with Alice in particular, Lottie was fighting a losing battle.

Didn't stop her trying, though. For what else was there to do? This was her job. More than that: right now, it was her life. There wasn't a lot else besides.

She eyed Alice's hand resting on the arm of the chair, veins protruding through the skin. It was close. So close. Then she shook her head. She wouldn't lay her hand over it. Not yet. As Alice wasn't her charge, maybe not ever. She'd tell Bobby what she sensed, as promised – the same as her, basically – then that would be that. She'd done her bit.

It was as she finished blue-tacking the final bit of tinsel, having promised Patsy she'd make good any damage if it should occur – again, in her own time and, again, at her own expense – that Diane and Mandy entered the room.

"You not finished yet?" Diane said. No 'Oh, that's nice. That looks more cheerful, doesn't it, Mand?' No thank-you from either of them. If anything, Diane seemed annoyed Lottie had even thought to decorate for the festive season, or rather decorate so lavishly. As for Mandy, she usually looked like a wasp had stung her, so Lottie couldn't complain there.

"I've finished now," she said, realising how long she'd lingered, more so than in any other room, even Bobby's, caught in the silence.

Bobby was no longer in the doorway of her room when Lottie returned to the corridor, had clearly tired of waiting. She could knock on her door, enter, and exchange notes, as Bobby had put it, but she decided against it, feeling…drained, suddenly. As if she had somehow aged too, had withered, not one ounce of energy left to expend. She'd go home instead, climb into bed, watch some YouTube, and fall asleep. Return the next day.

And the next, and the next. All the way to Christmas Eve…

* * *

"Wish! Wish! Wish! Wish!"

It was a cry Lottie would never forget, the agony in it.

Christmas Eve had arrived, and so far the day had gone well. Lottie's cousin Phil had come early and gone around with her greeting the residents, trying to persuade those in their rooms to come to the dayroom and, if not marvel at his efforts, then at least laugh at them. That's what was so nice about Phil; he was nothing if not self-effacing. Tall at nearly six feet, three inches, and a couple of years older than Lottie, they could be friends as well as cousins, and maybe, after this, they'd make more of an effort to see each other.

They got almost everyone down the corridor to the dayroom, even Hilda, where copious amounts of tea and coffee were waiting, along with a selection of biscuits, not the plain digestives Patsy dished out but ones Lottie had bought, shaped like Christmas trees and baubles and covered in chocolate. Bobby came too – Bobby who now had pink hair, having got Lottie to dye it for her one afternoon, much to Patsy's horror.

"You can't!" she'd told her. "What if there's a reaction?"

"Oh, there'll be a reaction all right," Lottie had said, deliberately misunderstanding her. "She'll start a trend, is what she'll do. We should maybe take out shares in hair dye."

It was Bobby's hair, though, and therefore Bobby's right, as Bobby herself pointed out. Having been an admirer of Lottie's blue hair, she wanted in on the action.

Lottie would never forget either what Bobby had said when she'd finally looked in the mirror, once the dye had been washed off and her hair blow-dried and styled:

"I am," she'd said. "*I am* that woman. She is me."

She'd looked lovely, the colour not as intense as Lottie's, more pastel. Lottie had squeezed her shoulders, knowing exactly what she meant, that what reflected back at her was the woman time couldn't touch, that would always exist as long as she did.

They'd talked about Alice, of course, several times.

"What did you think of her? What did you…feel?"

The way Bobby had asked had made Lottie frown – did she know she was perceptive, that she had an ability? Strange if so, because Lottie hadn't told her. Not yet.

"I just felt…sadness," Lottie replied. "A *crushing* sadness, actually."

Bobby had nodded. "Yes. Yes. As did I."

"I didn't touch her or anything, you know, hold her hand."

Why Lottie had thought to add that, she didn't know, but it made Bobby's eyebrows – the few wisps that remained – raise.

"Will you?" she'd asked. "Next time?"

"Next time?"

"I presume you see to her too sometimes."

Lottie shook her head. "Not really. She's Diane and Mandy's charge."

"Well, perhaps you should *find* a way."

Why Bobby was so keen for her to do that, she didn't say. Maybe, just maybe, it was because there was nothing much else to think about around here, and Alice *was* intriguing, although strange that a woman who sat and stared at nothing all day could be.

Alice, of course, didn't come to the dayroom whilst Phil was performing. Lottie hadn't asked her because Diane had told her not to. Dan didn't come either. He'd almost finished the snow scene he was working on and wouldn't budge till he did.

"Then what?" Lottie had asked him. "Have you got another one lined up?"

"Not another bloody snow scene," he'd grumbled. "That's for sure."

Overall, though, it was a good turnout, and Phil was pleased. It was the biggest audience he'd had, he told her, and actually with some of them grinning and nodding at him – Nelly and Tom in particular, the most enthusiastic.

The magic tricks… Lottie winced on his behalf when he failed to pull several off. Even the cups and balls he got wrong, but it didn't seem to matter. Those who faced him either didn't notice or cheered him on anyway, Hilda prodding Dot in the limbs and telling her to wake up, that she was missing all the fun. In response, Dot snored louder.

As Lottie flitted along, refilling cups with tea and coffee and handing out more biscuits, she couldn't help but smile. A genuine smile. Perhaps her first since Matt. It was just…so heartwarming to see people enjoying themselves, *these* people, ones who rarely smiled either, laughing as Phil turned his show into more of a comedy act, something she'd have to have a word with him about, albeit tactfully – that it was perhaps more where his talent lay. Despite this, and despite Hilda's claim that there was no magic left anymore, it proved a lovely afternoon, one befitting an occasion such as Christmas Eve.

When Phil was finished, he had a much-needed cup of tea too, pulling up a chair beside Lottie and the residents, all of them in a semicircle and some chat going on, James saying what a good job he'd done, being kind, so very kind, and Joan agreeing.

"Better than last year, thanks to you," another resident, Ronald, said. And Eve, who was beside him, glancing nervously out the window in case another storm might be on the horizon – something she seemed to do perpetually, as far as Lottie could tell – nodded too, even smiled, masking her nervousness if only for a few seconds. But they were *golden* seconds, Lottie's smile growing wider. She was having such a nice time, could almost feel a glimmer of excitement for the following day. The *big* day. Working towards it, anyway. Two years after Matt had died. Slowly, slowly recovering.

And then that feeling instantly vanished when the shouting began.

"Wish! Wish! Wish! Wish!"

The sound travelled down the corridor and entered the dayroom, all heads turning towards it. Even Dot had her eyes open, wondering what was going on.

"Wish! Wish! Wish! Wish!"

It was a strident voice, one you'd never associate with anyone at the rest home, at least not the residents.

More sound accompanied it as Eve made to rise, further agitated – that of feet running along the corridor. Where to? Most were in the dayroom.

Although Dan wasn't.

Or Alice.

A *shrill* voice, more feminine than masculine, Lottie realised.

So it was her. Alice.

Speaking at last.

Screaming.

Chapter Seven

Diane, Mandy, *and* Patsy were in room twenty when Lottie arrived, she having scampered all the way down the corridor too. First, though, she'd had to placate Eve, nervous, birdlike little Evie, treating her like the child she'd become.

"What is it? What is it?" she'd kept saying. "Is there a storm coming?"

"No, no," Lottie had said. "Nothing like that. It's…well, it's Alice, I think."

"Who?" she said, seemingly having no idea of who dwelt in the same building as her. But why would she if Alice never left her room, if she never spoke?

Until now.

Phil took over. "Eve?" he said. "Evie? Come on, why don't you sit back down again, and I'll get you a nice cup of tea?"

As he gently guided Eve back to Ronald's side, Lottie asked if he'd be okay.

"I'm fine," he said. "You go if you have to. I'll hold the fort."

Lottie chanced a quick smile. "If you ever need a job…"

But Phil, as helpful as he was being, shook his head. "They're a great bunch, best audience ever, but…you're all right. I'll leave it to people like you, the experts."

Bobby also joined in. "Go," she said. "See what's

happening. Can't report back if you keep standing there, can you?"

Lottie didn't need asking twice. What had set the normally mute Alice Danes off?

When she burst into the room, Alice was still shouting, was *fighting* the care workers, a ninety-one-year-old woman, with Lottie further stunned to see it. She'd thought her a frail woman – she was – but here amongst much younger women, she was lashing out.

Diane and Mandy were the ones trying to restrain her. Patsy, who *hadn't* attended the magic show but stayed in her office, doing God knows what – hiding, Lottie sometimes thought, not wanting to get her hands dirty – wasn't getting her hands dirty now either. She was standing back, observing, although definitely bewildered.

She noticed Lottie entering.

"What are you doing here?" she demanded.

"I heard the shouting," Lottie said, nodding at Alice. "Is she okay?"

"She does this," Patsy said, again tersely. "Apparently."

"Apparently?"

"We'd been warned," Patsy informed her, "by the previous care home, the one that had to shut down. This is what she does. Silent for years, but on Christmas Eve she comes alive. Shouts that same word. *Wish*. What the hell it means, we've no idea."

"Have you asked her?"

Patsy was further bewildered. "Ask her? Why?"

"Because you might get an answer!"

Their gaze held for a moment, employee and boss, and then Patsy dragged her gaze away and pointed at Alice. "You think she's in a fit state to answer anything?"

There was anger in her words, in her whole manner. What Alice was doing was an inconvenience to her. That much was obvious. Maybe she had another date lined up this evening and wanted to get away quickly, a Christmas extravaganza of some sort. Certainly, she looked all dolled up, but then she always did, tight tops, short skirts, and high heels as much a uniform for her as the burgundy tunic and pants she insisted her staff wear.

As Alice continued to fight akin to an alley cat being cornered, Lottie half expecting her to hiss and spit soon, she heard Patsy speak again, half expecting these words too.

"I'm calling the duty nurse," she said, stalking towards Lottie, then pushing past her. "She needs sedating."

Her answer to everything.

Her departure, though, gave Lottie an opportunity. With Diane and Mandy still struggling, she drew closer, still marvelling at the change in the woman, the *spirit* of her. What was it she wished for? And why now? Although wasn't Christmas a time for wishes? When you hoped and prayed with all your might for something to come true?

Patsy would be gone for a few minutes at least, especially if Eve, riled by the commotion, started with her keening again. If Phil or Ronald couldn't placate her, Patsy would have to do the honours instead and go see to her. It was time in which Lottie could wade in, could help, Mandy even now looking at Lottie with her vinegar face, as if beseeching her: *Well, come on, then! You're staff too. Bloody help, would you?*

"Here," she said, finally close enough. "Let me."

Diane was more territorial. "She's our charge," she said, her face bright red from the effort it was taking to restrain Alice. "Go on. Away with you. See to the others."

Lottie, however, ignored her and knelt in front of Alice

like she'd done before.

"What are you doing?" Diane continued, but it was as if her words were coming from somewhere far away, as if they were…fading. "Lottie? I said what are you doing?"

She'd knelt, but she hadn't touched her. Had felt nervous about doing so. And with good reason. Not just silence suffocated this woman, usually the darkness did too. For now, though, the silence had let go, if only for a short while.

"Wish! Wish! Wish! Wish!"

The woman was still shouting, but not as loudly as before, that sound continuing to reduce. Her hands, previously clawing at Diane and Mandy, became still too.

Her eyes were on Lottie instead, possibly as intrigued by her as Lottie was with Alice, a clear question in her eyes: *What are you going to do?*

She was going to reach out, take her hand, and enclose it in her own.

And listen. Really listen.

As she did, she heard her mother's voice in her head: 'Stop! Focus on the real world. That's all that matters. What happened with Matt was tragic. I know it hurt you; it set you back. But focus on life, not death. He'd want that too.'

And Jenny *was* pleased with her, how well she was doing at her new job, how seriously she was taking it, doing something useful rather than lying in her bed all day in the dark.

'You've made a good start,' she'd said, unspoken words hanging in the air: *Don't ruin it.*

Is that what she was doing right now in taking Alice's hand? Ruining it? Going headlong into the darkness again, not Matt's, not her own, but Alice Danes'?

"Wish."

The word was a whisper now, and yet it drowned out Jenny's voice; *easily* it did that. It became hypnotic, even, a word that swayed from side to side, that whooshed, that penetrated, travelling deep inside Lottie, reaching her heart, maybe even her soul.

Wish. Wish. Wish. Wish. What is it you wish for, Alice? Tell me.

She'd expected Alice's hand to be cold to the touch, almost like that of a corpse, but it was warm and soft. As the woman's other hand came over Lottie's and clung to her, as desperate a thing as Eve, *more* so, Lottie took a deep breath and raised her eyes. Alice was staring right at her, her mouth not open and shouting but shut tight, mute again. She was staring at her, and she knew – somehow, she knew – that Lottie was different to the others surrounding her. To the *many.* Always this woman had been surrounded by people in rooms as stark as this that had little to no furnishings, no comfort. No light.

There it was, the darkness. Rushing at her. So much of it and so complete, no chink in its armour. A *blinding* darkness. And Lottie was lost in it, as Alice was.

"Alice." Lottie had no idea if she was talking out loud or communicating merely by thought, but she saw something in Alice's eyes – watery now, opalescent, but a vivid blue once, she'd wager. An understanding in them that encouraged her onwards. *What's your story? Tell me how I can help too, because you need help, don't you? What is this darkness?*

Shouting. A screeching, actually, and Lottie was startled by it. That place she'd been, where Alice was, was a place of silence, a silence that had been...enforced? Now, though, there was shouting again, colours, someone else touching her besides Alice, hands that broke the connection – Diane's, colder than Alice's could ever be.

"I said, don't touch her. She is *not* your charge."

As Alice started screaming again, repeating that same word, Lottie got to her feet and wondered how much time had passed when she'd been in that other place with Alice. Seconds, minutes? It had seemed like she'd been stuck there for hours. But, of course, it could only have been seconds. And now there was another commotion quite apart from Alice. Not Eve, for there was no keening, but Patsy again, shouting for Diane and Mandy.

Younger, faster, it was Lottie who made it to the door first, leaving the other two no option but to stay with Alice until the duty nurse arrived.

No denying it, Lottie felt relief as she departed room twenty and left the darkness behind, the agony of it, which was something she knew about, but not in as much depth as Alice. What had she endured in her life? What did she wish had happened? Or rather hadn't?

The door on its closer slammed behind her as she entered the corridor, as if Alice too was glad to be rid of her, didn't want her entering the same hell she occupied, wouldn't inflict it on anyone, for no one, *no one*, should have to suffer like that. Fanciful. Lottie was being fanciful now. Fabricating what was already bad enough. Yet still she fled, faster than ever, down the corridor, all the way to Dan's room.

She entered. He was in there. At the desk where he did his jigsaws, slumped over it.

"He's dead," Patsy said, as blunt as ever.

Lottie stopped in her tracks, could only gaze at his back, a man who preferred his own company, who'd loved puzzles and solving them, a man with a history too that she knew nothing about and never would. It was too late now.

"Don't touch him! Stay there!" Patsy continued before emitting a heavy sigh. "Had to go and die on Christmas Eve, didn't he? Wanted to get away early, but no, I've got to wait for the duty nurse now and then the medics. There'll be no going anywhere, not for me, and not for you either, I'm afraid. We're stuck here until all paperwork's been completed."

"That's fine," Lottie whispered. "I'm happy to stay. Really."

A smell in the air. Not death, not yet. And not the musky sweetness of expensive perfume either. Whisky. The soured edge of it. She stared harder at her boss, noticed her eyes were almost as watery as Alice's, but not because of grief; it had nothing to do with losing a resident. A *moneymaker*. That was the only part of Dan's departure that might cause distress. Then again, where he'd come from, there were plenty more. Whisky…so that's what she'd been doing in her office, having a party for one. Maybe what she *always* did. As Dan had his jigsaws, she had whisky, their way of getting through the days, making it more bearable, even her, even Patsy.

Once again, Patsy rushed by her. "Think I just heard the buzzer, although God knows how over the commotion that woman's still making. Still, the duty nurse will put a stop to it. Thank God it happens but once a year. Stay with Dan, but as I've said, don't touch him. He can't be touched, not until the doctor's been. Until he's been signed off."

Signed off? Oh, she was all heart, was Patsy.

Alone in the room with another resident, a dead one this time, Lottie wandered closer to him. He was *freshly* dead. If she touched him, tuned in, what would she discover?

She was tempted, despite her mother's copious warnings, despite Matt, despite Alice, despite everything. She didn't, though. She kept her hands firmly by her side, leant over instead to peer at the jigsaw beneath him. A snowy country scene. A difficult jigsaw because it was mainly snow, one thousand pieces. Dan had been struggling with it but also determined to finish, the few spaces he'd had left now filled.

"You were a determined man," she whispered. "That much is obvious. A...proud man. Who deserved better. Well done, Dan," she continued. "Well done for finishing the jigsaw, and Godspeed. I really hope it's a better place you're going."

Chapter Eight

The residents were returned to their rooms after Dan's death.

"What's happened?" Bobby asked as Lottie walked along the corridor with her. "Another one gone and croaked it?"

"It's Dan," Lottie said, seeing no reason to sugarcoat things, not with Bobby. "He seemed to go quickly, though."

"But alone?"

Lottie nodded solemnly. "Yes. Alone."

"Poor sod. He had family, you know? I've seen 'em. A son and a daughter, grandkids. All too busy on Christmas Eve to come and see him. When you *should* see family."

"I know. I know," replied Lottie, for what else could she say? Bobby was right.

"And Alice, I see she's quiet now. What was all that about?"

"I don't know," Lottie answered. "It happens every Christmas Eve, apparently. That's what Patsy said. She seems to go a bit crazy."

"What was it she was saying? 'Wish'?"

"Yes."

"What does that mean?"

"No idea."

"She probably wishes she was somewhere else, like all of us in here do. Those of us who still know where we are, that is."

Lottie laughed. "Come on, let's get you in your room."

"All right, all right, I'm going. Hide me away whilst they take someone out on yet another trolley, why don't you? It's not a nice sight, but if you're staying, Lottie, it's one you'll have to get used to. One pops their clogs every month here."

"Not you, though." Lottie was fervent about it. She might not have known Bobby long, or any of the residents, only for a couple of weeks or so, but she was growing fond of her. Like Phil, and like Matt, she could be a good friend, the age difference of no concern.

"You okay, girl?"

How intuitive Bobby was! Every time she thought of Matt, sadness reared up in her. And Bobby sensed it, was gazing at her as if she could *see* the sadness.

"I'm fine," Lottie said. "Honestly. And I'm coming in tomorrow for Christmas Day, I've decided. I want to be with you all."

Intuitive and with a smile like sunshine on water, the *youngest* of smiles. "I'm glad," Bobby said, turning away from Lottie and going into her room, but not before Lottie had seen it, how misty her eyes had become. "*Really* glad."

She wasn't obliged to, but Lottie *volunteered* to go in Christmas Day. She did so because she'd found out neither Pasty nor Diane *nor* Mandy were going to be there, only Maja, who stuck strictly to the kitchen, didn't mingle. It would be bank staff going in, strangers, those on double or triple pay most likely. And, yes, they might do a good job, might be wonderful people, in it for the right reasons, but they also might not be, and so she cleared it with Patsy, said she'd come in from noon onwards after opening presents at home, wanting there to be some familiarity, at least, for the residents.

Patsy just didn't get it. "You *want* to come in?"

"Yes. Yes, I do."

"What about your own family?"

"My brother's got a girlfriend now. She's at uni with him but lives in Bristol, so no doubt he'll be FaceTiming her all afternoon and all evening too. As for Mum...well, Mum likes to watch all the old, nostalgic films on TV, *It's a Wonderful Life* and that really old version of *A Christmas Carol*, the one with Alastair Sim, both of which I've seen a dozen times already, so it'll be fine. They won't miss me for, like, a few hours."

"Suit yourself," Patsy said before walking away.

Christmas Day came and went. Lottie wanted to pop in to see Alice again, just to say, 'Merry Christmas,' words loaded with meaning but which could also ring hollow. For Alice they would, for what on earth did she have to be merry about it, a woman in her position? Yet Lottie didn't get a chance to, because Patsy had not only hired bank staff but also someone to sit with Alice, to make sure there was no repeat performance, so the way was barred.

Maja, though, created a decent enough lunch: a choice of turkey or beef as Patsy had said, with roast potatoes, parsnips, carrots, and gravy, albeit the packet variety, followed by plum pudding with custard. Some of the residents ate it, others pushed it around their plates or stared at it, Dot guilty of the latter, clearly not wanting to eat but return to her chair and sleep.

The TV was kept on all day in the dayroom, as bank staff rushed here and there, doing their job, nothing more, no going the extra mile in any way, shape, or form. There were some visitors during the morning to see Hilda, Joan, Gerald,

James, and Tom, but they didn't stay long, rushed off, Tom's two daughters barely there for twenty minutes.

A fair bit of Lottie's time was spent in Bobby's room, but Bobby was quiet that day, preoccupied. She kept dozing in front of Lottie, performing a great escape of her own.

Christmas passed, and New Year's came – a quiet day at Silver Birches and, again, poignant, Lottie knocking off shift and heading home for a quiet evening too with her mum, resolving to be in bed before midnight to let another year without Matt enter gently rather than with any forced fanfare. The January that followed was a cold month, bitter. They even had a smattering of snow at one point, which some of the residents cooed at, but it didn't settle, just left the pavements colder and damper.

January's death came – as Bobby had said, one a month on average. It was Dot, which was no surprise to anyone. Finally, she got to sleep forever. And once again, all residents were deposited into their rooms until she'd been transported out.

"Hasta la vista," Lottie whispered as the trolley with Dot was wheeled past her, one of the paramedics, a young guy called Harry, giving her a shrug and a rueful smile.

Two empty rooms – Dan's and Dot's – but they were soon filled by Jane and Valerie, eighty-seven and eighty-nine, respectively. Sweet ladies, who enjoyed the company of others in the dayroom but didn't particularly speak much.

"*The Walking Dead*," Bobby said one day on a rare visit to the dayroom, looking around. "That's what this lot remind me of. Do you know what I mean? A bunch of zombies. That's why I don't come in here. Won't tar myself with the same brush."

Lottie had been rushed off her feet that day, was feeling

a bit tired and fractious herself. "They're not zombies! They're old and, well…why patronise others if you don't like being patronised yourself?"

Initially, Bobby appeared startled by Lottie's admonishment, but then slowly, slowly, she relented and nodded also. "You're right. My bad, as you youngsters say."

"You could chat with some of them, get to know them," Lottie suggested. "Just like you, they've had lives. Still do."

"You think some of them'll actually make sense? Can string a word or two together?"

"Bobby! You're incorrigible."

"And I always will be," she assured Lottie with a wink. "But yeah, okay, I'll have a chat with some of them, do my best before I go back to my room, back into hiding."

Hiding.

Her use of that word made Lottie wonder: Was that what Alice was doing? Taking it to a supersonic level with this catatonic business?

There hadn't been a peep from her since Christmas Eve. She was back to her usual silent self. Not that Lottie had seen her much, had no reason to, Diane and Mandy still doing the honours. And so the reason why remained a mystery.

She'd tried to do some digging, had asked Patsy for further information on her as casually as she could.

"Strange what happened with Alice on Christmas Eve, wasn't it?" she'd said when in her company a few days afterwards. They'd been in the kitchen, Patsy checking stock. She'd just shrugged in response, so Lottie had pressed further. "But you say it's happened before, at other care homes she's been in?"

Maja was also there, busy chopping as always, doing her

job, only that, not getting involved further, certainly showing no interest in what Lottie had just said.

Lottie had to repeat herself before she got an answer.

"What? Yes, yes, it has."

"Always on Christmas Eve?"

"Apparently."

"I wonder how long she's been in the care system for?"

"For an age."

"Oh, really? A long time?" No real surprise there; she was ninety-one. "No family, then? I've not seen anyone come to visit her."

"Maja!" Patsy called out. "Do we need plain flour as well as self-raising?"

Maja lifted her head. "Tak," she said before adding in English, "Yes. Yes."

"Okay," Patsy replied, and then, as if remembering Lottie was there, an annoying little gnat buzzing around her ear, she added, "Look, I don't know if she has any family. It's not on her notes if she has, so I presume not. Now, if you'll quit with the twenty questions, I have to get on and get this food order in. This is something you can take over, actually, in the near future. From next week, I'll start training you up." She then shuffled off, leaving behind the smell of expensive perfume with a side of whisky.

Maja lifted her head and eyed Lottie. "The potatoes won't peel themselves, you know."

Lottie sighed. She hated peeling potatoes, the tedium of it, but needs must; it was all part and parcel of the job. What wasn't was being privy to any notes on patients, the ability to find out their history other than the laying on of hands. Hard, concrete facts as opposed to vague. How could she access them? Patsy was always there in the day, and when she wasn't, the door to her office was locked. Where did she keep the key? Lottie wondered. In her bag? If so, was there a spare? There had to be a backup, kept not in her bag but elsewhere in the building, perhaps. If she kept an eye out – not spy, exactly, although not far off – maybe she'd see where. It was a plan of sorts. Maybe also she could put into place yet another idea, one she'd been mulling for a few days now: swapping the day shift for the night shift, a time when there was less staff, less hustle and bustle.

"Ouch!"

"Lottie? Are you okay? Have you hurt yourself?"

"I'm fine. It's okay, a small cut. I know where the plasters are."

The peeler was sharp, and it had slipped. Nothing new about that; it had slipped before when she'd peeled vegetables. This time, though, it was the *moment* it'd slipped that was of concern, when she'd thought not only was there bound to be less hustle and bustle in the care home at night, but also, during the witching hours, *less life*.

Chapter Nine

February was grim, worse than January, always cold and always raining. But Lottie had done it, secured the night shift, was due to start as soon as her probationary period had ended and she was a bona fide member of staff.

Lottie knew that Diane and Mandy did some night shifts, plus another woman, Eileen, a skeleton staff just keeping check, making sure everyone was breathing still until yet another morning arrived, not in paradise – in Silver Birches Care Home on an estate in Watford – but a *bridge* to paradise, hopefully, and by that time well earned.

She'd told Bobby what she intended to do, and she'd approved.

"So you're going to spend some time with Alice, try to…understand her?"

"Uh-huh," Lottie replied, "and I also need to find out if Patsy hides a key to her office in the building somewhere. I've been so busy, though, I haven't managed to yet."

"Why don't you leave that to me?" Bobby suggested. "I'll gladly help."

"If you're sure?"

"'Course I'm sure! What else is there to do in this joint? I'd enjoy a bit of subterfuge."

Lottie smiled. "That's settled, then. Thank you."

"She likes a drop, you know?"

"Patsy?"

"Yeah, her, Patsy. You noticed?"

"Well—"

"And it's getting worse. I saw her stagger the other day on those stupid heels she insists on wearing but can't. Hasn't got a clue how to balance. Know what I reckon it is?"

"What?" asked Lottie.

"Man trouble. She wants one, just can't keep 'em. Doesn't matter how rich she pretends to be, ultimately they don't want to know."

"So, like, she's lonely?" Lottie said, with perhaps a touch more empathy.

"I've said, haven't I? But don't go feeling sorry for her! Don't make that mistake. There's such a thing as karma. And she's getting a hefty dose of it."

"Karma?" Lottie shook her head. "Don't believe in it. Won't." Because if it were so, then what about Matt, about all the people death took too soon? What had they done to deserve it?

Bobby's expression softened. "Oh, don't mind me," she said. "I'm just...oh, I don't know. Maybe I've lived too long. Or rather...lived too long *here*."

"How long have you been here, Bobby?" Lottie asked, surprised at herself for having not checked before.

"Four years."

"Four years!" Lottie repeated, surprised. "I didn't know. I thought..."

When her voice trailed off, Bobby shook her head. "Not too much longer, hopefully. Might get early release for good behaviour."

Lottie looked at her, shocked at first, and then she laughed. "Good behaviour? You?"

Bobby laughed too. "You're right. Looks like I'll be sticking around a while longer, then."

"You better. You're what I look forward to when I come here. What worries me about the night shift is whether we'll still spend as much time together as we do during the day."

Bobby quickly reassured her. "Never been much of a sleeper, so don't worry on that score. If anything, we'll have *more* time. I let no one sedate me like they do the others."

"And Alice, I'll have more time with her."

"Yes, we mustn't forget about Alice."

"No. Alice is what this is all about."

* * *

How strange it was reporting for work at 11.00 p.m., ready to do an eight-hour shift.

Her mum had also been worried when she'd told her about the change in hours.

"Try it for a while and see how you go. But, Lottie, too much working the night shift isn't good for you. One of my friends at the hospital who works those hours too, on and off, said it can be detrimental to your physical *and* mental health. Google it, you'll see."

"I'll be fine, Mum," Lottie assured her. "Like you say, I'm just giving it a go."

Jenny continued to eye her beadily, as if examining her. "You've been there a while now, but you never really talk about it. I know you're tired when you get home, but even so. Do you like it? Really? Can you see yourself making a go of it, getting some care qualifications or something? If you do that, you can work privately, make some proper money. Patsy can be a bit of a tight-arse when it comes to wages."

"Work privately?"

"Yeah, build up your own list of clients, tend to them in their homes, all those rich old ladies and gentlemen."

"Rip them off, you mean, Mum? Like Patsy does? Like the state does too? Take every last penny from them when they're vulnerable, when they've got no choice, money they've worked hard all their lives for, now going to line my own pockets instead?"

How stunned Jenny looked! "All right! All right! It was just a suggestion, don't get a cob on. I wanted to know how you were doing, that was all."

"Fine! Like I said. The people there are—" she searched for a word to describe them "—interesting. Take Bobby, for example. She's so feisty, won't stand any nonsense, not from anyone, especially Patsy, gives her a proper roasting sometimes. Then there's Hilda. She's sweet, used to be a nanny, looked after children as well as having three of her own. Now it's her turn to be looked after. There's also Eve, who's, like, afraid of storms. She thinks there's one happening every five minutes. Tom and Nelly are funny – they've struck up a bit of a romance whilst at the home. They're like kids, always giggling together. But some of them keep themselves to themselves, like Grace, who's the oldest there, and Gerald and James, who has problems with his memory; like, he's just beginning to. Ronald's a bit more social, though, likes a chat in the morning. And then there's the new residents, those that replaced Dan and Dot, Jane and Valerie. Again, they seem sweet."

It was clear from her face that Jenny was enjoying hearing about the residents, or maybe it was simply just hearing Lottie talk, something she hadn't done much of lately.

"Oh, love," she said, "they all sound so nice. And they're

lucky."

Lottie screwed up her nose. "Lucky? How?"

"Because they've got someone like you looking after them, someone who proper cares. It's a good job you're doing, you know. Worthwhile. It's one where you can make a real difference to people's lives, and what can be more worthwhile than that? Although…"

They'd been sitting at the kitchen table whilst talking over mugs of tea. Lottie had nearly finished hers, so she'd risen and was heading over to the kettle to make another when she heard her mother's voice trail off. *Although…* She knew what was coming.

"You're not doing that…thing, are you?"

Lottie swung around to face her. "What thing, Mum?"

She was being obtuse for the hell of it, too much Bobby rubbing off on her.

Jenny straightened. "It's just…being there, at night, in an old-people's home—"

"A *care* home."

"All right, a care home. Being there at night, *anywhere* at night, awake, I mean, your mind can start…wandering. You can start thinking stuff might be a good idea when it isn't."

Lottie had placed her mug down on the counter. "Is that what happens to you, then, Mum? Do you lie awake at night and start getting strange ideas?"

"No!" Jenny countered, but the way she said it, so defensively, Lottie could tell she was lying. A single parent whose husband had left her when their kids were young, she'd had to battle through some tough times. Lottie remembered how much Jenny used to cry after his abrupt departure, at night, always at night, when she'd thought the kids were in bed and asleep. To be fair, Jack usually had been, but not Lottie, no matter how small she was, four or five at the time? She'd crawl from bed to the landing and sit and listen to her mum, who was either downstairs in the living room or in her bedroom, just *be* with her, sharing the grief, the load, even though Jenny never knew she did that. So yeah, her mum knew about the nighttime hours and being awake for them, and Lottie wondered what strange ideas had entered her head then, how low with depression she'd actually sunk.

Bearing that in mind, she softened. "That thing that I can do," she said, "I haven't done it so far." A lie, but a white one. And it wasn't as if she'd done much.

Jenny relaxed. "Good. Good. Keep it that way. Because…you know…"

"I *do* know," Lottie stressed. "You've warned me enough."

Again, that defensiveness. "It's for the best, love!"

"I know that too."

"And it's nonsense anyway. All of it."

Lottie raised an eyebrow. If that were truly the case, why the concern?

"Mum, this thing of mine, it's not all the time, you know."

Jenny waved a hand in the air. "Oh, we don't need to talk about it anymore."

"But…whilst we are, I just want to say, it's *not* all the time. I seem to be able to read people by touching them. I get flashes of insight into their lives. But…but…" She hadn't told her about Matt, what she'd seen with him; she'd told no one. She wanted to, though, right there and then, share the load regarding that as well. The hurt. Was this the right time? "It's only if…well…if not at death's door, then people certainly on the way to it."

Lottie was stunned when her mother stood up, *abruptly* stood up, the expression on her face like the thunder Eve so feared. "Lottie! That's…horrible! That's…macabre."

"I didn't ask for it, for…*this*, Mum! It just…*is*."

"It's weird. Unnatural."

"So what you saying? *I'm* weird? *I'm* unnatural? Your own daughter?"

"Yes! No!"

"MUM!"

Silence followed. As heavy as that in Alice's room. A darkness too, blooming in Lottie's heart and squeezing hard. So many thoughts tumbled through her mind: *Am I dark? Am I weird? That stuff I saw with Matt!* No way could she tell her mum about it; no way she'd understand. And, actually, Lottie didn't blame her. She didn't understand it either.

Jenny was the first to break the silence. She drew closer to Lottie, reached out and rubbed at her arm. In her early forties, she was an attractive woman, with light brown hair and clear green eyes. But even on a face as young as hers, life was etched there, the harshness of it. *So much suffering*, thought Lottie as any anger in her dissolved.

"Mum, I'm not weird, okay? And I haven't been doing stuff. I don't know what it'll be like on the night shift. There'll be call bells to answer and more food prep, but hopefully people will mainly be sleeping, so I won't be going around tuning in. I'll make a point not to."

"Good. Good. That's all good."

"It's just…I must have got this ability from someone. If not you, then…" How she hated having to mention him, because every time she did, her mother would flinch. "Dad?"

Jenny's snort of derision was loud. "Your dad? You think your dad was sensitive?"

Inwardly, Lottie sighed. She shouldn't have mentioned him. Set her mum off again.

She reached out, and, as Jenny had done with her, she rubbed at her arm, trying to diffuse the situation. Her mum's anger – she could not only sense it but see it – it was like sticky black tar, coating everything. Inside her, inside Jenny. Her mum. A woman who knew hurt, absolutely, but this? There was such...*venom* there. The years having failed to dilute it. Not deep down. It remained as potent as ever. A wound still busy suppurating.

She snatched her hand back, and Jenny noticed.

"What is it? What's the matter?"

"Nothing, Mum. Absolutely nothing."

"Did you...see something?"

"No! Not at all."

"Shit! You did, didn't you? What does that mean? That I'm going to die?"

"No! It's fine! Everything is. I'm sorry for mentioning Dad."

"It's nonsense. All of it."

"It is. It can be."

Jenny's chest heaving a little, she visibly tried to calm herself. "Right. Well...look, I've got to go shopping. We're fresh out of everything, but...if you still want an answer to your question, if you must, you're not like your dad at all. And be grateful for that, okay? What you are is kind, caring, and considerate." Her mouth setting into a thin line, she added, "He didn't have a sensitive bone in his body."

Jenny turned on her heel and left the room, leaving Lottie to stare after her. Her mum was *not* close to death, somehow she knew that, relief edging its way in as she relaxed her shoulders. The hurt and anger in her mum was simply there in abundance. It *characterised* her. That's why she'd felt it. It was getting a chokehold on all the good stuff inside her, like bindweed, strangling it. Because of her own grief, Lottie had neglected her these past years, but that would have to change. Not overnight, but slowly, gently. She made a pact with herself about that. They'd spend more time together, chatting, *laughing*. Just…caring. Her lot in life right now, but it wasn't so bad.

This ability she had – and perhaps it was the care home responsible, being amongst people with such rich lives, such history, such…secrets, a treasure trove to delve into – far from shutting down, was developing further, expanding.

And Jenny was right: in the quiet hours of the night shift, it would come to the fore.

Chapter Ten

Tonight was it. Her first stint on night shift.

It was March, heading from winter into spring. Not that the weather seemed to realise it; it was still largely miserable, the wind howling as it had the first day Lottie had arrived at Silver Birches, and this time her heart sank because of it. If it was stormy, Eve wouldn't settle. Not unless she was sedated. Lottie was torn about that, knowing it was a fast route to bringing about some much-needed peace, but wondering also, was it used too liberally? Because it was easier not for the patients but for staff, meant they could have more tea breaks, more fag breaks too, chat idly with each other, whilst all their charges did was sleep or stare blankly at the ceiling. No attempt to engage with them, to understand.

Making a difference. That's what this job was about for Lottie, or rather, given her initial attitude, what it was about *now*. She felt passionately about doing so. Because of Matt? Because she couldn't make a difference with him? With him she'd felt so powerless. And now here she was, able to have another crack at it, albeit with different people. She couldn't stop fate in its tracks; when your time was up, it was up. What she could do, however, what she was trying to do more and more with her mum now she knew the extent of her pain, was just be kind. Even with Patsy she was trying, smiling at her more often, trying to engage her in more conversation, a bit of banter. And getting nowhere fast.

With Alice, though, curiosity was turning into a thirst. Sedation came but once a year for her; other than that, she shut herself down. For what reasons? What had she endured?

"Hello. Lottie, isn't it? I'm Eileen. Welcome to the night shift. For your sins."

As Lottie stood inside the doorway of Silver Birches with the night behind her, not just musing but realising too how different the atmosphere was, so silent, and because of that, so much heavier, the woman had come rushing down the hallway towards her. In her fifties or so, she was slim, her hair heavily peppered with grey, and she had a brisk, no-nonsense look about her, just as Diane and Mandy had, the job clearly attracting a certain 'type'. Lottie, young and with blue hair, was the anomaly. An anomaly full stop, if she were honest.

"Bad weather out there," Eileen continued, who was senior to her in rank also, the night-shift manager, as it were. "Evie's getting a bit riled, but we'll see how she goes before we call for the duty nurse. As for everyone else, they're in their rooms, tucked up and sleeping. Well, almost everyone. So we should be in for a relatively quiet night."

When she'd said 'almost everyone', Lottie had to suppress a smirk. She knew who wouldn't be: Bobby. She was waiting up for her, had promised.

As Lottie made her way to the staff room, Eileen followed.

"To make this easier," she said, "I've divvied the rooms up. It's what we do, standard practice. You take the first ten rooms, keep checking in. I'll take rooms eleven to twenty."

Bobby's room? Alice's?

Lottie swung round. "Oh, can't it be the other way around? Bobby's my friend. What I mean is, she doesn't sleep well, and…well, she feels comfortable with me." *Not you*, Lottie wanted to say, but only just refrained. Bobby had told her of her dislike for Eileen. 'She should be in the army, she's such a bossy boots, not a care home for genteel men and women.' The way she'd said 'genteel' so sarcastically had made Lottie laugh. But then Bobby had turned serious. 'Swing it, though, won't you? That you get me in your care, as well as Alice. That's the whole point of this, isn't it? To find out about Alice? To help her. And for me and you to have a little nocturnal fun as well. Stand your ground.'

"'Fraid not," Eileen said. "It's already been decided."

"By who?"

Eileen frowned. "Sorry?"

"Who decided you get rooms eleven to twenty?" She was standing her ground, as Bobby had told her to, but Eileen was clearly not going to give an inch, her glare steely.

"I've been working the night shift for two years now. *Two years*. And that's what I've always done, taken rooms eleven to twenty. So that's the way it's going to stay."

Before Lottie could utter another word, Eileen turned and stalked back down the corridor towards rooms eleven to twenty, laying claim, it looked like.

Entering the staff room, Lottie cursed. She'd still see Bobby, no reason why the dayroom couldn't become a night room, but how would she get to Alice? It was a shame the woman only kicked off on Christmas Eve – if she were more of a pain, she'd bet Eileen would readily swap the room quota round. As it was, Lottie had Eve, and, having changed into her uniform and left the staff room, she could hear it already, the sound of keening.

Eileen was back in the corridor when Lottie arrived at Eve's room. "Best check on her," she said, with no offer to help at all. "Calm her down."

"What about the—" She stopped herself before she went any further. In fact, it had shocked her what she'd been about to say: *What about the duty nurse? Shouldn't we just call her?* Because as she'd thought earlier, it'd be easier, and not only for Eve. A little over three months she'd been at Silver Birches, and she was changing, in more ways than one.

"Sorry?" Eileen said. "You were about to say something?"

Lottie shook her head. "It's okay. It's all right. I'll see to Eve. See what I can do."

Of them all, even Alice, Eve was the frailest. So tiny in stature, what flesh she had, shrivelled. There was a bald patch on her head too, the hair around it so fine it was wispy. It broke Lottie's heart to see it, wondering what colour it had been once and how she'd worn it – loose and flowing? Or neatly curled under, like old movie stars.

"Eve," she said, having entered the room and approaching her. "Evie, it's all right. It's just a bit blowy out there, that's all. It'll soon die down."

Eve's room was like all the others, but there were cards on a shelf, at least, several of them to mark a recent birthday, sent from family and friends. Perhaps if Lottie took them down and read out the messages inside, it might calm her.

On seeing Lottie, Eve had gone from keening to whimpering, clutching at the nape of her nightdress. Sitting up in bed, she was so frightened, so helpless.

"Look at these," Lottie continued, gathering the cards. "You got a fair few, didn't you? Who's Miss Popular—?" She stopped herself mid-sentence. *Change your tone. Don't patronise! She is* not *a child. None of them are.*

With the cards in hand, she pulled up a chair to sit beside Eve, the woman's eyes trained on her all the while, wide open and full of angst. Proceeding in what she hoped was now a more conversational tone, the kind she'd use with a friend, with Matt or Bobby, she tried again. "I think I heard Diane mention your children live abroad. You have two, don't you? One in Australia and the other in Singapore? Is that right?" When Eve only continued to whimper, Lottie shrugged. "I think that's right. Okay, let's have a look at these cards. I'll read them out."

Dear Evie, happy eighty-fourth birthday. Love, Winn and Lou.

Eve, hope you're keeping well. Look at us! We've reached a ripe old age. God bless, Agnes Marchant.

Dear Evie, happy, happy birthday. I hope you have a lovely day full of fun.

Like the furniture, the messages were pretty generic too, the handwriting sometimes scrawled, sometimes neat. At last, she got to one she thought might truly soothe her.

To Mum, it read. *Happy birthday. John.*

The words, or rather lack of them, made her frown. No 'dear', no 'love'? *No kisses.* She studied the card closer. It was pretty enough, flowers and butterflies embossed on it, but the printed words were rather plain too: *Wishing you a happy birthday.* Just that.

Another card *To Mum.* This time from Carol and with a koala on it. Clearly, she was the one who lived in Australia. Again, the words were plain, although Carol *had* put a kiss. Only the one, though. And it was tiny in comparison to her big, looped handwriting.

Lottie was so busy contemplating this lack of emotion, it

took her a moment to register that Eve's whimpering had grown louder, soon to become keening again.

Placing the cards down on the bedside table, she stood and bent over Eve, took her hand. "It's okay. It's all right—"

The words died in her throat as feelings, sensations, *images* took over.

A storm. And screaming. Not screaming because of terror, though, nor Eve screaming either, not initially. Others were responsible, and they were scared of something…something *like* a storm. A tempest. A hurricane. Then came Eve's screams, overriding everything. Such anger in them. Blinding anger. John and Carol the target?

Lottie had clutched Eve's hand with the sole intention of comforting her, but, as she'd done with Jenny, she now tried to snatch it back. To her surprise, Eve wouldn't let go. Frail, tiny Eve, afraid of storms, *was* the storm once, lashing out. Was that why she feared storms now? Because they reminded her of who she used to be? Someone out of control?

Still Eve clutched at her, the other hand too…pawing.

There was no choice but to look into the older woman's eyes as she continued to wail. Such a frail woman. Now. But once upon a time, she'd been anything but, had taken her anger out on those who were frail, her children. What part her husband had to play in the matter, Lottie didn't know. Had he even been aware of what went on? Had her friends and family? It seemed that people other than her children liked Eve; the cards she'd received were testament to that. But behind closed doors, had her smile slipped? Lottie could be mistaken, she hoped she was, but had there been a kind of perverted glee in her ability to make the children cower? Had she been drunk on the power of it? John and Carol had left. As soon as they were old enough. Got as far away as possible from her, the bruises on their skin healing, but not the scars inside. They'd sent her cards, both of them, for her birthday. Likely they did that year after year and at Christmas too. Because, despite everything, she was *still* their mother. Not a loving action, though, purely from a sense of duty. This woman – whatever she was now, however much her current distressed state tugged at the heartstrings – wasn't *deserving* of their love. And perhaps, just perhaps, they'd each made peace with that, resolving one thing: not to follow in her footsteps.

Still Eve pawed at her, not keening now but mewling, something so pathetic.

Lottie couldn't help herself. "Eve. Eve, let go!" she shouted, finally managing to extricate herself. "And…and…stop that noise, okay? Just…stop it. There's no storm. All there is, is memories. And I can't help with that. I can't take them away. Unless…"

She was an old, old lady, and because of that, vulnerable. Also because of it, Lottie had believed the best of her, knew she'd had a life but assumed it a normal, run-of-the-mill one. Not so. She'd been a veritable demon when younger, had showed so little mercy… Another vision erupted even though they were standing apart, as though the essence of Eve was in her veins, had polluted them. It was of a hand raised high, which then came crashing down, skin against skin, a beating, and for what? For nothing. That was what.

There'd be more to the woman's history than she'd tuned in to: the reasons behind why she'd lashed out, what she'd experienced that had made her want to do so. Had no one truly noticed, if not the father, then another family member, a teacher, even? The children had confided in no one? Oh, the way the woman was holding her hands out now! So beseeching! Those faded eyes haunted. She wanted Lottie to take them again, to…hold her, just hold her. And if she did, she might see further, get answers to those questions.

But those children, their fear and pain, she couldn't rid herself of the memory of it, nor how wantonly it was inflicted. She didn't *want* more answers. Not yet. But should she do it, show mercy when Eve hadn't? The children had flown, and, subsequently, she'd had so many years to sit and think about her behaviour. At Silver Birches, more than ever.

It must be torture. Ironically. Sheer hell.

It was karma, the very thing Lottie professed not to believe in, in action.

She took a step back, and another, Eve no longer mewling but back to keening, the sound growing louder and louder as Lottie continued to withdraw, becoming earsplitting.

Mercy. *Easy* mercy. That's what she'd bestow on her.

In the corridor, Eileen was approaching. Bobby too had emerged from her room.

"She's not settling," Lottie told them both. "No matter what I do."

"So, what do you recommend?" asked Eileen.

"That we call the duty nurse, get her here as quickly as possible. Sedate her."

Chapter Eleven

December 2023

"Blimey, pet. So that really happened? You…saw, you…felt all that?"

"I did warn you this was a weird story."

Tony nodded. "Aye, you did, and I'm not doubting what you say, not for a minute. I like to think of myself as pretty open-minded. Could be the reason I love ghost stories so much, 'cause I believe in it all, that there's more to this world than just what you can see."

"This isn't your run-of-the-mill ghost story, though, is it?"

Tony smiled. "No, granted. It's more interesting than that. I have to say, though, I'm wondering where all this is heading. What you found out about Alice."

"I'll come to it. I will. I've not really had a chance to go through everything like this before, from start to end. I'm realising how much there is to it, all the layers. Tony, I don't like nagging, and I know the weather's awful still, but can you go just a bit faster?"

"Hey, I'll leave the talking to you; you leave the driving to me."

"Sorry. Yeah, of course. Forecast says it's still better down south."

"Seeing is believing," Tony answered wryly before adding, "although in your case…"

Lottie laughed along before growing serious again. "I *did* see. With Alice. Plenty."

"But with this Evie character, you decided against delving further into her history?"

"That's right. I couldn't change it, and…so, we followed the sedation route. I believe now, I really do, that that was the best option for her too. Although I did take her hand again, just one more time and only briefly, and asked if she'd like to apologise to John and Carol. Because if she did, I'd get in contact with them. I'd let them know."

"And?"

"And as tortured as she was by her memories and her actions, she refused. She snatched her hand back, and she—" Lottie swallowed hard "—she, like, *hissed* at me."

"Hissed? Ye gods!"

"She's gone now. She's dead."

"When?"

"Springtime. Several of them went this year, actually, including one of the newer residents, Valerie. She passed peacefully in her sleep."

"What about Eve? How did she go?"

Lottie hesitated before telling him about the keening that had carried on right till the last, the hands that had grabbed at bedsheets, knuckles white with the effort, refusing to let go, because to do so might mean a reckoning. On the other side, she'd have to face further what she'd done, give reasons for it. Keening just wouldn't cut it.

Although she hadn't liked Eve, as old and as frail as she'd been, Lottie had found at her demise that she didn't wish her any ill. It simply wasn't her place to do so. She'd wondered who'd attend the woman's funeral. Not John or Carol, as it turned out; they'd merely sent cards again. Besides Lottie, it was just a couple of her friends, those who'd survived her and sent cards on her birthday. One of them, Agnes Marchant, saying to Lottie what a wonderful woman Eve had been. 'So kind and helpful. A wonderful mother too. John and Carol were always very smartly turned out, despite that no-good husband of hers never being around. Terrible they couldn't be bothered to travel for their own mother's funeral.'

Ah, what went on in public and behind closed doors, Lottie thought. They could be two very different things, and the face people presented merely a mask.

There was a burst of silence in the cab before Tony spoke again.

"This thing that you can do, you call it an ability?"

"Uh-huh. It seems to fit."

"And your mam doesn't approve?"

"She doesn't, no."

"But what you're doing, clearly trying to help this woman, this Alice, give her some peace, surely that *is* a good thing?"

"I hope so," replied Lottie, although in truth, she didn't know what Alice's reaction would be. Would the knowledge she had appease her? Surely, it wouldn't torment her further?

"Hinny," Tony said, seemingly aware of the sudden conflict within her, "you can only do what you think is best. And right now, you do think you're doing the right thing, don't you?"

"Yes," Lottie's voice was a whisper. "I do."

"Then this ability of yours *is* something good. But…"

When his voice trailed off, she had to prompt him. "But what?"

"Your mam's right, in a way."

Lottie turned her head to look at him. "Oh?"

"You're a young girl," Tony continued, "with a lot of life ahead. You have to strike a balance. Not get caught up too much with death, with too much…darkness, as you put it."

She'd thought this herself after what had happened with Eve and, to an extent, Alice. She'd worried the balance would tip, and not in a favourable way. And so, despite how much she'd grown to love Bobby, she'd looked for another job.

"Funny, isn't it?" she said.

"What is, hin?"

"That when you look at old people, you can be fooled."

"In the way you were fooled with Eve?"

"Yeah. Like, you know they've lived, they've got history, but because they're frail, so *clearly* frail, you think they're like children, as innocent. But they're not. They're as guilty as anybody. They've done great things and bad things, sometimes really bad things. You excuse them because they're of no harm to anyone, but, actually, age excuses nothing."

Tony was nodding, his hands on the wheel, clearly contemplating what she'd said.

"Anyway, that job I went for, it was for an admin assistant in an insurance firm. I didn't tell anyone, especially not Bobby. I didn't want to upset her. And it would, because as much as you might get attached to some of the residents, it, like, works the other way around too, you know? You become a sort of lifeline for them. Me and Bobby spent a lot of time during the night shift in the dayroom, the only time she'd happily go there, 'cause it was just me and her and not the 'elderly'. We got to know each other so well, but…I was young, I was in a conundrum. And this ability of mine, it wasn't going anywhere. If anything, it was getting stronger. In truth, it frightened me."

"Are you frightened of it still?"

More silence. It seemed to stretch in the confines of the car, become exaggerated.

"Sometimes," she eventually admitted. "I just wish I knew others like me. And maybe I will in time. Bobby says like calls to like, so maybe there's someone out there who can help me understand it. And maybe, after tonight, I might even feel better about it. Sorry, I keep going off on a tangent. So I went for this job interview, and I was sitting there opposite this woman, the manager, Shirley her name was, Shirley Seddons, and she was telling me about the job, how *wonderful* it was, sorting post, delivering it to the various departments, and copious amounts of filing. She said there was plenty of opportunity to progress, to become like her, a manager. If I played my cards right, it'd be a job for life. And that's when I knew."

"Knew what?"

"Nothing against Shirley, don't get me wrong, but she wasn't that much older than me, in her early twenties, and already she looked old. As if life had somehow passed her by. And yet, it was clear she loved nothing more than pushing paperwork around. Me, not so much. If I accepted the job – because she offered it to me there and then, on the proviso I changed my hair colour – in a sense my life would be over. It was a safe job, which she kept reiterating. And maybe I didn't want safe after all. So I turned it down and went back to the care home. Don't know where my future lies, but it's not in an office."

"You're young!" Tony insisted. "You'll figure it out. Know what you should do?"

"What?"

"Travel. Buy yourself a ticket to somewhere like Oz, work out there. *Live*."

"Is that something you'd have liked to do?"

Again, Tony laughed. "You keep presuming things about me. Who says I haven't?"

"Oh. Sorry."

"Don't be. I'm just kidding. But meanwhile…I think you're in the right job, pet. Helping people is meaningful, all right? I know there's many who dismiss caring for others as something menial, but it's not. It's *full* of meaning. It's essential. And someone like you who's willing to go the extra mile, you know what that makes you, ability or not?"

"What?" asked Lottie, feeling her cheeks warm.

"Special."

Special. That's what Bobby had called her too. Bobby who'd told her to help Alice, to validate her, who, like Tony, Lottie had told about her ability eventually and, unlike her mother, had encouraged it. 'So fucking special,' she'd said, with pride in her eyes.

A clap of thunder startled Lottie. Tony too.

"It's not directly overhead," he said. "It's behind us, the storm still giving chase."

They were coming up for Leeds when the heavens opened, rain rather than snow tipping down, beating at the windows as mercilessly as Eve had beaten John and Carol.

"Crap!" said Lottie. "We okay to continue?"

"If we take it slowly, like we have been." When Lottie didn't answer, he added, "We'll get there, okay? To the care home. Don't fret."

"I'm trying not to, honestly. Thank you, you know? For not giving up on this."

"Tony's Taxis," he said. "Never any need to look elsewhere. We're the best in Sunderland. Flaming 'ell! It's gone dark again. It's pitch out there!"

It was. But it was apt. Very apt. Because there was so much darkness to the story too.

Chapter Twelve

April 2023

It came out one night in April, all about Matt and his darkness. Lottie sat in the dayroom with Bobby at three in the morning and confessed. She didn't know *why* she did, maybe something to do with that time being the witching hour, when stuff like that seems more real, not just something you've conjured up through imagination.

Once the words were out, they both sat there in silence. And then she did something – maybe it was a test or just a desperate need for reassurance, but she reached for Bobby's hand. Bobby didn't snatch it away, afraid of what Lottie might see in her too, but held it firmly. And Lottie saw nothing, only her own grief, something as sticky and black as tar, tears pouring from her eyes and racing down her cheeks.

"There, girl. There, girl," Bobby kept saying. "That's it. That's all right. A problem shared is a problem halved. But, Lottie?"

"What?" Lottie said when she was able to.

"Matt dying was not your fault, okay? *That's* what you hold on to, not the guilt. Of course he was envious! It's only natural! He wanted to live. All young people do. And so…so he had a moment. Think of it like that. That's what you tuned in to. Just a moment. He took nothing over to the other side but love. Yours, his parents, and all those who knew him."

"Do you think that? Do you really think that?"

"I absolutely do. Don't beat yourself up about it anymore. Let it go. And don't…do that to yourself anymore either."

With her hands still in Bobby's, she looked down to where the older woman was gazing.

The sleeve to Lottie's tunic had ridden up, exposing what was there – some of the lines silver now, but not all. Some were redder, fresher, angrier.

"Oh," Lottie gasped, trying to pull away, but Bobby wouldn't let her.

"It's okay, I understand. The pain of loss…it gets too big sometimes. You have to distract yourself. But find other ways. Better ways. More positive. It's true what they say, time helps, but it won't make the pain disappear, not entirely. It simply becomes a part of you. Your history. Life's never a smooth ride. But let the blame go, and the guilt. Because that really shouldn't play any part in your history. Not with Matt or Evie or anyone."

"Thank you." It was all Lottie could do, whisper such words. This woman understood her when so many wouldn't. Never judged her when so many would, according to Jenny, anyway. Jenny, who hadn't seen the marks on her daughter's arms, who she'd managed to conceal them from, because if she did catch sight of them… Black sheep of the family, that's what grief had turned Lottie into. Jack the golden boy, who did things by the book, went to uni, had friends who stayed alive and abilities that were acceptable.

More than just thank her, Lottie threw her arms around

the person who'd become her best friend in Matt's absence, had stepped into the breach. How could she have thought about leaving this job and moving on? Leaving *her*? She wouldn't, not while there was breath in Bobby's body. She promised herself that, there and then. She'd do right by her.

Bobby's arms came out to hold her, and that's when she felt it, what was in her – a sadness too, just as big, a secret. One she'd stowed away in a box, then padlocked shut.

Maybe it was because she'd stiffened slightly that Bobby did also, then pulled away.

"Bobby…" Lottie muttered, confused. "Bobby, what is it?"

"I'll tell you." Her voice was little more than a croak. "I will. I'll do that. But not now, eh? Not…right now. I need just a little more time."

"Of course! Take all the time you want. I'm not going anywhere."

"Alice," she said, surprising Lottie. "For now, let's do as planned and focus on Alice. Unlike Eve, and unlike me, she's the one that *deserves* help."

* * *

Alice Danes was why Lottie had switched from day shift to night shift, so she could have more contact with her, get to know her better by touching her hand, this woman who Bobby believed deserved help. *Passionately* believed it. Because when she'd said it, there'd been a fire in her eyes again and a pleading: *You have to help her, Lottie, because if you do…it might absolve something in both of us.* Not Bobby's actual words, just Lottie's spin on them, but in which she was sure was a kernel of truth. Sometimes the only balm for your own turmoil was to look outside yourself, spot those in turmoil too and help them.

But the problem remained: Alice was hard to get to, Eileen proving herself something of a rottweiler when it came to guarding her charges.

April turned into May, and still Lottie and Bobby were getting nowhere fast. Despite surreptitiously stalking her, Bobby hadn't spotted where Patsy kept a spare key to the office. And Lottie hadn't managed to creep into Alice's room and hold her hand.

"How are we going to swing this?" Bobby asked Lottie one night in the dayroom, the pair of them munching on meatball marinara subs they'd ordered from Deliveroo.

"I don't know," Lottie muttered. "I just…don't know. Eileen spends a lot of time in Alice's room as far as I can tell. 'Tending to her,' she'll say if I ever ask, but the thing is, Alice *does* nothing. Not by day or night. So, want to know what I reckon?"

"She's grabbing a kip in there?"

Lottie nodded avidly. "Which is why she's so territorial about her charges, because she's having herself an easy time of it on the night shift by grabbing a bit of sleep right alongside her patients, and who's the quietest of them all? Alice Danes."

"We *do* see Eileen, though, going from room to room."

"Yeah, sure. Every half hour or so. It's likely she's on a timer. Worked the night shift for so long, she can sleep according to will."

"You have to get into Alice's room somehow," Bobby muttered.

"I know," said Lottie, wiping red sauce off her chin. "I know."

Wary after Eve, what she didn't let Bobby know was that she was growing warier too of Alice the more that time was passing. She wanted to help her, but was she capable of it? As she'd learnt, just because someone was old and frail didn't mean they always had been. The person they used to be was still inside them. *The monster.* If Alice herself wasn't a monster, then what monstrosities had she suffered? That's what Lottie was afraid of, that insight and what it'd do to her. Once she'd left Alice and the building, returned home, and tried to get some sleep, would the horrors follow?

She checked herself.

She was getting carried away. Being dramatic. And yet, even now, sitting there with Bobby, safe, quite safe, having now finished their subs and disposed of the packaging, her palms were sweating. Maybe she should be glad Eileen was such a rottweiler and pray she stayed that way. Maybe that old saying was true: curiosity really did kill the cat.

"Bobby," she began, about to say this, that perhaps they should leave it...it was *best* to... when Bobby brought her hand to her lips and hushed her.

"What is it?" Lottie whispered.

Soft footsteps. Approaching them. So light...so fleeting...almost like a—

"It's her. It's Eileen."

Lottie frowned. Not a ghost, then. "What's she doing? Tiptoeing down the corridor?" Normally she stomped along; you could hear her coming a mile off.

"A little loo break, probably, then back for a nap somewhere. Now's your chance."

"What? But she might only be in the toilet for a few seconds!"

Bobby turned to her. "She won't, believe me. Hurry. Go

now. To Alice Danes' room."

"But…I'm not sure anymore we're doing the right thing." *Interfering*.

Bobby would not be deterred. "Damn right we are," she said. "Go in there and leave Eileen to me. Just…see. Please. If we're right."

Lottie screwed up her nose. "Right about what? Her sadness?"

How solemnly Bobby shook her head. "Not sadness. *Tragedy*."

Chapter Thirteen

A room. A darkened room. And Lottie in it, unable to see. She *was* Lottie still, she had to be, but also someone else, as if hitching a ride inside another. Perhaps that was the best way to describe it. Seeing the world through two pairs of eyes.

And feeling it too.

Everything was about the feelings. In the end, that's what a person boiled down to, emotions both black and white and all the shades in between. She'd been right to suspect there'd been horror in Alice's life, and that she'd fill Lottie with horror too.

Where are you? Where are you? Tell me where you are! Not her own words, but words that repeated in her mind, such angst behind them, which kept building and building. *TELL ME WHERE YOU'VE GONE!* A dark room, and so anyone could be hiding in it, any*thing*, in the far corners, waiting to pounce as you drew near. To do what? Sink sharpened teeth and ragged claws into you? Devour you? A dreadful thought, but there was one worse still. That the corners were empty. That there was *nothing* there.

A scream. One louder than any keening Eve had been capable of, tearing through Lottie, who brought her hands to her ears to cover them. No use. The sound was coming from inside her. *Produced* by her. Or Alice. Screaming over and over.

She threw herself forwards, her hands outstretched.

Where are you?

Where was who?

There was desperation in her movements as she clawed at the darkness, at the walls that surrounded her. Nails scrabbling so hard, they'd surely leave trails of blood. No more screaming but sobbing instead. A body collapsing in on itself. A protest that kept falling on deaf ears: *You're wrong! Wrong! Wrong.* Fragments, really, and none of them drifting together. Someone had disappeared. Gone. Without informing Alice. And someone was wrong, she claimed. About what?

Previously, when Lottie had first entered Alice's room, it was dark as expected, but not like the darkness she now encountered in this other room, nowhere near as solid. All rooms in the care home had night-lights, which emitted a soft glow come evening time, meant to comfort. Not so in Alice's room. It had seemed eerie instead, and she wondered why it should be so different. But then *everything* about Alice was.

However Bobby meant to delay Eileen, she didn't know. Nor how much time she had. And so, despite her trepidation, her reservations, she'd hurried in there, straight to the woman's bedside, and stood for a few seconds, observing, before taking her hand.

Immediately, she'd been plunged into that other room, into despair. No preamble. Almost as if… *Were you waiting for me, Alice? You know what I can do from when I touched you before, that I can…see. And so you've waited for me?* If that was so, then Bobby was right – she not only needed help, she craved it. Someone to listen at last.

You're wrong! Wrong! Wrong!

The words came again, not aimed at Lottie, dispelling any notions she might have hatched, but screamed at someone else, someone as lost in the darkness as Alice was. Or…who was hiding behind it? Like Eve, wearing a mask?

She was running now, in Alice's mind. Had broken free of the room and was racing along a straight path; on and on it went, narrow like a corridor. Broken free but still trapped because the corridor led nowhere, was as dark as the room, and although more cries left Alice's mouth, the same as before – *Where are you?* – there was still no answer.

"Oh, Alice," Lottie breathed, confused and scared but also despairing, knowing how painful it was to lose someone, to have them ripped from you. "Who was it that left?"

Her past was indeed tragic, as Bobby had suspected. Could it be, however, that the sudden departure of someone, clearly much loved, had led to this – Alice Danes losing her grip on the precipice, on reality, and plummeting into freefall? *Still* falling.

Nothing from Alice, no murmur, no movement. Her hand felt limp in Lottie's, bone-dry.

"Alice, I'm not your carer. Eileen is. And she's coming back soon to sit with you. If you've anything more to show me, do it now. Help me make sense of what you've experienced. If I can help in some way, ease things, I will. I promise."

Nothing. Absolutely nothing. And she had to go, get out of there. She hadn't been in Alice's room long, probably just a few minutes, at least she hoped so. The thing was, she could feel time slipping the longer she held on to Alice's hand, her comprehension of it becoming skewed. In Alice's head there *was* no time. Her body had aged, but events were as fresh as if they'd only recently happened. The emotions attached as strong.

Tears stained her cheeks as she continued to stand there. What united them, other than the touch of flesh, was grief. It was there in all the residents. You couldn't live as long as they had and not experience it in some form. It was simply too much a part of life. Everyone lost at some juncture, be it when they were young or old. But for most it didn't cripple them; they could carry on, take part still in everyday things, smile even. They didn't retract from life, bury themselves alive, their own body the tomb.

"Alice. Oh, Alice. I'm sorry you—"

Another scream erupted in her head, rattled round it with so much force it made her teeth ache. More protests, more insistence. *You're wrong!* And the darkness wasn't so empty after all. There *were* others in it. Or voices, at least. Male. Superior. Cold voices that could turn blood to crystals. What were they saying? She strained to hear above Alice's screaming.

Two men? Three? Lottie imagined a crowd of them, all gathered around Alice, peering down as she looked pitifully up, as she struggled, tried to tell them what had happened, to garner some understanding. *You're wrong. You're wrong, and I'm right. I'm not deluded!*

And in their eyes was their response: *You are* highly *deluded.*

Cold voices and cold eyes. A cold manner that showed no mercy.

A battle. And Alice refusing to give up.

I'm sane. I'm sane. I...am.

Lottie listened to it all in the darkness, only able to

imagine the woman that Alice was – young, so young. As young as she herself was? Could it be? With so much life in front of her. Or like Matt, who *should* have had. But she'd been robbed too.

The men were speaking again.

And they were such familiar words:

"Sedate her."

* * *

"Eileen's ill? Oh, okay, Patsy. And Mandy's coming in tonight to cover? Yeah, that's fine, no problem. I'll be there at eleven, as usual. In just over an hour, in fact. And no, no problems with continuing the night shifts. At least for a while, anyway. I'm happy with it. It…suits me." A short laugh from Lottie, a *forced* laugh. "Yeah, you're right, it must be my age. More able to cope. Anyway, thanks for letting me know. See you soon."

Having ended the call, Lottie stared at her phone. Oh, one thing before you go, Patsy. Tell me where you hide the key to your office, will you? There must be a spare. So where is it? She could imagine Patsy's face if she'd gone ahead and said that, the frown that would try to develop, the lips that couldn't purse. If only she and Bobby knew, though, where it was and could get in there, find the files on Alice and read them. A couple of weeks had passed since she'd last gone into Alice's room, taken again into the darkness, into a room different to the one at Silver Birches – a corridor that was different too, an endless one she'd run down, then hunched on the ground with a circle of men surrounding her, intent on denouncing her. Sedating her. Just as they sedated patients at the care home when they got agitated, administering a little something to relax them. Eve was gone, but now Lottie was back to feeling guilty about what she'd done that night of the revelations, telling Eileen to call for the duty nurse. Too easy. Just…too easy, and the prospect of being even remotely like those men, like Patsy, Diane and Mandy too, painful.

A pain too big for her? Was all this simply too big?

Alice had been young when first sedated. That feeling had now become a certainty. Bewildered Alice. Scared Alice. But also brave Alice. Because she wouldn't be quieted. Not until they'd made her. A strange thought: Had she been quieted all these years, these decades? Had they ever allowed her to surface again?

That was something Lottie hadn't yet found out.

The first night she'd gone in to see Alice, Bobby had locked Eileen in the toilet, albeit temporarily. As a safety feature, all toilets in the home had locks that would release from either side of the door with the use of a special tool. A tool shaped rather like a two-pence coin, which Bobby had just happened to have on her, subsequently jamming it into the outside half of the lock to prevent it from opening.

"How I managed to stop from howling with laughter, I'll never know," she'd later told Lottie. "Eileen was cursing like mad in there. You should have heard what she was saying! Actually, scrub that, I'm glad you didn't. It was enough to make a navvy blush. Grabbed you a good ten minutes, though, didn't it? More if she hadn't tried to kick the door down."

"And she had no idea it was you?"

"I didn't make a sound! When she finally emerged, I hid in the broom cupboard!"

That faulty-lock scenario had worked in their favour a

couple more times, with Lottie on standby, hurrying to Alice's room but always to encounter the same scenario.

"Alice," she'd said, she'd pleaded with her, "you've lived a long time. There's got to be much more to your life than what you're showing me. Tell me."

She was not her carer, as she'd said; Eileen the Rottweiler was, but Lottie cared. That was the difference. Yet how to delve further into her memories?

Eileen had clearly complained to Patsy about the faulty lock, and Patsy had had it changed. It wasn't so easy to jam from the outside now, a tool more sophisticated than a two-pence piece needed and kept in as safe a place as any spare key to the office, which Eileen informed Lottie about with more than a hint of suspicion in her voice. With that ruse put paid to, they had to think of other ways to preoccupy her. Bobby, though, was going through one of her tired phases. A phase where all the sassiness inside her faded and she was as frail as everyone else at Silver Birches, frailer. Those were times Lottie hated, that made her afraid. Made her remember too the secret Bobby held close to her heart, that she'd said she'd tell her in her own time. Lottie could press for it. Had in a way.

"Bobby, are you all right? If you take my hand, I could sit here. Just sit."

"And you could read me too?"

"It doesn't just happen. I have to focus. And I wouldn't. Not without your permission."

"Sit with me, just sit with me. I'll be all right in a few days, you'll see. It's a wave, that's all. They come and they go. Just another wave that needs to crash to shore. Sit with me, and then go and sit with Alice. Find a way. Read her instead. From what you've said, I think she's given you permission. I think she wants this."

Lottie persisted with Bobby, however. "I thought we could tell each other anything." When tears formed in Bobby's eyes, immediately Lottie regretted it. "Oh, Bobby, sorry!"

"Me too," she replied. "Me too." And then she closed her eyes and slept.

Quiet nights. The residents sleeping, mainly, close to death some of them, but none dying, not during the month of May – there seemed to be a reprieve from that. In rooms one to ten, Lottie took a turn sitting with each resident, and, because she was unable to do so with Bobby and Alice, she reached out for them, having to steel herself.

Memories formed. Hazy. Those that belonged to others. A jumble of them. A confusion. Nothing clear. But nothing untoward either that caused concern. Ordinary memories. Days at beaches or in towns, both local and more exotic, with friends or family. Precious times, with tears and laughter. If there was anything extreme, she didn't detect it, the pendulum not swinging too wildly. And they faded quickly. Didn't linger. Didn't plague.

Was she plagued by what she'd experienced with Alice? She had to admit she was. By Bobby's secret too, which stole the shine from her.

Everyone kept sleeping, probably Eileen too in Alice's room. Lottie the only one awake, in the corridor, walking down it, not running as she'd been in that corridor in Alice's mind.

She'd walk alone and yet…not alone. There were people in the building, in their beds, but a sense of something else too: people behind her. Those who had come here to this glorified – or rather not so glorified – waiting room, then passed on.

Not an old building, it was new, purpose-built. Nondescript. Yet life had played out to the end within its walls, kept doing so on a loop. It was a new building ingrained with endings. And so it could well be them at her back, those who'd taken their last breath in one of twenty rooms. The likes of Dan, Dot, Valerie, and very possibly Eve, her mouth wide open still, keening, but silently. Real hauntings? Or merely shades, with no substance to them? The essence of such transient passengers taking time to dissipate. It was the unknown that people were afraid of, where they were going from here, to heaven, to hell, or neither, but into further oblivion. Perhaps that's why something of them lingered, because there was nothing out there, only darkness, a void akin to that which Alice was trapped in, in life, as opposed to death. One chance for the flame of existence to burn brightly, and for her it never had.

For a second, Lottie wondered if Matt would be in amongst the spectres. There because he was attached to her. Because he was…angry with her still. If she turned, would she see him, his mouth as wide open as Eve's, raging?

Or would she see nothing? Imagination having sprouted wings and flying.

She longed to turn as she continued down the corridor, so, eventually, she did. There was nothing. The air seemed to shimmer and waver, though, as if it were indeed alive, the space far from empty, crackling almost, with what…energy?

Perhaps if she was quicker next time…

She was due for another night shift that evening, and this time, because Eileen was sick, it was with Mandy on co-duty. Did Eileen know Mandy? Had she specified which residents she took care of, those in rooms eleven to twenty?

Alice Danes.

She'd find out soon, she guessed. But if she could gain access into Alice's room tonight, legitimate access, she'd do it, bend low and whisper into her ear:

"It's time, Alice. It really is. Be brave again, and I will too. Go beyond the black room."

Chapter Fourteen

Alice was coming round, gaining consciousness, trying to open her eyes, but the light hurt, so forced her lids shut again. Perhaps she should cry out instead, her lips already working to form words, but it felt strange, as if her mouth was stuffed with something…wet rags? She couldn't control her jaw, nor, when she tried, her limbs, wishing she could lift her hands and pull those rags out of her mouth, not cry out but scream.

Where am I?

And then to scream again.

Where did you go?

Memories surfaced, fast, too fast, a jumble of them and nothing clear. There were men standing around her, she knew not who, their faces long and pointed, their eyes dark. They were looking at her as if she were…deluded. That's what they kept calling her. Mad.

Then one had spoken, one whose eyes were particularly empty. 'Sedate her,' he'd said. And although she'd struggled, had told them no, a syringe had been produced, magicked out of nowhere, it seemed, scratching at her skin before driving deep, and then…then there was only darkness. A *world* of darkness. Darkness in which she'd lost herself, in which she'd run and run, searching. To no avail. The darkness was gone now, the stark lighting having replaced it, but there was no relief, only a sense of further foreboding.

"Alice? Alice? Good, you're awake. Sit up for me."

Someone was speaking. A woman. Was it her whom she was addressing?

"Alice! Come on! We don't have all day. Sit up so we can examine you. We need to make sure you're…clean before admitting you."

Admitting her where?

She couldn't move, felt so sluggish. Her mind the same. More memories were trying to surface, but it felt like they were pushing through treacle – a *wealth* of memories, yet for now this woman, this stranger, was prodding her, the tips of her fingers like ice.

It was cold, it was bright, and there was a smell too, acrid, that stung at her eyes and made her nose twitch. Disinfectant? If so, it had been liberally used.

More hands. More women's voices.

"Is she clean? We're not at risk here?"

"She seems to be."

"What a way to spend Christmas, eh?"

"Christmas? Ha! It doesn't exist here! You're right, though. This is no way to spend it. Next year, no way. Oh, come on, Alice! For God's sake! Move yourself."

The women were stripping her! Removing the dress she'd worn, her undergarments, leaving her naked and shivering. Still they prodded, searching, it seemed. For what?

"Hose her down."

No sooner had those words left one of their mouths than she was pushed against a tiled wall, a blast of water on her skin, an *attack* of water that was freezing. At last, a scream escaped her. Forced upwards from deep within, unstopping what else was there. More screams, crying and begging, but it elicited no sympathy, no understanding whatsoever; indeed, the women appeared to be smiling! Having some fun after all.

By the time they'd finished, she'd collapsed again, was in a corner, her hands brought up to her mouth, her teeth chattering and lips mouthing nothing but gibberish. She was hauled to her feet, and they dried her with towels that scratched at her skin, then a dress was forced over her head, nothing like what she was used to, the material as rough as the towel, every bit as uncomfortable. Then, with the women standing either side of her, dressed in white like angels, but far from it – nurses? – she was half carried, half marched from the room they'd been in into a corridor, also tiled, half green and half white, *grubby* tiles, a black mould in the cracks, and dragged down it, such a long, long corridor, until they reached a door at the end.

One nurse detached herself briefly from her to push at the door, holding it open so they could pass through. That was when something other than the stench of the place hit her, the *noise*. It was like an explosion in her head, making her long for the corridor again, for that room in which she'd been kept, far, far away from it. It was a hellish noise, comprised of crying and shouting.

Disorientated, she was now terrified. Why was she in a place like this? She didn't belong there! And if not, if that was the case, then where did she? Because inside her was a sense of…displacement. Was that it? She'd lost things. *Vital* things. Things she should never have lost. Because without them, she'd go mad. Quite mad. As mad as those in here were.

That was where she was: a madhouse. The noise proved it, that of the afflicted. The scene that met her proved it too.

It was a room, large and square, not tiled but plastered, cracks running through that too, a light in the middle of the ceiling which only cast further gloom.

There were chairs, high-backed some of them, others more like stools, scattered haphazardly, no cohesion to them. There were tables, some empty, some with cups on, and plates, other plates on the floor, as if hurled there. And there were so many people. Either sitting on chairs or slumped over tables, or milling around in circles, their mouths open as they cried, their misery unbearable. One girl, one young girl, just as she herself was young, drew her attention more fully. Not on a chair or walking, she was at the far end, slumped against the wall there, and she was tearing at her hair, tearing and tearing at it, her efforts successful given the bald patches. She was wailing too, her mouth stretched open and her eyes as wide as could be, leaking tears. It was a silent wail, though, as if her voice had given up, shrivelled inside her from too much use, so she went through the motions, only that. Would her tears eventually dry too? Or was the well they were drawn from bottomless?

A scene of horror that you might suspect existed, for the mad must be put somewhere, but never acknowledged. For why would you trouble yourself in such a way? Their plight was their own. It could never be yours.

When she could drag her eyes from the girl, she noticed something else.

A tree! In the corner. A pine or a fir, placed in a tin bucket. A tree whose branches might have been luxuriant with needles once, the green of it resplendent, but which was now greyish in colour and sparse, the needles having not just fallen off naturally but been *raked* off by eager hands, troubled hands, intent on destruction.

Hands belonging to those around her.

The tree might once have been adorned with baubles too, silver or gold, strands of tinsel adding further glitter and sparkle. There were *still* baubles, or rather evidence of them, the golden strands they'd hung from, plus one that twirled round and round, perfect from one angle, and then from another you saw it was caved in, for nothing perfect could exist here. Yet someone had tried, because of the season, to make it special.

The season. Christmas. It prompted another memory. Someone had wanted to make it special for her too. Had tried so hard. And now this. *This*. An asylum. And no sign of that someone.

The nurses had hold of her arms, squeezing so tight she was sure they'd leave bruises. They seemed to revel in this, a patient's first sighting of what awaited them, their fate.

That tree. That poor tree. Ripped from its roots and put here. For what? To die.

Exactly that.

They were holding her arms, but still she managed to break free, to reach up just like that girl in the corner and grab at her own hair and pull and pull at it. Unlike the girl's, her voice was not used up; it returned with a vengeance, and she utilised it.

"NO! NO! NO! I do not belong here. I don't."

As the two nurses grappled with her, her fist shot out, making contact with the slighter of the two, with her jaw, a cry escaping her too, which she welcomed, which she gloated over, just as they had gloated seconds previously. They deserved to scream and cry just like the patients here, poor, poor patients, whom they had not one iota of sympathy for. They were not responsible for that tree. If there was someone kind here, it wasn't them.

Nor was there sympathy in who was heading towards her as the scuffle continued. A man, his stride determined and one hand held aloft as patients scattered in his wake, turning away with hunched shoulders, trying to make themselves smaller. No crying now. No wailing. All were silent, apart from her. "No! Don't. Get away from me. All of you! Get away!"

What he held aloft was by now familiar to her. It was what the long-faced, dark-eyed doctor had held in his hand too, waving it in front of her before he plunged the needle deep into her arm. Should she really fight against it? For she also knew it would deliver some respite, if only for a short while. From this. From hell. Perhaps darkness – her last thought before the scratch of the needle, so sharp, before more cold fluid rushed into the corridors of her veins rather than pummelled at her skin – was all there was now.

And she should be grateful for it.

* * *

"Incarcerated! So young! And in an asylum, it sounds like. A nuthouse."

As usual, Bobby didn't pull any punches when Lottie visited her later and told her what she'd found out, in need of a bit of comfort, if she were honest. For what she'd seen – what she'd experienced alongside Alice – she was reeling from it.

"I wonder what she'd done to invite that?" Bobby continued to muse.

Lottie's voice was harsher than intended in response.

"Invite? You really think she *invited* that on herself? Those places…were they really like that? So…cruel?"

Bobby looked more contrite as she nodded. "Never seen the inside of one, but you hear tales, don't you? They could be pretty harsh. Like prisons. Worse, even."

"What was her crime, then? Why was she locked up? As far as I could tell, she had no idea why. Was as confused as we are."

"Oh, the things they could lock you up for back in the day!" At last, Bobby's face was as anguished as her own surely was. "The conditions they tried to cure you of! Hysteria. That's one of the reasons women were locked away through the ages. *Hysteria.* What the hell does it even mean? If you raised your voice, if you dared to disagree with someone, *showed temper*, you'd be diagnosed with hysteria? And your husband, the man in charge of you, could lock you away for it? In one of them places. Men! I'm glad I never…well, I'm glad I never married. Although, I'm telling you, people looked askance at me because of it, couldn't figure out why. 'You're a woman, so you *must* get married. You *need* a man.' That was the intimation. Women don't. They're better off on their own!"

Whereas Bobby had received the news of what Alice had gone through fairly objectively, she was now growing as riled, as affronted, as Lottie.

"Bobby?" Lottie said, reaching out. "Are you okay?"

Bobby moved her hand just before Lottie made contact, and Lottie tried to conceal her hurt about it. This woman knew of her ability and had encouraged her to use it, had said she was special because of it, like Matt had, that she was someone with the potential to help others in a unique way. So why retract her hand the way she had? So harshly. As if

Lottie wasn't special at all but someone worthy of locking up too? *In a madhouse.*

Bobby must have noticed the confusion on Lottie's face, because suddenly she smiled, waving a hand in the air as if to dismiss what she'd done, what she'd said.

"Sorry, sorry, sorry. Ignore me. Just getting carried away, that's all, at the way society treats some people. It's…a bugbear. But this isn't about me, it's about Alice. So she was in an asylum, eh? And at a young age. At *your* age. Or thereabouts. I wonder…"

"Wonder what?"

"How long she was in there for. Or…"

Again, her voice trailed off.

It was nearly 5.00 a.m. Another couple of hours and Lottie would be clocking off. Before that, she'd need to go and check her quota of residents, make sure all was well. With Mandy on tonight instead of Eileen, Lottie's were those in rooms eleven to twenty. It'd been easy to switch it up; Mandy hadn't questioned it at all, looked as if she couldn't care less, in fact. For why *would* it matter? The woman would simply do her job, *perfunctorily*, getting double pay, thank you very much, then she'd go home and forget all about it. Sleep until the next shift. Normal dreams, hopefully. Untroubled. But for Lottie…she knew what her dreams would revolve around later. Not a darkened room full of mystery, in which some kind of loss had occurred. They'd feature a room full of *people*, who wailed, who screamed and tore at themselves. For whom the only respite was enforced oblivion and a different kind of darkness. Would Eileen be back on duty in time for the next night shift? Or would she remain ill? Mandy there again instead?

Because if it was Mandy, then, once again, Alice would

be Lottie's responsibility.

She returned to the moment. "Sorry, Bobby. Or what? You were saying?"

"Oh, yes. Yes, I was, wasn't I?" she replied quite airily, before her expression once again darkened. "What if…Alice never left?"

"Never left the asylum?"

"Uh-huh. That's right. Not until she had to because asylums were being shut, so many of them, up and down the country, that 'care in the community' business replacing them instead. Dispossessed. Yet again. Also, she was older, more docile. *Catatonic*. So she was transferred to places like this. *Care homes*." Bobby spat those last two words out, her face a perfect picture of disgust before continuing, sadder more than anything now. "What if she's spent all her life in care? Institutionalised. Or rather, from what you've seen, all her life *not* being cared for." After a sigh that was deep and protracted, she focused on Lottie, her gaze sharpening. "Can you bear to do it again? Hold her hand and tune in? In a sense, hear her, when clearly she's not been heard for a long, long time."

Lottie couldn't deny it; she'd been half hoping that for the next shift, Eileen *would* be back. And so she'd have an excuse not to. Even so, she agreed. "Yes. Of course. Although…I'm not sure what good it's going to do. Apart from satisfy our curiosity."

"Oh, I think it'll do some good." Bobby was emphatic. "I think she has to be heard. Before it's too late. She has a story. We *all* do, but hers…well, hers may be a little more colourful than most. And I'm sorry about that, Lottie, I really am. I'm sorry for all of it."

Chapter Fifteen

The dark room with no one there – *no one*. A place of horror, or rather a place where horror had begun, but, for Alice, that started to change. It was a place she returned to again and again, if only in her mind, because as dreadful as it was, it was better than the place she was in – a *succession* of places. And each one worse than the last. More brutal.

No kindness at all in some of them. And yet there had been in that first one, even if what their kindness had resulted in, a tree decorated for Christmas, had only served to drum home the cruelty of her situation, the unfairness of it. But it had *still* been a kindness, and she'd never found out who was responsible for it, not in all the time she'd been there – couldn't, her mind too addled from the tablets they made her swallow, holding her jaw shut as soon as they were on her tongue and pinching at her nostrils until she had to swallow. Medication that left her lifeless almost, a passenger trapped inside a body, unable to call out, beg for help, for understanding. *This is a mistake! You know it is. I shouldn't be here.* And such, such confusion as to why she was! She tried so hard to remember what was before. Because there *was* a before, a before that was…wonderful, and a before that *wasn't* wonderful, a whole mix of memories, a muddle, those that populated them wispy shadows. She must continue to try, though, because if she could remember, and remember clearly, then she could explain. Succinctly.

Without hysteria. Her eyes remaining dry. That's what she must strive for. *To appear sane.* Because only if she was sane would they listen, would they stop the tablets. Surely?

She was upright but had no idea how. She'd been lying down previously on a long, thin stretch of bed, the mattress hard and lumpy, making her bones ache. But now she was upright, on her feet and shuffling forwards. Going somewhere.

"Hey! Hey, don't wander! Get back in line. Take your lunch. Eat it."

Were they calling to *her*? The voice stern. *Eat your lunch. Eat it all. Don't waste it. We'll have no waste. There's punishment for waste.* Punishment for everything. But most of all for being alive, for breathing, for being nothing more than a burden. Surely better not to eat, then? Why press her? Better that she starve and die.

No!

She mustn't give up! She mustn't because…there *was* someone else. Someone whom she had to help, rather than the other way around. That they'd taken away too, but where? Not to the same places she'd been. She hadn't seen them again. Someone who was…

She doubled over, the pain in her stomach as sharp as a knife, causing her to retch.

"Danes? Danes! Stop that! Get out of line. Step away."

Get in line. Get out of line. What did these people want? Nothing she did was right or could appease them.

There were hands on her as she retched, pulling her towards the corner of the room, where whatever was in her stomach, something meagre, could be emptied. Vomit spewed from her mouth, a stream of it, burning at her insides. It hurt, but her pain was clearly amusing for some, for whooping accompanied her plight, clapping, and a sound like that of a hyena, high and excited. It didn't amuse the nurses, though, for she'd splashed one of them, and for that a cane was snatched and the backs of her legs whipped until she buckled further onto the floor, lying in the mess she'd created.

A bucket and a mop were thrown at her, a harsh clatter as they hit the floor.

"Clean it," the nurse demanded. "It's your mess, so you can clean it."

Scrubbing and scrubbing. Such a small amount of water in the bucket, not enough to do the job properly. More whipping. And more of that hyena laugh. The darkness. It was all she could pray for. To go back to that room. And keep searching.

* * *

"An ideal candidate, don't you think?"

"Possibly. I don't know what else to suggest. She seems so…hopeless otherwise."

"I agree. And prone to outbursts of aggression, thus putting our staff in danger. We can't have that. This should be a safe place to work."

"It's a shame, isn't it? She's a reasonable enough–looking girl. Fairly young. It's simply terrible how diseased the brain can become."

"Shall we book her in?"

"Of course. Of course. I'll consult the diary."

"And in answer to your question, yes, it is a terrible shame when such diseases strike, how they reduce a person thus, eat away at all that is human. But what you propose, the operation, it may well be the answer – transform her, give the woman her life back yet. Although…her original notes state, 'permanent state of disorder', yet they also only go so far back. I wonder if she was like this in childhood? Born this way, even?"

"Perhaps. But nothing ventured, nothing gained."

"Absolutely. It's her only chance. For her benefit and for ours, whatever the outcome of the procedure."

Procedure? What procedure were they talking about? She had no idea. Was too afraid to open her eyes, to see who was talking. Doctors, of course. The kind that *always* talked about her. That stood over her, peering down, examining the specimen, looking so interested sometimes, *fascinated*, but always talking, never listening. Not once.

No matter, for she'd forgotten what she'd wanted them to listen to, the point she had to make. It was in there still, but too deep; she couldn't reach it or understand it, understand the point of anything. They were talking about a procedure, one they intended to perform on her. To help her? The 'ideal candidate'. Could it possibly?

They'd said she was aggressive. But if she hit out, it was only because she wanted to make them listen. If words were no use, she'd use actions instead. And what about those who were aggressive towards her? She'd been hit, whipped, slammed into walls, had her hair yanked so hard she thought her neck might snap, and bones broken. She'd heard the snap of them, seen blood exploding from her nose, a fountain that sprayed over everything. Yet *she* was the aggressive one? People needed to be protected from *her*?

This procedure, would it render her harmless? And if harmless, how long would she last where she was with the *harmful*?

There were those amongst them who would rock to and fro. Rosie, in particular. And Eammon. The nightshirts they wore riding up and exposing what should stay private. She knew that she remained still, but she was rocking too, in her mind, back and forth, back and forth, growing so agitated. *I don't want the procedure! I don't want anything you have to give.* They wanted to cure her because she was mad. And perhaps she was now. But not always. Those notes they'd talked about, *her* notes, they only went so far back, so as a child she might not have been mad? Not until here, where they'd driven her towards it.

Think! Think! It's all inside you. Somewhere.

Not madness, not that, but something…something terrible. Something that *could* have driven her mad, the grief of it. But before that… *Think!* Before that…laughter…is that what she could hear? And if so, whose? A child's laughter! So innocent, so beguiling that it made you want to laugh too. She could do that, laugh along. Use muscles in her face disused for so long. Try to reach whoever it was that life *hadn't* broken. Who saw the…*magic* in everything. That was it! The child was laughing because everything was magical. But what specifically? What could possibly be magical in this world?

"Is…is the patient laughing?"

"I'm not sure. Laughing…or grimacing. It's hard to tell."

"That's the trouble with them, isn't it? Even they don't know the difference."

A tap against her forehead was as unkind as she'd expected it to be.

"The stuff that goes on in there! The brain really is so complex."

"And we know so little about it. But as long as there's

people like her…"

More laughter, his not hers. "Indeed! At the very least, they help us to learn."

At the very least…

No more laughter in her throat, and no more digging for memories. Memories didn't matter. Not here. All that mattered was the room, the blackened room, which was another prison, but so what? *They* weren't there, these people, no one from the asylums were. It had become her only home, a sanctuary, and so she'd go back there. Such a dark room with dark corridors leading to it. No tiles beneath her feet as on the floors in the asylum, against which the nurses' shoes made such a racket, but softness, no noise at all. She'd be alone. The very thing that had inspired this dread. Yet now it was the only thing to give comfort. There'd be nothing and no one. A void she'd be lost in.

After the procedure, perhaps forever.

* * *

Untethered before. Now even more so. Adrift, in darkness, and no clear route back.

The procedure had been performed. On some level she knew that, had been told.

"A great success, Miss Danes! We believe we have restored your soul back to you and that you will continue to improve. Miss Danes? Alice? Can you hear me? We will monitor you, keep a close eye, but as I've said, we're confident you will continue to improve. In time." Laughter that seemed familiar, a bellow of it. "You may even be able to live independently. Again, all in good time. We shall see. Certainly, we know patients that have been able to after the procedure, been restored to some semblance of sanity, enough not to cause a problem to society, at any rate. To disrupt it. Until then, you'll stay here. You're comfortable here, I've been told, while we watch for signs of improvement."

Did they watch? she wondered. Over the years? Certainly, people entered her room, came and went, came and went. Some stayed longer than others and did indeed seem to be watching. There were others that…touched her, which she was used to, although not in this new way, their touch accompanied by strange grunts, their breath on her cheek, fetid.

No matter. Not when she had the room to escape to. There she could hide whilst they touched, they grunted, they watched, leave them to do whatever it was they desired. She couldn't feel it so couldn't contemplate it. A blessing. Such a blessing. Only when they'd gone would she unfurl in that dark room and start wandering the corridors, her arms flung out either side. How tightly the darkness wrapped itself around her! It carried her. Sometimes she would open her mouth, to utter what words, she didn't know. She *used* to know. She'd be calling for someone. *Where are you? Where are you?* But no longer. Her mouth was open but otherwise silent. Words had dried up after all. Tears certainly had. Long ago. The well empty of everything. Any…ambition. Really no matter and, because of that, a freedom in it. The only freedom she'd known in so long. Freedom but not happiness. Happiness was forgotten. Magic was. Perhaps they'd never existed, any prior memories false. No happiness, but peace. The black room both a torture and a joy.

In the end, it might become nothing too.

Chapter Sixteen

December 2023

"I know I told you I wanted a scary story, pet, but I was talking about ghosts and ghouls, the regular kind that jump out at you from the wardrobe or behind a closed door. Spectres that hover over you whilst you're asleep, that disappear when you open your eyes – although not straightaway, a split second after, just enough time to let you know that they *were* there and would be coming back as soon as you closed your eyes again and were vulnerable. Honestly, hinny, I did not expect this. The kind of horrors that happen in real life. Flaming 'ell! If what you're saying is true, then you're right, this woman has truly suffered. What they did to her, the procedure, we're talking about a lobotomy, aren't we?"

Lottie nodded. "We are. Performed when she was twenty-eight. *Twenty-eight*! I've since read up on it, me and Bobby did. It's where they drill into the skull, into your brain, then push a sharp instrument in, sweeping from side to side to sever the connection between the frontal lobe and the rest of the brain."

"Ouch! That's bloody barbaric!"

"It was, and it was outlawed in the seventies because they realised more were suffering from it than being cured.

Effectively, they were turning people into zombies."

Tony took his eyes briefly off the road to look at her. "Like in *The Walking Dead*?"

Lottie smiled. "You know that show? Bobby liked it too. I started watching it, but…it kind of lost its appeal since finding out about Alice. But like we were saying, it was barbaric, it made matters worse, but actually there were some doctors who genuinely looked upon it as, like, a miracle cure. They started performing it back in the nineteen thirties, and it was considered 'the new surgery of the soul'. They called it that 'cause they thought that's what they were handing back to the patient, their very soul, restoring them, not destroying them. And maybe with some people it did improve them. Got neuropathways firing again."

"Not with Alice, though?"

"Not with Alice. But…"

"But what?"

"I think she *chose* to stay hidden, inside herself, I mean. I think she just believes she's safest that way. Even now. Even at her age. *More* so, maybe. Because they can't destroy people, the doctors, not in the way they think they can. Everything you've ever said and done remains inside you; it's logged somewhere, a kind of blueprint, and it doesn't fade. They didn't hand her back her soul – they handed no one back their souls – but they never took it from her either, because the soul, it seems, is untouchable. Jeez, this weather! It's not letting up, is it, like it's supposed to? The rain and wind are ferocious still."

"We're still moving. That's what counts," Tony reminded her. "All of us are. The holiday traffic. The determined. People don't let a little thing like weather put them off, not when it's Christmas, which comes but once a year. So did you dig deeper? With Alice?"

"I did. I tried. I dug and dug and dug. I became…very protective of her when I realised what she'd suffered, the abuse…"

A moment of silence. "Aye, I was coming to that. I know you didn't say it in so many words, *she* didn't, but she was…abused in the asylums? In a particular way, I mean."

"I shouldn't be shocked by it. That kind of stuff goes on, back then, anyway, and there were times I thought I had to let it go, what had happened to her, but…when I realised *that* had happened too, then no way. I'd help her like I'd promised, listen, no matter how hard it got. And I'd find out the truth, why she was put in the asylum in the first place, which I have. I really think I have. We all deserve peace, but her more than anyone."

Even though he didn't know the whole story, not yet, Tony was nodding avidly. He didn't doubt her, think her as insane as Alice had been accused of being.

"You're a gift," she said, before quickly adding, "Sorry."

"Sorry? For what, pet? For saying I'm a gift?"

"Yeah. Well, I'm sorry for saying it like that, for blurting it out."

Tony laughed, a belly laugh, like the doctors used to laugh around Alice when discussing her, but, unlike them, with no hint of malice in it, no sense of superiority or self-satisfaction. It was genuine, heartfelt, as were his next words. "I think I quite like being called a gift," he declared. "But you know what, by the same token, so are you."

"Me? In what way? For Alice, you mean?"

"For Alice, for Bobby—" a slight hesitation before he continued "—and for me."

She frowned. "For you? I'm ruining your Christmas!"

"You've ruined nothing. You see…I hate this time of year."

"Hate it? Why?"

"Because I've no one, that's why."

"You said you had family in London."

"I have."

Lottie was genuinely confused. "Well, then you have got someone!"

"They're family, but I haven't seen them in a long while, in years. Cousins, that kind of thing. Who've got their own thing going on, who won't want to see me."

"Why not?"

"Why would they? I'm as good as a stranger to them. Why on earth would they want someone to gate-crash their Christmas Day?"

She thought about it. "Christmas is a time to welcome family. To welcome everyone. *We'd* welcome you at our home. My mum, brother, and me."

"Thank you, hinny. Thank you so much. But I'd soon as turn around and go back."

"But the weather…?"

"We're managing now, aren't we? So I'll manage on the way back as well. I'm just your cabbie, pet; don't feel responsible, and I'm sorry, I shouldn't have said anything. It's just…I wanted you to know, to realise. *You're* a gift too. You want to save Alice, and you've saved me. Tomorrow, I'll be too tired to realise how lonely I am, and if you *do* save Alice, give her some peace, I'll feel happy too, warm inside. Knowing I played a part in it."

Lottie smiled. "I suppose we're both gifts together," she said at last. "And I know you're just my cabbie, and I'm just your passenger, but I'm glad we met, Tony of Tony's Taxis."

He glanced at her and winked. "Aye, me too. And I'm enjoying your story. But do me a favour, will you?"

"'Course. Anything!"

"Give Tony's Taxis a good rating online afterwards. It all helps."

"You'll get all the stars in the sky, I promise."

"There's a good g—"

"Jesus!"

It had gone from sleet to snow and back to rain again the further south they got, but they'd been dealing with it, managing – slow going, as Tony had said, but still eating up the miles – not even stopping for coffee, although both might need a loo stop soon. Doing well, really well. They'd reach the care home in plenty of time, perhaps even before Alice kicked off, which by last year's reckoning, would be around six o'clock. Lottie could perhaps *prevent* her from kicking off and the distress it caused her, soothing her, saving her, as Tony had said, as Bobby had, that poor, poor woman in whom there was a world of pain and all of it inflicted on her.

Yes, they'd been going great guns, when someone just had to come along and spoil it.

A driver in a BMW in the outside lane, going way too fast for the wet weather, had lost control and careered across the motorway, aquaplaning. Missing them, but only by a hair's breadth as it slid across the lanes, not hitting anyone, miraculously, but flying into the hard shoulder instead, then spinning back out again as Tony and all the other motorists slammed on their brakes, everyone coming to a shuddering halt.

Lottie had hunched over and screwed her eyes shut, sure,

absolutely sure they wouldn't escape carnage, that they might even be killed outright.

Time slowed right down in those seconds, images flashing before her eyes. Her life, no one else's, just Lottie Beck's, aged nineteen. *Forever* nineteen, at this rate. And in it there was laughter, plenty of it, with her mother, her brother, her friends, but most of all, Matt.

Dear Matt. He was at the heart of everything. Her sidekick, her sounding board, her fellow adventurer. She'd forgotten they'd gone so often to a patch of barren land at the back of the rec to play when they were younger, there to build dens they could hide in from the rest of the world. He was such a great architect! Talented in every way. A loss. Such a terrible loss. And yet all she could see was him laughing. No evidence of any darkness in him at all. And it was wonderful. In such a terrifying moment, it was magic.

Matt. Oh, Matt! I miss you.

He laughed again, the blue of his eyes twinkling. So very young. So cruel what had happened. To him, to Alice, to so many. And yet…there he was, laughing. And it did something to her; it lessened the pain she felt at such cruelty. Blew it clean away.

He was mouthing something: *I'm all right.* Was that it?

Something else too. Something clearer.

And I miss you too, you crazy girl. But you're doing great. Keep on. Just keep on, okay? You can open your eyes now. Go on. Open them. You're all right too.

"Open your eyes. It's okay, pet. It's all right. We're not in any danger."

It was Tony speaking, not Matt, although Matt *had* spoken; she was sure of it.

"We're okay?" she checked, tentatively peering around

her. The BMW was moving back towards the hard shoulder, against a backdrop of people blaring their horns at him and gesturing, but otherwise driving by. Tony put the car into gear and started driving too.

"Bloody beamer drivers. They're as bad as those in Audis, I swear it," he said. "Think they own the road. Who the hell drives like that in conditions like these? Hope he's giving himself a good talking to. Are you okay, hin? We'll stop for coffee soon. I think we could both use it, settle our nerves before we carry on. A pit stop, though. We won't be long."

"Yeah, sure. That's fine."

"This journey takes 'Driving Home for Christmas' to a whole new level, don't you think? Chris de Burgh should have counted himself lucky. Oh, hinny, I'm sorry. So sorry."

"Hey! It's not your fault! You reacted brilliantly and in the nick of time." Because he no doubt would have hit them, the man in the beamer, if Tony hadn't been so swift. *Matt, I could have come for you. We'd be together again. Can you imagine?*

The near-crash was over, was just another memory, and they were cruising forwards again under stormy skies on Christmas Eve, their destination Silver Birches in Watford. Still in this world. Rooted. And yet she could hear Matt's voice again, answering her.

I can imagine. I'm counting on it. One day. But not yet. Not for a long while. Until then, listen to me: like I said, keep keeping on. I'm all right. It's like you said, it's fun.

She didn't realise she was crying, not until Tony reached out and laid a hand on her shoulder. "Hey, hey, hey! Come on! It's okay. We're fine. Oh, hin, you're trembling. That was a terrible thing to happen. Really awful."

She pulled away, looked at him, and smiled through her

tears.

"I don't think it was, actually," she said.

He looked confused. "What?"

"I don't think it was a terrible thing to happen. I think it was a gift too. Another one. You're right, you know. What a Christmas this is turning out to be!"

Chapter Seventeen

June 2023

Eileen didn't come back. Lottie had no idea why, and Bobby professed not to know either. At first. But Lottie knew Bobby well enough to know she wasn't quite telling the truth; it was the way she averted her gaze when declaring she'd had nothing to do with Eileen's departure, concealing a slight smile on her lips.

"Bobby? Come on! What is it? What did you do?"

"I may…or may not…have dropped some vodka in her coffee, on one or two or three occasions. And I may…or may not…have filed a complaint about it to Patsy, who we know drinks on duty, who reeks of whisky sometimes. She's such a hypocrite, isn't she? When we find the spare key, look for the bottle, okay? Just to confirm."

"And so she got fired?"

Bobby hunched her shoulders. "She must have done. We've not seen her since."

It was true; they hadn't. It had been either Mandy on night duty or bank staff, and, therefore, Lottie remained in charge of rooms eleven to twenty. She had easy access to Alice now, but although she'd finally got beyond the black room, she was now back there, given an insight into the woman's time at the asylums, but brief. Alice hiding again.

"The thing is, there was a start point in all this," Lottie said to Bobby, the pair of them back in the dayroom, the residents sleeping – her lot, anyway – during her last round of checks. As it was warm, the summer in full swing, they had a fan in front of them to keep cool. "She wasn't always in asylums. She was taken there around my age, definitely around my age. So she came from somewhere, and…she did something."

Bobby nodded her head thoughtfully. "Something that brought the doctors to that room, that saw them encircle her, and she was protesting, shouting for someone."

"That's right. Someone who'd disappeared. So who was it, and where'd they go? But when she continued to protest, to insist on it, there was only disbelief in those doctors' eyes. They saw only hysteria. Someone who needed to be locked up."

"And the key thrown away," Bobby said, sighing. "That's what I don't get. There appears to be no crime here, unless…"

Lottie was quiet when she spoke. "Unless she murdered them, you mean? The person that disappeared. And then she couldn't accept it? Went straight into denial?"

Bobby nodded. "Unless she really is mad."

The chair squeaked as Lottie reclined. "I know it's easy to be fooled by those who look vulnerable. We forget that that sweet old lady or gent sitting in a corner or lying helpless in a bed was young and robust once, was capable. But I don't know, Bobby…Alice as a murderer? I've sat with her in the dead of night, and…like…I don't feel she's that."

"But it *is* possible," Bobby said. "Because in life, frankly, anything is. And…you know…sometimes there are reasons for murder, if not good reasons, then…justifiable. If people suffer at the hands of others, sometimes, just sometimes, they'll hit back."

Bobby made a good point. Alice could have committed an act of retaliation or a crime of passion.

"So if she did murder someone," Lottie continued to muse, "then the asylums she was in would be for the criminally insane?"

"That's what you'd need to find out. From her records. Records that must have followed her here to Silver Birches. A paper trail."

"I need the key to Patsy's office. Which we still haven't found."

"We will," Bobby assured her. "Meanwhile, keep trying to push past the barriers."

"Break them down."

"Bit by bit."

"She wished for something, remember? Last Christmas Eve, that's what she kept shouting out, over and over, before they sedated her. Maybe she wishes to confess?"

Another possibility. That was the trouble; there were many avenues they could wander down trying to make sense of her history, many conclusions to draw.

"Bobby?"

The old woman looked at her. Her brave, strong, yet at other times frail best friend. Was it Lottie's imagination? Was she looking even frailer this night? She was a good weight yet, not painfully thin like some others, her hair still a pastel shade of pink – Lottie making sure she refreshed it regularly – and her cheeks had colour in them too. It was in her eyes she saw an increasing weariness, the flame trying to burn bright but struggling.

"Were you going to ask me something, duck?"

"Oh, sorry, yeah, but it's a weird question."

Laughter from Bobby made the flame burn brighter. Funny how it did that, stoked the fires. "I'm used to weird from you, let me tell you! But…it's a weirdness I love. That I admire. Go on, speak up, girl. What is it?"

"Okay. All right. Here goes nothing. What I want to know is, in the life you've lived, such a brilliant life, so different, so colourful, have you ever wanted to kill anyone?"

* * *

Lottie used to like long, hot summer days when she and Matt were young. They'd spend so much time outdoors, in parks, by lakes, just mucking about, whiling away the hours, which seemed to melt into one another, hazy days that lasted forever. It was on a hot summer's day that he died, the sweat dripping off Lottie as she sat at home with her mother and waited for the news, just his parents and siblings with him, and Lottie's terrible relief that that was so. After that, she hated summer, kept indoors in the confines of her room with the curtains closed, shutting any light out, no matter how determinedly it tried to find its way in. And when the pain got too much, when it built and built as it always did, that was when she'd cut herself to get some relief from it all. Bobby knew; she'd seen the scars. If Jenny did, she'd never said, had chivvied her up in different ways.

'No more being alone in there,' she'd said. 'Enough now. Matt died, and I'm sorry about that, so bloody sorry, but you didn't. Lottie. You *have* to live.'

And so she'd tried for her mum's sake. She'd gone to school, failed her exams, then got a job, or rather her mother had got her a job in a care home, of all places, a place that dealt with death, failing to see the irony in it. And it was there, on hot summer days and hot summer nights, that more deaths occurred, a spate of them, so she was right for hating the summer. It wore a mask too, seemed so carefree, so nourishing, but the heat came for those that were vulnerable, was relentless in its pursuit, stole them clean away.

A busy summer. Checks on the patients at night doubling and trebling. No respite from high temperatures, not even after dark, and so fans whirred in each room, sometimes two. Yet still they died. Hilda went. Dear, sweet Hilda, whom Lottie had sensed only good things about, her love for her children and grandchildren, wishing they'd visited her more, because, oh, how her face lit up when they did!

James went too, tears pricking at Lottie's eyes when she had to put the call in. And then Nelly, followed a couple of weeks later by Tom, who simply gave up without her. Four over the summer on the night shift. Three in her charge – only James in Mandy's.

And because of it, she and Mandy were asked to attend a meeting in Patsy's office, during daytime hours, of course.

Lottie had been feeling nervous about it, like a criminal, topically enough, as though she or Mandy or one of the other carers were being held responsible for the deaths. As if they too might be murderers. Not such an outlandish thought; she'd seen true-case documentaries where those in care had put themselves there for a reason, to indulge their psychotic tendencies. Just what would the meeting be about? What would Patsy…imply?

"Come in, come in," Patsy said when she'd turned up promptly for the 'chat', Mandy sidling in, also looking wary.

Another hot day, but the sweat forming on Lottie's forehead had nothing to do with the heat this time. Shit! She'd done nothing wrong! The four who'd died had died of natural causes and without drama. It was this heat…it *killed* things. Outside, the grass in the local park she walked through to get to work was yellow instead of green, bald in places, even. People everywhere were just…wilting. The elderly did. Everyone knew how lethal this weather could be for them, and the fans they had at Silver Birches just didn't cut it. Patsy needed to invest in better ones, those Dyson ones, perhaps, that also looked really cool. Perhaps if she wasn't such a tight arse, creaming off money for herself, she could even think about installing air-conditioning.

Defensive. That's what Lottie was being. Fidgety too. Taking a seat, then shuffling in it. She was guilty of nothing. Mandy couldn't be either. Or the bank staff. And yet there she was, getting all het up.

Have you ever wanted to kill anyone?

She'd asked Bobby that a few weeks ago. And Bobby hadn't answered. She'd gone quiet instead, very quiet, then stood up, declared she was tired, that she needed sleep and was going back to her room. When Lottie had offered to fetch her some water or a cup of tea – they'd long since finished the ones in front of them – Bobby had shaken her head. 'I'll go on my own, thanks. You busy yourself with those in need, because I'm not.' And off she'd gone, leaving Lottie mystified. It was a stupid thing to ask, and she'd berated herself for it. Wanted to rush after Bobby and apologise. But she hadn't; she'd stayed put, just staring after her friend instead until she'd disappeared from sight.

Bobby hadn't done anything as dreadful as killing anyone. As with Alice, Lottie would have sensed it before

148

now, surely? Although, Bobby, by her own admittance, was holding back something. And whatever it was, it caused her pain, could even be responsible for her 'frail' episodes, flooring her. But it was nothing like murder. Of course not! In that respect she was innocent, as Lottie herself was. She really must sit still and stop fidgeting!

"So…" Patsy began. "Four deaths in as many weeks."

"Over five weeks, actually," Mandy corrected, also shuffling slightly.

She sounded defensive too, Patsy's eyes narrowing, and Lottie had to admit hers did as well when looking at Mandy. How easy it was to condemn without a trial!

Patsy sat back in her chair. "We can't have any more. Not for a good while."

Lottie almost laughed. "We can't *stop* people from dying! Not if it's their time."

"We have to! This kind of thing attracts attention. The wrong kind. And that's the last thing we want. Greater care needs to be taken. I've checked medication levels, and all seems to be present and correct."

"Of course it is!" Mandy grew more indignant. "We do our job, and we do it well."

"I might have to oversee," Patsy decided, neither denying what Mandy had said nor confirming it. "Pop in, just to check."

"There are bank staff too," Lottie said.

"I'm perfectly aware of that, thank you."

"And it's been so hot. The air at night is stifling in here."

"We can't help the weather. You have fans trained on the clientele?"

"At least one in every room," Mandy replied. "Sometimes two."

"I was wondering," began Lottie, "about more modern fans, whether they'd be better than those we've got. You know, those Dyson—"

A commotion in the corridor, some kind of yelling, interrupted her.

"Oh, for goodness' sake!" Patsy swore. "What the bloody hell's going on now? If this hot weather polishes the clientele off, I swear it riles them up before doing so."

Mandy started to rise. "D'you want me to go?"

"No, stay here. I haven't finished talking to you both. I'll go."

With her face a perfect picture of exasperation, Patsy stalked from the room, leaving Mandy and Lottie sitting there. Should she turn to Mandy? Lottie wondered. Say something like 'Scary, isn't it, how you can be held accountable for something you didn't do?' She refrained, just continued to sit there, gazing ahead, until Mandy rose.

"What you doing?" Lottie said, curious. In the corridor, a fuss was still being made.

"I need a fag. Cover for me, okay? Say…I don't know, say I've gone to the bog or something." She then shrugged. "Actually, you know what? I don't give a toss what you say. I'm going outside, having a fag, and when I come back, I'm gonna tell Patsy to shove it. They don't pay me enough to have doubt cast on me like this. It isn't right. And you, if you've any sense left, should think about jacking this job in too."

Lottie was aghast. "But if you leave now, wouldn't that look…suspicious?"

"Don't care about that either. I'm guilty of nothing." And then a sly look at Lottie. "What about you? You confident you've done everything right?"

Lottie cursed how high-pitched her voice was, akin to a squeal. "Yes! Of course!"

Mandy's frown increased. "And still it doesn't matter. In jobs like these where you're in charge of people, it's so easy for the finger of blame to get pointed in your direction. Everyone needs a scapegoat, see? Well, I won't be one. I won't give them that satisfaction. No, fuck it, I'm leaving. I've made my mind up. I'll go and get a job in a supermarket or something, where the only thing you can be accused of is stealing the goods, not someone's life. Well…see ya. Have a nice life and all that. Make the most of it whilst you can, before you end up in here too, and I don't mean in a work sense."

Having delivered that statement, Mandy left. Lottie now alone in Patsy's office.

Alone, as she'd wanted to be, as she *needed* to be if she was going to find out any more about Alice, where she'd come from and how many asylums she'd been in.

On a deep breath, she looked over her shoulder, then rose and first made her way to the door rather than the filing cabinet. Just what *was* going on out there? And, more to the point, how long did she have before a red-faced Patsy came bustling back to her office to find only one of the accused sitting there?

Minutes. Maybe not even that. If she was going to act, she had to be fast.

Almost slipping in her haste, she reached the cabinet and pulled at the top drawer, praying it wasn't locked, that it would open readily. It did, paperwork galore stuffed inside, divided alphabetically. Patsy had a computer, of course, and this stuff should be on there – everything was computerised nowadays – but what if it wasn't? If Patsy was a bit old-school or just remiss? Lazy, even.

If so, it worked to Lottie's advantage, was a damn sight easier than having to crack a password. The first drawer covered *A* to *C*, and under *Eve Crown*, there it was, handwritten stuff about her, including notes on her death a few months ago – the relevant paperwork attached to those notes, including a death certificate.

Alice Danes, by rights, should be in the drawer below, and so she slammed that one shut and opened the next, surprised at how big the *D* section was.

"Come on, Alice. Where are you? You're in here somewhere. You have to be."

So many files, so many deceased, such a quick turnover. But as Lottie'd said, she had to be there. Notes and notes on her that went back decades, passed on from institution to institution. The filing was in alphabetical order by first letter, but that's as far as Patsy's orderliness went. People within *D* weren't filed in order or Alice would have been near the front.

Lottie cursed. Why couldn't Alice have had a surname that ended in *X* or *Y* or *Z* rather than *D*? Still she flicked her fingers through files, all too aware of the seconds passing, the minutes, the sounds from outside dying down, whoever it was being subdued. *Sedated.*

Alice Danes.

At last!

Gotcha!

A huge file. A file she couldn't possibly hope to get through in the time she had left. Already she could imagine, if not hear, the clicking of Patsy's heels as she stalked back towards her. And if she found her doing this, rummaging through the files, then there would be more questions, more suspicions. *So easily the finger of blame can point at you.*

But she had to have this file. And her bag, by her seat, was thankfully big enough to conceal it. She could take it home and read it at her leisure. Patsy would never notice.

As for returning it…

Before she could talk herself out of it, she grabbed the folder and stuffed it in her bag, noting something else, a folder on the desk, wondering too what it contained. Her hand shot out, unable to resist. Receipts, dozens of them, recent ones for more fancy meals, champagne, and cabs, Patsy truly living the high life. She also opened a desk drawer to find more paperwork in there and, underneath it, a bottle half filled with whisky.

A clatter of heels, and Lottie shoved the drawer shut and hurried to her seat.

"That Bobby…" Patsy said as she entered the office. "That…*infernal* Bobby."

Lottie smiled to herself. So it was Bobby who'd caused the commotion? Got Patsy out of her office. Maybe she'd seen Lottie arrive and seized her chance. As had Lottie.

Their *only* chance.

As Patsy fussed and complained, as she wiped the sweat from her face, as she noticed, finally, Mandy was missing – Mandy who would *not* carry the can, who'd left Lottie to do that for both of them – the small matter of returning the folder would have to wait its turn.

Chapter Eighteen

So many institutions. That's what shocked Lottie the most. Alice Danes had been moved from pillar to post. And all in locations in the north.

"See, look here, I've made a list of the places she was in, in Newcastle, then Durham, Middlesbrough, up to Glasgow for a spell, then down again, near Leeds. I've listed the names of the places too, the asylums: Craigsmore, Dunhaven, Heathside, Low Stanton, the names go on and on. They sound awful, like prisons. Don't you think? Bobby?"

"What? Oh, sorry. Yes. Yes, I agree. They don't have the most…enticing of names."

Lottie had taken the folder home and studied and studied it. A paper trail indeed, although the information provided was sometimes scant, especially from the earlier years. She'd been right, though, in guessing Alice had been around the same age as herself when first admitted. She'd been eighteen when she'd gone to Craigsmore just outside Newcastle, *not* an asylum for the criminally insane, as far as Lottie was qualified to tell, and the date was 25 December 1949 – Christmas Day. What a day to be admitted! The happiest day of the year for some, but not Alice, Lottie remembering the images she'd seen, the room she'd been taken into after being hosed down and dressed in rough clothing, the people milling about in there, some railing against their fate, others hopelessly resigned, and the tree that had been in the corner, wrecked. Christmas Eve, however, was when the normally mute Alice, the allegedly *catatonic* Alice, kicked off, so that was the date when events were likely to have been set in motion, leading to incarceration.

Lottie continued. "It says the reason for her admittance initially was persistent delusion. Later, it claims stuff like 'agitation', 'hysteria', and 'alogia', which I looked up and means 'poverty of speech'. That happened in her mid-twenties. When she withdrew from life, just…gave up, maybe? I thought there'd be more detail, to be honest, psychiatric reports trying to come up with solutions, but there's nothing. It doesn't say 'hopeless', exactly, although I kept expecting to find that word, but the feeling I get, handling these papers, is that no one looked too deeply into her disorder. They simply accepted it. There's no mention of *why* she was deluded. I mean, what about?"

She'd been so engrossed in what she was relaying, had been engrossed for days, poring through the file in minute detail, expecting to find something more concrete as opposed to sketchy. How could notes this vague be kept about someone who'd been locked away so long? The state had imprisoned her, therefore didn't they have a duty to explain carefully and thoroughly as to why, giving examples of behaviour, especially the behaviour that had led her to the asylum in the first place? That was yet another thing. Before arriving at Craigsmore, she was 'of no fixed address'. A vagrant, then? Off the streets?

Her lobotomy had been mentioned, a prefrontal leucotomy, which Lottie had also read about independently, surgeons drilling a hole into either side of the skull and cutting through brain tissue with an instrument resembling an ice pick. It sounded horrendous, barbaric, not a cure, for how could it be? All it did was shut you down further, more effective than drugs and a damn sight cheaper. A *lifelong* solution that had been deemed 'successful' in her notes. It had taken place in 1959, when already she was becoming less and less vocal.

Later, the paperwork for Alice Danes changed. As Bobby had said, asylums were closing all over the country, huge, drafty, and foreboding redbrick Victorian buildings that were either left to rot, abandoned as their patients had once been, or razed to the ground, housing estates replacing them, *luxurious* accommodation in some cases. Care homes took over the responsibility for those in need at a certain age. By that time, Alice Danes was indeed old, a woman who'd been subdued *medically* whether it was her will or not, who could be tended to relatively easily if she didn't speak or barely moved. Barely ate or drank too, Lottie would bet. Although she'd never fed her, that wasn't her task, she could imagine Diane pushing food between her lips during the day, mashed up as you would for a baby, some of it being swallowed, some of it dribbling out of her mouth to run down her chin. No need to feed her during the night to test that theory, for she slept, or gave the impression she was sleeping, but those times Lottie had taken her hand, she knew that behind her closed lids was life enough, crammed in there.

"So she could have been a vagrant," Lottie surmised, referring to the mysterious life *before* the asylums. "Maybe she pretended to be deluded as a way off the streets. Then got admitted and got more than she bargained for. Never found her way out again. It really could be as simple as that.

And every time she tried to protest, they called her deluded. It makes sense. Kind of. Although, the black room, it doesn't explain that."

All throughout her musings, she'd expected Bobby to comment further, Bobby who was just as determined to find out about Alice, solve the mystery surrounding her, was passionate about it, had caused a ruckus so that Lottie could get these notes in the first place. All for one purpose, one mutual purpose. So why so quiet now?

Lottie laid Alice's notes on Bobby's bed and examined her friend more carefully. She wasn't sitting up in bed, the glow of the lamp illuminating her. She was…slumped. And instead of having colour in her cheeks, she was pale, like those Lottie imagined sometimes followed her around the building – the ghosts, the wraiths, the imprints.

"Bobby?" she whispered, and then with increasing alarm, "Bobby!"

Patsy had said no one else must die on the night shift, not for a while, anyway, that there had to be a 'decent gap', and as well as riled, Lottie had been derisive. How could you prevent death if it was due? Some of the residents here, even those newly admitted, were simply too close to it. You could make what time remained comfortable for them, see to it they ate enough, were hydrated, kept cool when it was hot and warm when it was cold. You could also chat away, coax a smile, easy with some, not with others, show them that all-important kindness, but ultimately, ultimately, you could not prevent death. But all was well at Silver Birches that evening; the atmosphere was calm. The night shift set to pass without incident. Or so she'd thought. But perhaps she was deluded too, because right now there was something about Bobby's pallor other than a paleness. She looked *waxy* in the lamplight. Her demeanour that of the defeated, of someone who'd fought enough.

Panic threatening to overwhelm her, Lottie shot to her feet. The other person working tonight was Caroline, bank staff, but one of the more regular ones who knew the ropes. Patsy had threatened to come in, just 'pop in' ad hoc, all the better to catch them out if they were slacking at their job, but so far hadn't bothered – not wanting to disrupt her lavish nights out, no doubt. Lottie could run, grab Caroline, get her to call the duty nurse or, better still, an ambulance, get Bobby out of there. Tear her from the only home she had, hers for several years now. A bloody care home in Watford!

Bobby raised an arm. "Lottie! Lottie, where are you going? Come back. Don't panic. Oh, for goodness' sake, Lottie! Wipe that look off your face. I'm not going anywhere, not yet." And then a sigh as she repeated those words, reinforced them. "Not *just* yet."

"But…but…you don't look well, Bobby." She'd seen that waxiness before in other residents, knew what it meant. "I'm going to call an ambulance. I think we should."

With great determination – and clearly a little pain too, as she winced – Bobby pushed herself upwards into more of a sitting position.

Lottie rushed to her. "Here, let me help. Oh, Bobby, I'm so sorry! Patsy warned us about being slack, about taking our eyes off the ball, and I was cross with her about it. But she's right. I've done just that, taken my eyes off *you*, too preoccupied with Alice."

"Will you stop fussing, girl! Go on, take your hands off me and just…sit back down. She deserves your attention, Alice, because by the sounds of it, from everything you've said, you've discovered, she's had none. For the longest of times. I'm pleased you're so concerned with her, and I want you to continue, okay? Do you hear? You *must*."

"I will," Lottie promised. "*We* will. You and me. This is our…" Our what? *Project* seemed too cold a word, although it was the first one that sprang to mind.

"It's a battle," Bobby said with a small smile. "That's what it is. Always a battle."

"Bobby." There was a crack in Lottie's voice. "Are you really okay?"

"Truth?"

"Yeah. 'Course!"

"I don't know. I really don't. It's a strange thing, you know…to feel whatever's in you start to run out. You *don't* feel it, actually, not for a long while. It just…it creeps up on you, is suddenly there. You might look all wrinkly on the outside, like someone elderly"—she spat that last word out—"but as I've told you before, you still feel young inside. *Full* of life, invincible." Only briefly did her eyes dart towards the door to look beyond it, to Alice's room, perhaps. "Some of us, anyway. I was lucky. So lucky. I managed to have a bit of a life, but I've deluded myself too. Worse, I've deluded others."

"Bobby, I really think I should call an—"

"Don't call anyone! Not yet. That's not what I want. There's things I have to say, and…and I want you to listen because I've never said them before. I've never…admitted."

Lottie reached out and took Bobby's hands, held them in her own. She could read her, she supposed, if she really tried; the barriers were down between them, so it should be *easy*, but no need, because Bobby was going to tell her anyway, in words, not visions.

There were tears running down the old woman's soft cheeks, the lines there providing something of a trough for them. A wonderful woman, a woman who'd lived, who'd experienced, who'd done life her way, or so Lottie had thought. But everyone had secrets, *she* did, Bobby, and she'd carried them through life with her. The fact she no longer wanted to showed she was truly close to death, more so than the waxy sheen on her face and the body that couldn't remain upright but which slumped again. She needed to absolve herself, not take it to her grave, for in death it would prove heavy too.

Lottie should call an ambulance; really, she should. If she did that, and did it right now, they might be able to help Bobby, pump her with drugs or whatever it was they did, snatch her back from the jaws of death, which seemed to hang forever open.

Why did people have to die? Young or old. Why couldn't everyone last forever?

"Lottie? Lottie, darling. Don't you start crying too. It's all right, it's okay. I'm ready now. I want this to end. It has to. It's…time. I'm so lucky to have had you in my life the last few months. You've made it all so much easier. You're a true angel, and…and I love you. If I had ever had a daughter, I'd have wanted her to be exactly like you. Blue hair and all."

That drew a small burst of laughter from Lottie, who sniffed back any further tears, trying to do exactly as Bobby had asked.

"I love you," Bobby repeated. "And I hope you don't mind me unburdening myself."

"No! No, of course I don't."

"We all need to be heard."

"I know."

"Me, Alice, and even that dreadful Eve."

"I know, Bobby. I agree."

"The good stuff…and the bad. It's all part of us."

Lottie nodded. "I love you too, Bobby," she said.

A smile that so effortlessly swept away the years appeared on Bobby's face when she said that, and for a moment, one sweet, sweet moment, they were simply two girls together, sitting there with so much ahead of them still, so much adventure.

And then her smile was gone.

"You asked me once, in all the years I've lived, whether I ever felt like killing someone."

Lottie blinked. That's right, she had. When they were discussing the possibility of Alice being a killer, hence her years of incarceration.

"Yeah?"

Bobby's smile this time was full of heartache. "There was someone I didn't *feel* like killing, but I did anyway. All because I didn't live life my way after all. I was just too scared."

Chapter Nineteen

December 2023

"Bobby was a murderer?"

Tony sounded shocked, and with good reason. She should explain, quickly, but for now more words just wouldn't come. Remembering what had happened that night, still far too recent, hurt so much, piling grief upon grief, a mountain inside her. That's why she did what she did sometimes, cut herself. If she didn't, she feared her heart would shatter.

It's all right. I'm okay.

Desperately she tried to remember what she'd just heard and seen in Tony's cab, Matt's face and him mouthing those words at her. And she'd seen Bobby's face too in dreams afterwards; she mustn't forget that. Bobby's *smiling* face. It *was* okay. It *was* all right. They were. Now. The dead. But for the living, for her and Alice, the trials continued.

"There, there, hinny. Take a moment. Take a breath. Just…breathe."

All during the journey from Sunderland to London – outrunning the storm and the storm never quite letting go, snapping at their heels every bit of the way – they'd either been talking or there'd been bursts of silence. And so came another one, Tony allowing her the time and space she needed to find her way out of yet another struggle. Understanding.

He kept his eyes on the road and continued driving, the wind still fierce out there, the rain having stopped for a short while but now starting again, the windscreen wipers doing as valiant a job as the driver, the way they hurtled back and forth.

What a kind man Tony was. Benevolent. Surreptitiously, she turned her head, just a fraction, to look at him. He was bald, rather thin too, and lonely, definitely that. As so many were. People who didn't deserve to be. If she reached out, if she touched his arm, would she be able to see why, a wife or a partner who had died, perhaps, and children far-flung? The same old, same old. Stories she'd come across so many times since working at the care home. Or, like Eve, like Alice, like Bobby herself, was there more to it, more...depth?

She shook her head, albeit imperceptibly. Everyone's history was not hers to discover. People had a right to privacy. Another thing: she could only carry the weight of so much.

The tears had come, the second time they'd done so during the journey, and no way to stop them, but Tony made good his word and gave her several moments, an entire collection, as many as she needed. Then she did indeed take a breath, inhaled slowly and deeply, then exhaled, feeling the grief rush out of her that way rather than in blood and pain.

"Bobby *wasn't* a murderer," she said at last. "But does that matter when you think you are anyway? When you've *convinced* yourself of it? When it destroyed your life? My poor, lovely Bobby. Before we continue with Alice, I'll tell you more about her, the *ghost* of her."

* * *

August 2023

Bobby, when younger, had been wild. She'd ridden a motorbike, drank copious amounts of whisky, and owned a hotel in Brighton, where life had been one long party. Lottie had loved hearing the story of her life, that which the older woman had imparted willingly, the good stuff, always the good stuff. But no life was ever wholly good. Bobby's wasn't. Like a tapestry, it was compiled of many threads, and not all of them golden.

There'd been one who was golden within it, however, the very sight of them as they'd walked into her hotel on Christmas Eve, of all days, enough to dazzle Bobby, who, hovering at reception, whisky in hand – anticipating the night to come, the gathering that would take place in the bar later – had been rendered speechless.

Not a man. A woman. Elspeth.

Who'd been crying, clearly, her big blue eyes red-rimmed and mascara staining puffy cheeks. And yet to Bobby, she was the most beautiful person she'd ever seen.

Elspeth had come to the bar after she'd checked in, and Bobby's hand had trembled as she'd poured her a gin, although Elspeth hadn't seemed to notice, her eyes still swollen and downcast. But when Bobby handed the gin over and their hands brushed, she'd felt it too, the frisson that passed between them, lifting her head finally and their eyes meeting.

A small chuckle from Bobby. "Did I just describe it as a frisson? It wasn't. It was a great big bloody electrical shock! It surged through me, and it surged through her too. It was like…I don't know…waking from a dream, from death, even, and feeling so *alive*."

She burned brightly again when talking of Elspeth – at least initially as she described their love and how deep it was, the passion that consumed them. *Privately* consumed them, as Lottie was to find out.

"Elspeth, or Ellie, as I called her, had run away from an abusive husband, couldn't stand it any longer so finally decided to go on Christmas Eve, and it was to me she came, my hotel. Fate connected us. That's how it felt. We were meant to be, she and I, two halves of a whole. She came for Christmas and didn't leave. That night, I spoke mainly to her, left the other revellers to their own devices, and then, when they'd either left, gone to their rooms, or passed out right there in the lounge, slumped over the tables, I walked her to her room – number thirteen, it was, lucky for some, for me definitely. Nothing happened between us that night. Not even a kiss. Although I wanted to take her in my arms and soothe all the hurt that was in her, that he'd inflicted, her husband, make it vanish. And the strange thing? I knew I could. That I had that power within me. But…"

"But what, Bobby?" Lottie said, noting how the woman's hands clutched at her blanket.

Bobby answered, although not for a few seconds. "Don't you see? A miracle had happened, but a…warped one. We were two women. In love."

Lottie frowned. "Oh, Bobby! That doesn't matter. No one cares about that kind of thing."

"No one cares *now*," Bobby amended. "In your day. And that's right, that's the way it should be. Love is love. But back then, in my day, there was still such stigma attached."

"But…surely you must have known you liked women before Elspeth?"

Bobby nodded. "I knew I didn't like men, that I'd never cared for their touch. I wasn't a virgin. I'd had men, but I'd also begun to avoid them. Lottie, I was no looker, okay? No, no, don't do that, deny it. That photograph on the sideboard, it's not me. It's her! It's Ellie! I *hated* having my picture taken. I wasn't tall enough, I wasn't slim enough, my features were…doughy. Men barely looked at me, so I could easily avoid them. And that other yearning in me, it was easy to ignore too, to just…pay no heed to it. Until her." A sob escaped Bobby. "Bring the picture closer, would you? Let me hold it." When Lottie obliged, Bobby just stared at it for what seemed like an age before speaking again. "She was so delicate. So trusting. She'd never felt before like she had with me, had presumed she liked men, men who took advantage of her, who beat her. Her own husband! When I found out how he'd abused her, I wanted to find him, kill him, but she persuaded me against it. 'It's about us now, not him. He can rot in hell for all I care. Bobby,' she said, 'I'm telling you, I won't waste another second thinking about him. I've left him, and he won't come looking. He doesn't know where. What we have is precious. We're lucky to have found it. Please, please, don't let him tarnish another day of my life, *our* life, together.'"

"Delicate," Lottie whispered, "but strong too if she'd left him, if she'd found you."

"Yes, yes, yes," Bobby said, her voice also barely above a whisper. "Despite appearances, she was always the strongest of us both."

"Bobby, what happened?"

Bobby began blinking, causing more alarm bells to ring in Lottie's head. She looked around the room as though surprised to be there, like she was searching too, not just for Elspeth in the picture but the ghost of Elspeth.

As tempted as Lottie was, she didn't turn her head to check for that also but nudged Bobby gently, brought her back to the moment.

"We said goodnight on Christmas Eve," she duly continued, "and I returned to my room in the hotel, but as morning dawned, a cold, crisp morning with the sky so blue, I had to do it, leave my bed and run to her, down the corridor, down the steps, to the lower floor. She was waiting, Lottie, as if she knew I was on my way. She was there in the doorway, holding her arms out to me. My love! My dearest love! No one was about – it was far too early – and so she pulled me inside, and we fell onto the bed, our lips touching, our bodies so close, and, Lottie, I'm telling you, I knew heaven that Christmas Day." Her voice cracked as she added, "I knew heaven *every* time we touched."

Lottie wanted to hug her. "That's beautiful, Bobby. I'm so happy you had that."

"I did. I did," she replied. "But then I destroyed it. Destroyed *her*."

"Oh, Bobby." No use giving her a reprieve; time was running out. Bobby needed to confess, and as she continued to scan the room, desperately, she needed to know too if she would be forgiven by the one person who mattered. Lottie could only pray it'd be so.

"She came for Christmas and never left. Not for a long while, anyway. She started working at the hotel as well as living there, living with me, but we were discreet, always. *I* was. I insisted on it." A wail was quickly stifled. "Different times! Different times! And I had a business to run. If people knew about me and Ellie, that she was more than my employee or my friend, if the world knew…I'd be shunned, my business ruined."

"No! It wouldn't have been! Your true friends—"

"They weren't! They were clientele, the very thing Patsy calls me. They came because of the hotel, because of the bar, the camaraderie, because I was one of the boys, ironically, accepted. Oh, this goes deep, and we're running out of time, but I wanted to make my parents proud, despite the fact they were dead, my parents who were very old-fashioned, would never have condoned a relationship between two women. I'd heard them, when they were alive, denounce homosexuality, calling it an 'abhorrence', and I grew up with that, the church we attended every Sunday calling it that too. Despite my natural leanings, I *imbibed* it. And the clientele at the hotel that I was so proud of cultivating, they openly abhorred it too, just…couldn't understand it. I wanted to live life my way, be different, but not *that* different, it seemed. I failed, on so many counts. Failed Ellie. Ellie? Elspeth? Is it you? In the shadows? Are you there? Waiting? I'm sorry, so, so sorry. Do you hear? How could I have ever been embarrassed by such perfection?"

Lottie reached out to hold Bobby and drew her into her arms, felt the conflict within her, that still raged even now, a part of her, a tiny part, still believing she was abnormal.

Bobby shuddered as Lottie held her, an outpouring of grief that had to happen, as though a boil had burst, the poison draining. *Let it.* Of all people, she had to die in peace.

"How did you kill her?" Lottie forced the words through

her teeth. "What did you do?"

"In continuing to deny her, that's how," Bobby answered, the words slightly muffled as her mouth was pressed into Lottie's shoulder. Eventually, she drew back. "I was so careful not to display my affection for her in public, only behind closed doors. And she at first agreed, was as furtive, but then she disagreed the more that time went on and we became more established. Our love was pure, she said, purer for her than love had been with a man, so why shouldn't it be recognised? More than that, *celebrated*. We weren't the only ones who loved women, and there were men who loved men. We should make a stand. Normalise it. But I couldn't. I just couldn't. And in the end…well, I did something terrible. Truly terrible."

"What?"

"I told her to leave. She was growing angry with me, and I was growing angry with her too until anger was all I could see, a red wall of it. I forgot – so easily I forgot – what had been between us. The love. Such love! And I ended things, refused to see also her heartbreak, her sheer bewilderment, her utter disappointment. She did as I asked, packed her bags and left. Again, to disappear. And I was relieved, God forgive me, *Elspeth* forgive me, but I was relieved! Years later, I found out where she'd gone."

Was it Lottie's imagination, or had the room gone cold on that sweltering August night? Or was it simply her blood freezing because she knew Elspeth's destination. Could see it through Bobby's eyes when she'd found out by accident, quite by accident.

A man had told her. A man staying at her hotel, and they'd got talking one night. A stormy night, the curtains in the bar shut tight against it.

This man had made mistakes, Bobby could tell. A businessman, well spoken but angry at the world, at the cards life had dealt him. A man who spoke of broken relationships, one after the other. Perhaps that was why Bobby continued to listen; it wasn't because she liked him. She didn't. She felt…repulsed by him, actually, but they had one thing in common, at least, for she was angry too at the cards life had dealt her, for making her feel the way she did. So she'd poured the whisky, and the man had talked and talked of those who'd let him down. One woman in particular. A long time ago. His wife.

"Left me, she did. Just packed her bags and ran out on me, frigid little cow, after all I'd done for her too. I plucked her from the life she'd lived, a squalid little life, let me tell you, offered her so much, a good home, respectability, but she left me. They all did, in the end. Two other wives after her. Couldn't see what they had, refused to. And yet I gave all of me."

A whining, measly little man was how Bobby thought of him, constantly throwing himself a pity party. Three wives? What a revelation! She couldn't for the life of her work out what any woman would see in him. How they could be so stupid. This man was what society called normal. The travesty. Yet still she sat there and listened. She could shut the bar, she supposed, retire early, lie in bed and listen to the rain as it battered the windowpanes, the whisky that she was drinking more and more of finally kicking in and allowing her to drift. But she didn't. She remained where she was. A sounding board.

And that's when he'd told her in more detail about his first wife, who'd left him on Christmas Eve, of all times, a cruel, cruel woman, the 'frigid little cow'. Never found out where she'd gone either, not until the police had notified him.

Elspeth, her name was. Ellie. *Bobby's* Ellie.

"She'd drowned herself," Bobby whispered. "That day she left me, full of anger, and me so full of anger too, she'd caught a bus along the coast, all the way to Hastings, and there she went into the water and drowned herself. The *very* day she left me. I raged at the man when I found out, when I put two and two together, when I realised." In Lottie's arms still, Bobby's voice rose. "I threw him out of my hotel. He was so shocked, so confused, and every right to be, because still I couldn't tell him why. I wanted to kill him, drive a knife right through his heart, but I didn't. I merely put him out in the storm and told him never, *never* to come back. It was her I killed. Ellie. She took her own life because I'd denied her, because I was a coward, because I ruined something pure between us. And I remained a coward! Sought solace in whisky, made sure I lost everything but still continued to live and breathe. Never told a soul about her. Until you, Lottie. Until you."

She pulled away from Lottie then, looking not beyond her but into Lottie's eyes, deep within, the room so chill still. "Ellie's here. She is. And she's still so angry. But she has every right to be. I did it in the end, though, told someone about her. Denied her no longer. And so maybe…she won't be as angry as she could be. Yes, yes, I'm coming, Ellie! I am! And I'll spend an eternity making it up to you. I promise, but first…Lottie. Thank you for listening. For holding me, the very worst of people, a murderer and a coward. And yet still I see the love in your eyes for me. And that gives me hope that she might love me still too. I was so weak. I'm weak now. If only I could rewrite what happened. But at least now I've told it. That's what makes you special; you listen. *That's* your magic ability. Remember that, okay? And keep listening. All stories need to be told, beginning to end. One day."

The breath left her. The chill in the room dissipated.

Elspeth had flown. And taken Bobby with her.

Chapter Twenty

After Bobby, Lottie returned to her old ways, lying in her room day and night, curtains shutting the light out, just…lying there. Lost. Utterly lost.

Bobby had died in her arms. A tortured Bobby, who wasn't the woman she'd portrayed herself as. Never had been. Was Elspeth truly there at the end? Was she responsible for the chill in the room? Her presence? It had been *so* cold. And because it had, did that mean she was not just angry but *furious*, an entity seeking revenge? Bobby had sworn she'd make reparation, would spend an eternity doing so. But would it be enough? Or was it simply too late? Which meant that Bobby – who was good at heart, Lottie would not have it otherwise, but too much a product of her time – was in hell?

So many questions! If Bobby was in hell, so was Lottie. Or it felt like it. The hell she'd descended into when Matt had died, a place as dark as the room Alice was trapped in.

Alice?

She couldn't help her if she couldn't help herself. Indeed, Alice was fading, the memory of her. Because Lottie wouldn't go in anymore to the care home. Refused. Left the morning of Bobby's death and hadn't gone back.

Her mother was beside herself. Kept trying to talk to Lottie, to *reason* with her.

"Darling, why have you taken this so badly? I know Bobby was a favourite of yours, but she'd lived a long life; that's one thing to be grateful for. You have to expect these things."

She knew that, accepted that, but this was Bobby. And she missed her!

Jenny'd had to call Patsy and explain. God knows what Patsy had said in return; her mother didn't say. Didn't know what to do with her daughter either. She let her wallow, for a while, anyway, the look on her face as she entered her room, bringing in tea and food that often went untouched, one of despair. If so, that made two of them, as Lottie knew she was letting Bobby down being this way. *Being as weak.* Letting everyone down.

She didn't care. Refused to. Refused to see a doctor too, to take pills, *happy* pills. They'd done no good after Matt, so why would they now?

Maybe Jenny would have forced the issue if Bobby hadn't. If Alice hadn't too.

Dreams. That's all they were, dreams, but they felt so real. After Matt, she hadn't dreamt. She'd fallen down a black hole, and that was where she'd stayed, at the bottom of it. But now, after Bobby, dreams came thick and fast. *Good* dreams. Surprisingly. Of Bobby and her and the times they'd shared, all those nights in between room checks and kitchen duties, sitting in the dayroom together, sharing a Deliveroo, not even chatting sometimes, just being together, friendship as powerful a relationship as any.

In the dreams, she'd turn to Bobby. "Are you happy now?" she'd ask her. "Is everything all right? Over there. On the other side."

When Bobby continued to gaze straight ahead rather

than at her, smiling but not answering, she'd beg her. "Bobby, tell me!"

She *seemed* happy, but that wasn't enough, not for Lottie.

So she did it, reached out and touched her arm, trying to glean more information that way. That was when the dreams changed.

Alice was the one who turned to her, not Bobby. Her mouth moved, but there was no sound. Even so, she could hear it. Two words.

I am.

"I am what?" Lottie said. "And where's Bobby?" It was her she wanted to hear those two words from, and more: *I am happy. Everything is good here. I'm forgiven.*

Bobby was gone from her dreams, though, for now, and Alice just kept repeating those words: *I am. I am. I am. I am.*

Lottie tried talking to Bobby when she was awake too. "It's you I want to see in dreams. Just you I'm concerned with. You died in such…torment."

And again, the tears would overwhelm her, the descent into darkness worse than before, deeper. What did 'I am' mean? What was Alice trying to tell her?

"Bobby, if you're there, sit with me again tonight when I sleep. Only you."

Her prayers were answered. Bobby came back, not Alice. And in dreams they'd sit, and it was like old times, Lottie happy again. But still, Bobby wouldn't answer her question. "Are you happy now, Bobby? You be the one to say, 'I am.' Please."

But she didn't.

Two weeks Lottie remained in her bedroom with the curtains closed, or was it three? In a dark room time can become meaningless. She could see it, though, the growing impatience on her mother's face, the frown that replaced dismay. No way she could stay there forever, wouldn't be allowed too, time not so meaningless after all, but running out.

Bobby *did* turn to her, eventually, when Lottie begged her again.

"I am," she said, although not in answer to her question, rather to reiterate something she'd said when she was alive. "I am proud of you. I am proud because you'll do the right thing. Because you're different. *Better.*"

In the dream, Lottie vehemently shook her head.

"I can't go back there. Alice isn't my problem."

Bobby agreed. "She's not anyone's."

"Exactly!" Lottie continued to rail. "I don't want to go back. I don't want more unhappiness." She sobbed in the dream, ground her teeth. "Don't you understand? I'm fragile too. Can only take so much! I can't do it. I won't. Bobby, are you okay?"

Again, those words. "I am proud of you. Listen."

More words. Whispered in her head. Those whispers getting louder. Bobby or Alice responsible for them? Perhaps both. *I am. I am. I am.*

Finally, Lottie shouted out, screamed. "You're what, Alice? What are you?"

She'd asked, and as she'd done so, it was Bobby's face in front of her. In the dream. Only the dream. And the pride in her eyes, the belief in them, was unmistakable.

Listen.

* * *

No more night shifts for Lottie; she was back on the day shift. Whether it was because there had been another death on her watch – Bobby's – or not, no one said, but those were the conditions of her returning to work. The night shift was the realm of others now; she was to be there when the place was livelier, when she could be kept an eye on, no doubt.

Under any other circumstances, Lottie would have done as Mandy had and told Patsy to stuff her job and her suspicions, her worries that the care home would be investigated, that *she* would, Patsy herself. Was that more like it? Oh, what did it matter? Patsy was not her concern. Alice was. Bobby wanted her to be, and so Lottie accepted it, that she needed to find an excuse to get into her room again, take her hand, and listen.

But her room…it was opposite Bobby's. And she couldn't do it, go that close, the last place she'd seen her friend alive. Not for days that turned into weeks. An empty room now. For a while. But then, inevitably, her replacement arrived: Millie Atkins. And, like Alice, she was in her early nineties. Not Lottie's charge, Diane's, just as Alice was, but Diane got ill, so one morning in early October, it was Lottie who went in to see her.

Beforehand, in the corridor, she felt caught between a rock and a hard place. Millie wasn't her only responsibility that day, but also Alice. Alice's door was to the left and Bobby's to the right. Where should she go first?

Alice. She'd see her first. Doing so, she found her in the same space as before when she'd been on the day shift, in front of the window, in a chair, staring at nothing.

"Alice," she said, forcing brightness into her voice. "It's me. It's Lottie. You remember me, don't you? I'm sorry I've not been in for a while. Stuff…happened. I'm here now, though. Oh, Alice, look at you! You've slumped down. Here, let me help."

The moment she touched her – the *very* moment – it happened, the visions, the insight, the turmoil was shared. More scenes from the asylum, more noise, screaming and crying, the utter, utter hopelessness of human beings whose treatment included scant empathy.

"The room, Alice, what about the room? What happened before the asylum and before the room? Alice, come on. That's where the key to all this lies."

No use. She was entrenched, either in the asylum or the room, had never left either.

She couldn't stay with Alice, not with Patsy on the prowl, had to do her job and see next to Millie. Had to do something else too as soon as she could – put Alice's notes back in the filing cabinet. She still hadn't found an opportunity to do so before it was noticed. Letting go of Alice, she rose to her feet, then decided to take her hand again.

"I wish I could help you. I don't know how, but I want you to know I wish I could."

About to let go again, something happened that never had before, not with Alice.

A squeeze of the hand.

"Alice?" Her heart was racing at the gesture. "Alice, what is it?"

Another strange sensation, connected with Alice or not? It was like the ground was moving beneath her feet, fluid instead of solid, making her feel quite ill, quite nauseous, in fact. And then a whisper, when before, last Christmas Eve, it had been a wail.

"Wish."

Chapter Twenty-One

Getting somewhere. Getting nowhere. Being with Alice was like that; you'd think you were making progress, then you'd slide back into the same old memories she harboured.

What did she wish for? And how could she, Lottie, grant it?

Was she a fool for even trying?

Such a frail old lady, so damaged. Caught in a web whilst waiting for the final strike of the clock. She was so unlike Millie, who was the same age but so full of life. Full of joy. When Alice had squeezed Lottie's hand – the first time she'd ever done so – Lottie had tried to seize the moment, repeating that word to her over and over, *wish, wish, wish,* to gain more of a response, but there was nothing; the woman sank back inside herself again. Lottie had left her, gone to see Millie instead, steeling herself for what she might find, more frailty, someone barely holding on, and Lottie asking herself yet again, *why?*

When she'd knocked on the door, a voice called out, much brighter than expected.

"Come in!"

On entering, there was a flash of resentment. Millie had arrived and settled in, all surfaces covered with her things now, Bobby erased.

"Oh!" Millie continued on sight of Lottie. "Someone

different to Diane. A young lady! Come in, come in," she repeated. "It's lovely to see you. I'm Millie, and you're…?"

"Lottie. I'm Lottie Beck. Diane's ill, a cold, I think, so I'm here to see you're okay."

"Lottie! What a lovely name. And I love your hair! I'm very pleased to meet you."

Resentment faded, and so quickly. Faced with such beaming positivity, she simply couldn't hold on to it. Lottie ventured further into the room, part of her aching for the previous resident yet also happy to encounter someone who was not only joyous but so full of light. What a lucky, lucky person! She'd been told Millie was ninety-two, the same age as Alice was now. What a blessing to get to that age and be that way. What an achievement.

She liked Millie. From there on out. If anyone was going to occupy Bobby's room, she was glad it was her. She gave respite from the visits to Alice's room, which yielded no further results or information. From Millie, though, she received plenty.

Every person had a history, and Millie loved to share hers. As well as framed photographs of herself through the ages – always with someone, whether her husband, Douglas, who'd passed; her children, who visited often; her grandchildren, who did too; or her sisters and brothers – she had photo albums, several of them, that she and Lottie would flick through, Millie pointing out who was who and giving a potted history of them as well.

It was her choice to be in the care home, she'd told Lottie, even though her eldest had wanted her to come and live with them.

"Wouldn't hear of it," she said, "my eldest works full-time, has a good career, as do all my children. My husband

and I worked hard to send them to the best schools and universities, and now they want to give it all up to look after me. Absolutely not!"

No blame in her, no expectation. She was happy to be at Silver Birches, went to the dayroom when she could and mingled with the others, a real breath of fresh air. No need to take her hand, to tune in; there'd be nothing but contentedness. Lottie loved being in her company, as did others. Even Patsy found time to sit and talk to her – a miracle in itself – all of them leeching from her what was lacking in themselves, trying to make it better.

Lottie didn't wish ill on anyone, but she dreaded Diane's return, Millie and Alice going back into her care, but that didn't happen, not for a couple of weeks, two *fortuitous* weeks.

She was sitting with Millie again, flicking through more photo albums, this time discussing the various holidays she and her family had been on, the many and impressive sights in the world this woman had feasted her eyes on.

"Travelling's good for the soul," she said. "It nourishes you. We worked hard for the children's sake, and then after they were off our hands, we worked so we could travel, Douglas and I. Do you love to travel, Lottie? Is there that desire in you?" Before she could answer, Millie laughed. "Oh, you're young yet, and the world's a big place. But make sure you do it, travel as far and as wide as you can, so that when you're my age, you've no regrets. See the pyramids of Egypt, the Great Wall of China, the skyscrapers of New York, the cherry blossom in Japan, and the mountains in Asia. Leave no stone unturned."

Lottie laughed too. "I'll certainly try! And, Millie, I love that you have no regrets. No sadness."

"Ah, there's sadness for everyone along the way, even me. But you're right, I've *chosen* happiness, even in the darkest times." She then pointed. "In that chest of drawers, there's another photo album. Fetch it, dear. It's of a life that was lost early. Not on these shores, but far away. I was sad when we lost that. When we had to leave."

"Had to?"

"Fetch the album, and I'll explain."

She did as she was asked. Opening the bottom drawer, she saw the album straightway, sitting on top of some jumpers. It was made of wood, *carved* wood, two mighty tusked elephants depicted. It gave off a slight smell as she retrieved it, the mustiness of age.

"That's right, dear, bring it here," Millie said.

Seating herself again beside Millie, she handed the album over, carefully because it was a weighty thing, settling it down gently on Millie's knees.

For a moment all Millie did was stare at it, such a wistful expression on her face, and then, on a sigh, she opened it before beckoning Lottie to come a little closer.

Unlike the photographs in the other albums she'd seen, these were black and white, and somewhat faded too, stuck onto pages that looked equally delicate, so much so that Lottie feared the entire thing might crumble if handled too regularly.

"What are these?" she said, aware of the wonder in her voice.

"Old photographs of my childhood, taken, as I've said, in a far-off land, the place I lived before England. India."

"India? You came from India?"

"I did." Millie beamed.

"But—"

Millie burst out laughing. "I wasn't Indian, dear! *We* weren't, my family. Which is why we had to leave. We were the British in India. And rightly or wrongly, we lived the high life there. It was such a beautiful land. A beautiful life. And then it was over. The Raj fell. Oh, I can't complain. Perhaps it deserved to. I don't know. I don't do politics." She imparted a cheeky wink. "Now *there's* the secret to a long and happy life: steer clear of politics. As I say, it was over, that life, and so we left eventually. I'd never been to England before. My parents hadn't or any of my siblings, but we made an adventure of it, you know? Turned grief on its head and made it exciting. Look, that's them, Mother and Pops, and that one there is of my dear sister Lucy, who lived to a ripe old age too. We were all lucky in that respect; only Son wasn't. That was the family nickname for our brother Robert. Sadly, he died as a young man on a cricket pitch, of all places, from a burst appendix." Another glimmer of sadness, no matter how brief, before she added, "They were winning, though. His team. That's something, eh?" She returned her gaze to the photo album. "I think…I think that's where I got my love of travel from, from how excited our parents made us feel about new pastures ahead. Even though, if I'm brutally honest, the reality was a little disappointing at first. Do you know what it was doing on our first day in England?"

Lottie shook her head. "What?"

"Bucketing down! The skies were grey and miserable. And it was cold. So cold."

Lottie pulled a face. "Oh, Millie, I'm sorry, so sorry. That's just typical."

"It is rather, but hey-ho, we got on with it. Pops found work, and Mother did too. We coped. But oh, I missed the sights and sounds of India, now more than ever, the *aroma* of India, so heady with spices, a land with the brightest flowers I've ever seen and the greenest grass, the mountains in the background always covered in such a fine layer of mist, like gossamer. It's the one place I never returned to, only in memory, only through these photographs. I wanted it to remain special. Unchanged. And yes, untarnished. Do I sound like a silly old fool for saying that? Perhaps I should have gone back. Had a trip down memory lane. Too late now, but at least I have this to look at, a veritable treasure trove."

"It is," Lottie said. "It's precious."

Millie continued to turn the pages, losing herself down memory lane after all and taking Lottie along for the ride. She was there, seeing everything through the woman's eyes, no psychic ability needed when it was all so freely shared. How she was loving this experience, lamenting coming to the end of the photo album, for the journey to be over.

"And that's it! That's my life before England. I'm sad to leave India again, but life on these shores turned out to be pretty good too. It really is what you make it."

"I'm glad," Lottie answered. "But it turned out well because of your attitude. You're just one of those people that look for the silver lining. An inspiration."

"Bless you, dear," Millie said, patting her hand. "But it's not hard. Even in the toughest of circumstances. You have to *look* a bit harder, granted, but it's still there. Always. Oh, look, just one more photograph, the final one, the boat we travelled over on. So many of us. Refugees. I'll tell you something, I never went back to India, and I never travelled by boat again, not after that journey. It was horrendous! The seas were so rough. For weeks we were on that boat, and I was so sick! Confined to my cabin for most of the time, my poor mother having to tend to me, although she looked rather bilious too on several occasions. Okay, hands up, that's one time I couldn't see a silver lining, that I wasn't excited or happy. I was just plain miserable. I wanted to die, actually, that's how ill I was. I just thought it'd be easier than continuing to suffer. Yes, that put me off boat travel for life. Not even sure why I kept a photo of that dreadful vessel. As if I needed the reminder!"

Her finger was still pointing to the photograph as Lottie leant forward for a closer look. It was a boat in dock, Liverpool Docks, it looked like, a building in the background which Lottie recognised, the Liver Building. She knew it because Jack was at uni in Liverpool, and when she'd Googled the place, that's what had come up, it being a city icon.

There was a name on the side of the boat, painted in tall black letters but somewhat fuzzy, drizzle on the lens of the camera perhaps distorting it.

"What does that say?" Lottie said, also pointing. "The name of the boat?"

"Oh, that. It is rather blurry, isn't it? But I've never forgotten. It was the *Wish*. Rather ironic, really, as most of us were wishing the Raj *hadn't* fallen, that we were still back in India. The HMS *Wish*. The year was 1949. Just before Christmas. A *few* days before."

Chapter Twenty-Two

"Alice! Alice! I think I know what you mean. I know what the *Wish* is!"

Coincidence. It could be, of course. Solely that. But then, as she made her excuses and rushed from Millie's room, across the corridor and into Alice's, Lottie remembered how she'd felt when Alice had uttered that word, *wish*. The ground had shifted beneath her feet, as if she were not on terra firma but something like water. And the sickness that Millie said she'd suffered because the seas were rough, Lottie had felt a burst of it too.

Admitted to the asylums in 1949 on Christmas Day, Alice Danes had been eighteen. In terms of paperwork, that was where her life had begun. And ended. For it was no life being in those kinds of places, locked up. She was in a care home now, had been in a succession of them, just as she'd been in a succession of asylums, moved from place to place, *of no fixed address*. She'd moved *country* to be there, forced from it, had been let down all her life, one way or the other. Ousted. Wronged. Never listened to. Never validated.

Lottie hadn't known what to expect when she'd burst into her room, knelt in front of her and said what she had, but part of her was disappointed. She knew what the *Wish* was, a boat that had sailed into Merseyside from India, that Millie and her family had been on, and Alice Danes too.

With her family? Lottie knew she was right, had the courage of her convictions, so why no reaction from the woman? No…nothing?

Lobotomised. A procedure that had helped some people, yet with others – too many, way too many – it had caused complications. They could neither walk nor talk after the intervention, requiring lifelong medical care. Alice had been described as catatonic. But she could talk, at least, she'd proved it, not just on Christmas Eve when she'd become frantic and screamed out loud, 'Wish! Wish! Wish! Wish!' trying to tell someone, anyone, about her history prior to the asylums, but also when she'd whispered the word to Lottie. One single word, which could be interpreted in a thousand different ways or disregarded as nothing but a baseless rant. Even Lottie had misinterpreted it, wondering what her wish was and how she could grant it. Hadn't realised until now that it was Alice trying to cling to something *other* than the dark room and the asylums.

"Alice," she continued, "no one's listened to you, not in decades, but now you have to listen to me. There's a woman in the room opposite yours, room nineteen. It used to be Bobby, but now it's Millie, and she's the same age as you. She's lovely. We were looking at photo albums, *old* photo albums. She grew up in India, in the days of the Raj, when India was under British rule, she explained, part of the empire, but the Raj fell, and so those that were British had to leave. They came over on various ships to England, the country of their heritage, but which many had never been to before, the younger generations especially, the ships docking in Liverpool. That was where the HMS *Wish* docked, the boat Millie was on. Were you? Who with? She was sick on it, so terribly sick, felt like she wanted to die.

Did you feel sick as well? When you whispered 'wish' to me, I felt it for a moment, like I was on sea, not land, and a wave of nausea. Alice, I know you can talk. I know that inside you there's buried an entire world, but history begins when you take your first breath, not at eighteen, when your history was stolen."

Lottie sighed. Such impassioned words and spoken so desperately to get attention, *hers*, Alice's, and failing. The woman continued to look past her, out the window, at buildings as nondescript, as soulless, as the one they were in. If only she had one of the rooms on the other side that overlooked a patch of garden at least. Maybe...maybe the next time someone died on that side, Lottie would raise that possibility with Patsy. This woman deserved better than she'd ever got, and a patch of garden might count for something.

"India must have been such a hot place, the temperatures soaring in summer. It must have been...beautiful. Did you live by the sea, close to a city, or in the countryside like Millie, surrounded by mountains? What was your house like there? Can you remember it? Your bedroom? Did you have it all to yourself, or did you share it with a brother or sister? Millie said she'd wake every morning to a chorus of birdsong, so loud it was deafening, but she loved it so, the rhythm of it, the high, clear notes. She said there were snakes too, and she *hates* snakes! Did you hate them as well? One morning – this is funny, so listen up, Alice, *listen* – she woke and swore there was a snake slithering over her! From the corner of her eye, she saw something long and black and thin on her chest, going towards her shoulder. She lay still, perfectly still, barely even breathing, hoping that whatever it was would continue to slither away; only then would she sit up, dash out the room and away from it. Scary? Don't you think? So scary! Anyway, the seconds passed, the minutes, and whatever was on her was going nowhere. Millie was about thirteen or fourteen at the time. Upshot is, she got bored. Can you imagine? *Bored.* I'd have, like, screamed the house down! Finally, she moved her head, just a fraction to the left to get a better look, and when she saw what it was, well…she was in stitches! She had long hair that she plaited at night, and that's what it was, one of her plaits, laying across her! Nothing more sinister than that! Alice, Alice, did that kind of thing ever happen to you? Did you have long hair? What colour was it? It must have been crazy to live in a place like India, but a good crazy. So different to here. Was it, Alice? Was it?"

Damn it! Nothing from her! No movement of lips and no squeeze of the hand.

"Alice, please! Give me something. Am I barking up the wrong tree here?"

Flashes of images. At last! Transferred from flesh to flesh, entering Lottie's mind. The asylum. Again. The same wailing, the same screaming on permanent play, each day the same as the other and equally hellish. That girl in the corner, the one Alice often fixated on, there she was again, her mouth wide open in a silent scream, tearing at her hair.

Lottie didn't want to see those images again or for Alice to relive them.

"Who came over on the *Wish* with you, Alice?" she persisted. "You must have been accompanied, so who was it?" And did they disappear? *Suddenly* disappear, with no warning whatsoever. "Dig deep, Alice. You have to, because…because…" She almost let go of Alice's hand, *flung* it from her. Because she could sense it, death so clearly waiting, as ravenous as ever, wanting to swallow the mystery of Alice Danes, gobble it right up. And Lottie could let it happen, the inevitable, couldn't stop it, but for Bobby, for the pride in her eyes – Bobby, who'd wanted her to listen, to help, because if not, the black hole Alice would fall into would be just another nightmare, one without resolve.

Dramatic thoughts, but thoughts which fired her further.

"Forget the asylum, Alice! I know about that. There was life before the asylum, and it can't have been all bad! No life is. Tell me about India, tell me how you felt when you had to leave your home, the journey here, your first impressions of this country, whether you were excited, afraid, or both. Tell me about that room you were in, before it went dark, and who you were with. Who you later searched for. You tried to tell so many people long ago, and no one listened. But someone's listening now. I am. Tell me!"

More screaming, more wailing. Lottie's heart sank. Was it the asylum again? Maybe. Although…there was something different about the scream this time, as if coming from someone younger, a child? They didn't lock children in asylums with adults, did they? Or was it that Alice had been in an asylum when young too, as a child in India? Had *always* been mad?

If so, perhaps there was no helping her, no validating. Madness had too great a hold.

Lottie was about to unhand her and step away, try again another day or perhaps – despite Bobby's pride in her – not try at all and let her die, go from one hell to another, for what power did Lottie have, really? She'd never felt so power*less*. But when trying to break loose, Alice's hands tightened. Just a fraction, barely perceptible, imagination even, but it stopped her, kept her tethered, kept her seeing.

A body swinging! An adult body. A...man? And the screaming still, a girl, that girl turning and running, shouting at the top of her voice for help. Vague, vague images, but more followed. A house. A beautiful house. With a veranda wrapped round it. Mountains in the background, wrapped in mist, like Millie had said. That house...imploding. Actually or metaphorically, Lottie didn't know, then decided it didn't matter; they were the same thing. Sobbing. As wretched as the sobbing in the asylum, the sound of loss, a great, great loss. Suitcases. Piled high. And a ship. Definitely a ship. Ready to carry the displaced elsewhere. To carry *them*...a young girl and someone else. That someone else still too vague to see, more of a...shadow figure. Why? Because that's what they'd become over the years? A shadow? *Everything* about that former life was shadowy.

Lottie smiled. It was *still* a former life, as tragic as it might have been. A suicide and dispossession, but no madness, other than the madness of grief. And then came a repeat of the body swinging, the house imploding, and the asylums.

"No, no, no," Lottie said, clutching at Alice now. "Tell me something good. Let's latch on to that, not tragedy, although...I'm sorry there was so much of it." How different two lives could be, Alice's and Millie's, girls with so much in common but who'd been dealt different cards. Yet both roads ended at Silver Birches, a further hell waiting for one of them if Lottie couldn't get her to remember something other than torture. "Alice, there must have been something good in your life. Remember it. No matter how small. *Those* are the things we have to hold on to. Especially now. That we take with us. Only the good."

How hard the body had swung from side to side from

the rafters. A man. Definitely a man. The vision was becoming clearer, but she didn't want that, to see the eyes that bulged, the skin so badly discoloured, purple and grey. Alice had seen it, and her childhood was lost that day. Was it her father? The loss of his home, career, and status too much to bear? If so, he wasn't the shadow figure with her on the *Wish*, so was it her mother? Both of them bereft.

She was seeing through the lens of another woman, and that lens was zooming in.

"Don't show me him again, Alice! Don't! Because I won't be able to unsee it either."

Letting go of Alice's hands was no longer an option; the woman had almost preternatural strength, was lost in herself, truly lost in the madness.

Bobby, help me! What do I do?

Begging a mad woman and begging a ghost, did that make her mad too? Was her mother right when she'd said her ability would lead her into murky waters? Rather than develop it, she should follow the lead of others who'd never listened at all.

"Let go, Alice! If you can't show me anything good, let go! Alice! Stop this! Stop! I don't want to see him hanging. Your father. Oh God, Alice! Stop! Your life was not all bad. I won't believe it. There had to be some happiness somewhere. ALICE! LET GO NOW!"

"Lottie! Lottie! Let go! I said...let go!"

Screaming. Wild screaming. Like that in the asylum. But this time, herself adding to the cacophony and...someone else? Alice?

Disorientated, she whipped her head round.

Not Alice. That shriek belonged to Patsy.

She'd entered the room to find Lottie shouting at Alice.

With lightning-quick speed, she crossed over to Lottie, clearly intending to force her hands from Alice's, not realising it wasn't Lottie who held on tight, not this time.

She did it, separated them. Uttered more furious words too.

"In my office, Lottie Beck! Now!"

She was in trouble. Big trouble. But instead of afraid, she was exhilarated.

One of the bank staff came in too, glaring at her as she also rushed to Alice's side.

Alice, who was sitting still again, perfectly still. Who'd finally listened too. Because just before Patsy had forced them apart, Lottie'd seen it – a room. A room usually filled with darkness but, before that, something else. Joy.

A room of nightmares and a room of dreams.

One and the same.

A *hotel* room.

Chapter Twenty-Three

December 2023

"I lied to you."

Tony turned his head. "Oh?"

"I said take me to the care home, where I work."

"Aye, you did."

"I *don't* work there. That was the day I got fired. Mid-October."

"Oh," Tony said again. "What happened?"

"You remember I had the file on Alice?"

"Aye."

"Well, the reason Patsy was looking for me was because she found the file. In my bag, in my locker. I was still intending to put it back, waiting for a chance. Would haul it into work every day in order to do that. And there was either no opportunity or I'd forget and have to haul it back again. Well, that day, I forgot to lock my locker too. To be fair, it wasn't the first time. It's not as if I had anything you'd want to steal. So yeah, I forgot to lock it, forgot about the folder, and Patsy was in there and clearly, like, couldn't resist snooping. I was hauled over the coals for it. Fired. There and then. And if I argued, caused a commotion, she'd have the police in to accuse me of *attacking* Alice."

"Flaming 'ell! It sounds like Alice was attacking *you*.

With visions, at least."

"She was, but that last one, that glimmer of something different, something good at last, it gave me such hope! And then…more frustration. *Weeks* more. So, I had to go, couldn't say goodbye to anyone, to Maja, to Millie, to any of the residents. I was literally chucked out on the street, with Holier-than-Thou Patsy standing in the doorway, blocking any attempt at reentry, her arms crossed over those inflated breasts of hers."

"You didn't fight your corner?"

"Oh, I did! I told her she was wrong, but…the police being involved…that's quite a deterrent. I thought I'd get my mum to speak to her and explain. What I didn't expect was that, whilst I was on my way home, Patsy called her instead, and, once again, all hell broke loose as soon as I got indoors."

Tony sighed. "You've endured a lot for this woman, haven't you?"

Lottie was quiet for a moment. "For Alice? I suppose."

"That's nice."

Lottie turned to him. "What? Really?"

He nodded emphatically. "Aye. No matter what your mam says, and that Patsy woman says too, I'm Team Bobby all the way."

Lottie laughed. Felt relieved to hear it because with her mum, even now, relationships were strained.

Jenny had screamed at her! 'I know what you were doing! You were trying to read this Alice woman, weren't you?' she'd said. 'In that bloody stupid way of yours. That's why you were clasping her hands. Using that ability I've told you to get rid of! You've let me down. You've embarrassed me. Patsy gave that job to you as a favour to me. I just don't get it. Why d'you want to know more about these people? What business is it of yours? It's wrong, Lottie. So wrong. You're like a…Peeping Tom. The worst kind!'

It hurt, what she'd said. And it hurt too to think Lottie might not see Alice again, or Millie and some of the other residents she'd grown fond of. But could she blame Patsy for what she'd done? Both actions – the way she'd raised her voice, shouted at Alice, and stole her file – could be easily misconstrued.

In the office, with Patsy ranting at her, slurring her words, actually, from time to time, she'd been called corrupt and a fraud. Someone who could clearly not be trusted. Lottie had tried to interrupt but was shouted down at all attempts; even so, she'd had the strangest feeling… Patsy hurled these accusations at her, but it was like the woman had been looking through a glass darkly, because all those things – corruption, fraud, and untrustworthiness – were things *she* was guilty of, not Lottie. When she'd come forward and started bustling Lottie out of the office, her hands on Lottie's shoulders as she did so, those suspicions became more stringent. She already knew Patsy cut corners in terms of food and drinks for the 'clientele', in terms of décor, bedding, and any comforts at all; staffing, even, was kept at the bare minimum. Yet Patsy drove a posh car, a Jaguar, and kept augmenting herself with her lips, her breasts, and her Botox, kept dining out, lavishly. *Bobby* had known Patsy was conning them, had called her out on it. But for how long?

"I could have said something," she told Tony, "there and then, like, thrown her accusations back in her face, but I didn't because, despite seeing the receipts I had, *petty cash* receipts, it'd still be my word against hers. And now I no longer work there, which means I'll be going today as a visitor, nothing more. Somehow, I have to find a way in because even though I don't see Alice anymore, I didn't give up on her. Even when I hit another wall."

"Another wall? How do you mean?"

"If she was on the HMS *Wish*, she'd be on the passenger list, wouldn't she? I tried to access it online but got nowhere fast, so I rang the Archives Centre in Liverpool and got them to check. My brother's at uni there, and he did me a favour, paid them a visit, got them to double- and triple-check, not just the HMS *Wish* but other boats that docked that year and if Alice Danes was on them, or anyone in the Danes family, but they weren't listed."

"So you got it wrong? Alice didn't come over on the *Wish*?"

"I *thought* I'd got it wrong, and it was so disheartening. I questioned myself, my ability, my mum's disappointment in me, even when I tried to explain to her too what had happened, the basic details, anyway, questioned again whether I was deluded continuing to think Bobby was proud of me, even in death. It was late October, and…well, to be honest, I went into another decline. With no access to Alice, always clutching at straws, I tried not to think about her, but dreams – and Bobby – had other ideas."

"Bobby appeared again?"

Lottie nodded. "Did I tell you this was weird?"

"Only about a hundred times."

"Sorry."

"Don't be! Life *is* weird. This world is, when you think about it, what we're all doing here and why. What our real purpose is. There's a lot of things I can't get on board with, hin, but if you have an ability and you're using it to help, well…I can get on board with that."

Lottie nodded again, still wondering if she was clutching at straws with what she'd found out; only when seeing Alice would she know.

"I started dreaming of Bobby again, and this time, she just kept nodding at me. Nothing more. Just that. I asked her for help, *prayed* for guidance, but that was all I got. Mum was back to threatening me again by this point, telling me I had to get another job. Not in a care home, in a shop or something. I couldn't go back to the care home anyway. My job had been filled by another of Mum's friends, a much older woman than me, Gillian. Mum's like a recruitment manager for Patsy, I swear it. I had to come out of my own dark room and make an effort. I managed fairly quickly, actually, to get a job, not in a shop but a bar, which is actually where I work now, not Silver Birches.

"I kept thinking about Alice, though, about HMS *Wish*, about the hanging man, about how broken her life was before England and how much worse it got after she arrived. I wanted to piece those bits of the puzzle together but kept going around in circles. She was in a hotel room. There are *thousands* of hotels in England, in the north, where they landed. Which one had been a mixture of horror and joy? And if I found out which one, how would that help? I kept asking Bobby, and Bobby just kept on nodding. I screamed at her, 'Stop nodding! Do something more concrete. Give me a sign.'

"I was so preoccupied with everything, I nearly got fired again for not pulling my weight, for constantly 'daydreaming', adding up the rounds incorrectly, stuff like that. I'm on a warning right now, but you know what, if I get fired, I get fired. Probably will anyway because of going up north to find out more about Alice. I had to throw a sickie, see, to do it, and they weren't happy. Christmas is the busiest time of the year, and I'm not there 'cause I've got Covid. That's what I told them. But, you see, all that screaming at Bobby worked. She's rooting for Alice on the other side; she really is. Oh, Tony, look at the clock on the dashboard! We're only an hour away now."

"So where've you been? And how did you know to go there?"

"That's the best part. The…weirdest part. I was going home on the bus, having finished a shift. I was angry at my boss for threatening to fire me, angry at Bobby for her incessant nodding, angry at my mum for siding with Patsy, and angry at Patsy too for not giving those people in her care the comforts they paid for. For not letting me be there either to treat them with a bit of kindness, especially at Christmas. That was when I saw it."

"Saw what?"

"A two-for-one offer."

"A what?"

"In a supermarket window, one of those two-for-one offers they run."

"I don't get it, pet. So what?"

"Exactly! That's what I thought. *Absentmindedly* thought. *So what?* But I'd been thinking about something else on that bus journey, the usual, the hotel room, wondering where the heck it could be. And that's when I saw two-for-one."

"I really don't get it," Tony confessed, shaking his head.

Lottie laughed. "Nor did I. Until I did. Two-for-one: two, four, one. Room two forty-one. Want to know the next thing I saw, directly after that?"

"Go on, pet. Hit me with it."

"A poster for a band."

"A band?"

"Yeah, one of those posters advertising a pub band playing in one of the locals. Their name was The Abingdons."

"The Abingdons?" he repeated. "So...room two forty-one. The Abingdon."

"That's right. And the final thing I saw just before I reached my stop was Bobby's face. Not in a dream but when I was wide awake, right in front of me, as vivid as in a dream, though, and she wasn't only nodding, she was laughing and clapping too!"

Chapter Twenty-Four

Three days before Christmas Eve. A hugely busy time for pubs, restaurants, shops, for all kinds of businesses, even care homes. How Alice was, Lottie had no idea. She asked her mum to ask her friend who worked there now, but Jenny glared at her.

"Mum, please!" she persisted. "Just find out if she's still alive. Can you do that much?"

"Alice Danes has nothing to do with you!"

"I wasn't hurting her! I was trying to help. I've told you this. Something bad happened to her a long time ago when she was young, my age, something really, really bad. And…I just wanted to help, to find out what and to tell her something."

"What?" Such mystification in that one word.

"That she wasn't mad like they said she was. That I don't believe it for a second. And that I'm sorry. For what happened to her. Because, you know what? Someone has to be."

"Bloody hell, Lottie, I'm worried about you, you know. I'm—"

She didn't get to finish what she was about to say, because Lottie's brother Jack walked into the room, home from uni for the festive holidays.

"Mum, why've you got such a downer on Lottie? She's

only asking a question, and if your friend works at the care home, then you can find out. Simple."

Jenny threw her hands in the air. "Fine. Okay. I'll ask Gillian, then let this be the end of it. The care home and its residents have nothing to do with you, Lottie Beck. They did once upon a time, but not anymore. Honestly, I rue the day I got you that job. I really do."

Alice Danes *was* alive. Lottie found out later that day, relief flooding through her at the news. But Millie – bright, happy Millie – had gone. It was a blow to hear it, but she could only wish her well on yet another voyage, hoping the crossing was much calmer this time.

"Alice isn't well, though," Jenny continued after a few moments, as if she'd been contemplating whether or not to share this news. "She no longer gets out of bed to sit in her chair." And then, perhaps a little more gently, "I think her days are numbered too."

Room 241, the Abingdon. Lottie ran with that information and Googled the heck out of it. It was the name of a hotel, a real live hotel near Sunderland, over one hundred and sixty miles from Liverpool, or rather it had been. The hotel was shut now. Derelict. The windows boarded up on Google Images, with signs saying *Keep Out* on posts in the grounds. A haunted hotel. It was that too, allegedly, although abandoned places tended to attract that kind of reputation. It was set on the headland overlooking the sea, in amongst much greenery and woodland. Haunted because of a suicide there. In room 241.

Lottie's heart quickened. Was it Alice's travel companion? *Another* suicide in the family? Enough to send anyone mad! Further research, however, disputed that. The suicide had taken place in the fifties, was a young man who'd shown signs of being troubled on arrival, then was found in there the day after check-in – *hanging*.

Coincidence. It had to be. Alice had been incarcerated by then. But the hanging part…could she have influenced it somehow? Was she not only mad but…evil?

Bobby's face again in her mind. Not nodding but perfectly still.

She mustn't get carried away, sidetracked. The hotel had a reputation as being haunted; people broke in there, hence why it was boarded up now.

Should she go there and try to break in too? Head straight to room 241? Or should she go back to Silver Birches to room twenty, try to see Alice, the *dying* Alice, take her hand and soothe her? Tell her she was sorry anyway, even if she didn't know exactly what for.

Bobby – no nodding, but not still either. She was shaking her head.

She'd go to the hotel, then. Uncover – somehow, someway – the full story. Because therein lay the only justice, the only peace for Alice. And she had to go straightaway.

If she caught a train that afternoon instead of reporting for work, she could be there and back again in two days, in time for Christmas Eve, when Alice would stir.

Quickly she packed a bag and left a note for her mum. During the train ride north, Jenny tried to ring her several times, demanded, in fact, she return, that she was in trouble again.

How furiously Lottie texted back, stabbing at her screen.

I'm nineteen, Mum! I'm nineteen, and I have an ability. I am using my ability not to hurt Alice but to help her, before it's too late. She needs help, but more than that, she deserves it. She's dying. You told me that yourself. Fading fast. Millie was her age, and she died too. There isn't long to go. All I've ever tried to do is help Alice. I wish you'd believe me, I wish you'd listen. I got fired for trying to help her. Patsy accused me of all sorts of things, but she's the one guilty of stuff, not me, and I've told you about that too. That she lives the high life at their expense. I know she's probably lonely, but it doesn't make it right. And she drinks, Mum, on the job. Whisky, the hard stuff. Again, I've told you. But again, you don't listen. Won't believe me. All you ever do is condemn me. And you know what? It feels horrible. I couldn't help Matt at the end. I was too frightened because...well, I'll tell you why, face-to-face. But I'm not frightened anymore. He was proud of me, Bobby was, and I'm proud of myself. I really hope one day you will be too.

Before she could change her mind, she pressed the send button, and it was gone, Lottie sitting back in her seat and expecting a full tirade back.

There was nothing. Not for the longest of whiles. And then came the reply. One word. That was all. And a kiss.

Okay. X

All she could do was stare at it. *Okay?* What did that mean? That her mother accepted what she'd just said or something else? That she was so angry by the written words her daughter had just hurled at her that she couldn't trust herself to say anything more?

She guessed she'd have to wait and see regarding that as well.

The Abingdon. An abandoned hotel in a supposedly scenic spot, but which felt totally isolated to Lottie, cut off. On reaching Sunderland, she caught a cab there at vast expense, asked the cab driver if he could wait too whilst she took a first look.

He was no Tony, the cab driver. He barely spoke a word to her as they drove, just kept glancing at her suspiciously in his rearview mirror. She wondered if it was the blue hair, lifting a hand to smooth it, or whether it was because of the address she'd asked for. Who in their right mind would want to go and see an abandoned hotel?

When it came into view, set high on a hilltop, lawns leading down from it to the clifftops and the ocean, once manicured, now overgrown, she gasped.

A splendid hotel! That's what it would have been, once. A hotel with history, that had opened, then closed, then opened its doors again on Christmas Eve, 1949.

After the cab driver pulled to a stop, he reached over to the passenger seat, on which a newspaper lay. There was a pertinent ruffle as he opened it, then proceeded to read. Her cue to leave, she realised, to exit the car and stand there, gawping.

It was miserable weather, the sky above her the colour of granite, and a mizzle in the air. In London it had been crisper and the sky bluer. Christmas in a few days and there was no excitement in the air, not here. Not anymore.

The hotel first opened its doors in 1867, a beautiful Victorian building, whitewashed and full of character, set on a stretch of coast just outside Sunderland, close to the village of Crooklow. As well as sweeping views of the ocean, there was undulating countryside and sumptuous rooms, two hundred and fifty of them, attracting the notable people of the day, those who wanted to immerse themselves in luxury.

The 'Jewel of the North' the Abingdon had been called, its service and attention to detail second to none. They did indeed come from far and wide, the rich, the industrialists, the elite, and the famous too. Movie stars had stayed there!

People Lottie had never heard of but who were adored in their day: Mabel Normand, Mary Pickford, and Douglas Fairbanks. There was also the Vivien Leigh Room, an actress Lottie *had* heard of, but only because her mum loved *Gone with the Wind*, had made her sit through it twice.

During World War I and World War II, the hotel had fallen on hard times; people had other things to occupy them. There was also mass unemployment in Britain, the Great Depression, which hit those in the north the hardest. It had fascinated Lottie reading about it, realising how much the people had suffered, their hopelessness and anger as poverty became more and more widespread. Such a dark, dark time and for so many. Returning to wartime, Sunderland was a key target of the German Luftwaffe, the bombs that were dropped claiming nearly three hundred lives and devastating local industry. Through it all, the hotel tried to carry on but was eventually commandeered in 1942 as a temporary hospital to treat wounded soldiers. After that, it fell into decline, no longer something glittering but as bruised, as weary, as disillusioned, even, as its last occupants.

Lottie drew closer, her feet crunching over gravel and then the softness of grass, sinking slightly because the mud was so slushy. A temporary hospital…she could imagine it all too well, the pain and shock of those being tended to, the screaming caused by trauma that would have rung through the corridors, able to compete with those in the asylums, the *death* as men succumbed, lost their final battle. Not just room 241, the building in its entirety was a place of glory and tragedy. The war had ended in 1945. And the country was desperate for glamour again, some…frivolity, and so a tarnished jewel was polished.

December 24, 1949 was the date set for the grand

reopening of one of the finest hotels in the country, an old lady, a *grand* old lady that had survived so much and would return stronger, better, with all modern luxuries. Once again, people would come in their droves, put Sunderland back on the map, tourism able to replace industries permanently in decline – the shipbuilding, the glassworks – offering event after event and vast opportunities for employment. No more depression, no more grief; the north was done with it, would embrace change and rise again, the phoenix from the ashes. The reopening of the Abingdon was only the start of such dreams.

Nothing could go wrong. Would be allowed to.

The reopening was a gift for all.

And joining the merry throng that set foot over the threshold that day was a young woman who'd sailed the oceans to get there, who'd experienced such turmoil, such upheaval, her own personal tragedy – the death of her father by suicide, she being the one who'd found him. She'd fled a country that hadn't yet declared peace, was still caught in the grip of conflict, had *had* to, she…and another. Lottie squinted her eyes, focused on the entrance to the hotel, now boarded up. They'd walked through the doors, and despite everything that had happened to them, experienced excitement. *She* had. Alice. She was happy to be there. The only happiness she'd known in so long.

And then…

Then the darkness came for her again. *Rushed* at her.

And this time, it didn't let go.

Chapter Twenty-Five

Under cover of the darkness…that was when Lottie returned to the Abingdon, not that same night but the next, spent all day preparing for it, summoning up the nerve.

That dark room, inky black, with corridors that led to and from, was room 241. A room that still existed, both physically *and* in Alice's mind.

The room she was still trapped in, that she haunted too.

If Lottie succeeded, if she entered it *physically*, what would she find? she wondered. What would come rushing at her? And, unlike Alice, would she be able to leave it?

The cab driver that first day had got bored waiting and beeped his horn at her. Instead of mizzle, it had turned to hard rain. She'd had to go; it wasn't as if she could break into the hotel in front of the cab driver. He'd have called the police, and she'd be in even more trouble. So she'd got back inside the taxi, and another wordless journey began, this time to a small hotel in the heart of Sunderland, a city preparing for Christmas, shop windows twinkling with lights and decorations, and trees glittering from the windows of houses.

"Thirty-eight pounds and fifty pence."

Those were the only words the cab driver spoke to her, demanding the sum of money with menace, clearly believing a blue-haired young girl like her might be on the make, might just open the door and run from his cab, refusing to pay at all.

She pulled her purse out from her bag and gave him two crisp twenty-pound notes.

"Keep the change," she said. "And Merry Christmas."

The hotel she was staying in was modest, more of a B and B, as far from the Abingdon as it was possible to get in terms of luxury but without the price tag either. As she stood on the pavement comparing the two, she noticed a Christmas tree in the window there as well, just a small one, a little shabby even from where she was standing, but at least it had a few twinkling lights on it, flashing green, yellow, and blue. A token gesture.

She shook the rain from her hair, then hurried inside to reception. The carpet beneath her feet, with a swirling red pattern on it, was worn, and on the walls either side of her, woodchip wallpaper was painted magnolia. It was called the Harper, after the road it resided in, Harper Road. Nothing to overstretch the imagination. There was a smell in the air, that of all things old-fashioned, furniture now as much a part of the building as the bricks and mortar. What her room would be like, Lottie had no idea; she just hoped the bed was more comfortable than a plank of wood, if only by a fraction. As soon as she saw who was behind the reception counter, however, she felt comforted, knew she'd chosen the right place. Even offered a small smile to the heavens. *Is this your doing? Did you guide me here?* She'd chosen it primarily on price, or thought she had. But there in front of her was an older woman, in her seventies or thereabouts, yet with that same feisty look in her eyes that Bobby'd had, another proprietor. She had the very same grin.

"There you are, pet! Wondered what kept you. Ready to

check in?" The woman bustled out from behind the counter, brandishing a key. "Hey now," she continued, "what brings you to Sunderland, this time of year?" Beckoning for Lottie to follow her towards a flight of steps, she wheezed a little as she climbed. "Is it family you're seeing?"

"No, not exactly. I've come to see…a friend."

"Oh, grand, that's grand. We're busy here. We've only twenty rooms, but they're filling up. They always do over Christmas. It's that time of year."

As the woman continued to chatter about why it was some people only visited family at Christmas, didn't bother otherwise, Lottie couldn't help but smile. Like Bobby, the proprietor of the Harper had her opinions and didn't mind sharing them. A force of nature too, refusing to give in to old age, to let it slow her down. And yet…what lay beneath the exterior? Heartaches? Regrets? Disappointments? Everyone had those, particularly those who'd survived year after year; they had a story to tell. Peg, however, as the woman introduced herself, and as Lottie would soon find out, also harboured the stories of others.

For now, though, after climbing yet another flight of stairs as steep as the last ones, making Lottie wish for an elevator even if Peg didn't, it was simply a matter of showing her to her room.

"There you go, room nineteen. Hope you're gonna like it. No fuss, no nonsense, but it's clean. And you've a small en suite."

Her own grin as she entered the room clearly delighted Peg.

"Ah, you *do* like it! There are those that complain, you know, first about the lack of an elevator, as if they haven't got legs to carry 'em, then they say the en suite's too small or it stinks of cigarettes and that the furniture's not from IKEA. The list goes on and on. I tell 'em, what they've got here is a bit of character. If they want a Premier Inn, somewhere with no soul, then clear off. I do, pet! I come right out and say it." She smirked. "Depending on what mood I'm in, of course, and how much my arthritis is playing me up." Then, perhaps just a little more shyly, a little more…beseechingly, "But you do like it? It'll do ya?"

Lottie looked around at the dated décor, smelt the stale scent of smoke, which did indeed cling to the atmosphere, much like the presence of Peg herself, and the presence of someone else: Bobby. She *had* guided her here. Because this was what her hotel used to be like, no frills, no fuss, but honest. Even if Bobby herself hadn't always been.

Oh, Bobby, she breathed, missing her so badly despite feeling her close.

"Pet?" Peg said, clearly waiting for an answer.

"It's perfect," Lottie told her, beaming. "In fact, you know what? Being here feels like all my Christmases have come at once!"

* * *

According to Google Maps, the Abingdon was just under two miles from the village of Crooklow, so that's where Lottie got another cab to the following day rather than the hotel itself, making like Patsy and preferring not to attract attention of any kind. It wasn't late; she left the hotel at around three, Peg on reception, calling out to her.

"Have a good day, pet. Going somewhere nice?"

"No…I mean, yes. To see a friend."

211

"A good friend, I take it?"

"Erm…yeah. You could say that."

Was Alice a friend? Could she be classified as that? She wasn't a friend like Matt was, like Bobby, like some others from school she'd since lost touch with, but Peg calling her that – a friend – and Lottie playing along, warmed her heart. Alice was a woman she'd tended to for the best part of the year, catatonic, mostly, the only words she'd ever uttered *wish* and *I am*. The first phrase Lottie now understood, the other heard only in dreams, admittedly, and still so intriguing. It reminded her of when she'd dyed Bobby's hair and she'd looked into the mirror at her reflection and said, 'I am. I am that woman. She is me.' How proud she'd looked, and how sad. She was someone different, but some of those differences she'd hidden. Had she been born in another time, though, she wouldn't have. *So forgive yourself, Bobby. That's what's important. That* you *do the forgiving.*

Alice *was* a friend. She was a friend because Lottie cared about her.

And that was all it took.

"Anyway, have a fun evening," Peg continued. "There'll be more checking in today. Most of 'em single men. Now there's a story if you've a mind to hear it?"

The Uber was six minutes away, but Lottie nodded as Peg elaborated anyway.

"Lonely people," she continued. "People on their own. And, sadly, it's normally the men. Family have flown, wives have divorced 'em or died, you know?"

"Yes," Lottie said; having worked at the care home, she did.

"A lot of regulars, actually. People that come back year after year, at Christmas especially. I do a dinner in the dining room on the day. Howay, it's not much, a bit of roast chicken, roast pots, a bit of veg too, but it's something. It's *company*, even if most of 'em don't speak to each other but sit there in silence. Company for me too, to be honest, since my other half's gone. Ten years ago, the big C. Aye, it's for my benefit too. No judgement why anyone's here alone for Christmas, no questions asked. Although Reggie White, who'll turn up in a minute, you'll see, he's a character. Furtive, I'd call it. Might come down for Christmas dinner, might not. What he does in there, in room eight, who knows? It's not my business. Not if he doesn't want it to be. But you know what I think?"

"What?" Lottie asked. It was only two minutes now to the Uber; Peg would have to be quick.

"He cries, that's what I think. Aye, I think that because when I wander past his room sometimes on my way to do some cleaning or something – I do have cleaners, by the way. I'm not Wonder Woman, but they're not always up to my standards, so I sometimes go behind 'em, have a little check. Anyway, I've heard it. Crying. But then…"

Lottie prompted her. "But then what?"

"This is a hotel; a lot of people have stayed here. I've been running it for forty years. Sorry, forty-*two* years, get it right, Peg. People always leave something of themselves behind. But what happens behind closed doors sometimes stays there, if you know what I mean. I've heard crying from that room when it's been empty, heard stuff from other empty rooms too. Voices and whispers. Now, I'm not saying this place is haunted, I don't want to scare you, but…stuff lingers. Aye, that's it, it lingers. And it's fine. It's really all right. Part and parcel of the business. I really hope I haven't scared you, hinny?"

"No! No, you're fine."

"All right, because despite it being considered by some to be a bit shabby round the edges, the Harper's a good place. A haven. And if there are ghosts, it's safe for 'em too."

Lottie smiled. "A care home."

"Sorry, pet? What was that?"

"You take care of people, people like Reggie. You let them be who they are, who they've *become*. Like you say, there's no judgement. Just care."

Peg not only smiled, she let out a bellowing laugh.

"A care home! Aye, I like it! It sounds…*kinder*. Mind you, wouldn't want to end up in one. I've heard stories about some. There's no care at all. Reckon you're better off at a place like mine. That's what's wrong with the world, don't you think? People don't have the time nowadays. But if you can stop the ride for a bit, slow it down, think of others and not just at Christmas either but all year round, then it'd all be so different." Again, another chuckle. "A care home indeed! Now go on, howay. That's your taxi. I just heard it beep."

Chapter Twenty-Six

It was nearly five by the time she arrived at the Abingdon, having walked from the village, and full dark already. A place in a rural location, wild and windswept, the kind you read about in books, that attracted ghost hunters. Would she find any there? Doing what she intended to do, breaking in and poking around, calling out, *baiting*?

Hopefully not. If there were any intending to make the journey to this outpost, they'd do so later in the evening, by which time she'd be gone. No way would she stay there longer than necessary, especially not with Peg's words ringing in her ears – that stuff lingered in establishments such as these from those who'd gone before, leaving something of themselves behind, their essence, just as they did at Silver Birches. Yet wasn't that exactly why she'd come? To find out more about Alice, more than she already knew?

So desolate, and the wind picking up speed. A coastline she was getting a feel for too, that might well be beautiful in summer but in winter was a different story. It was hard to imagine *anyone* beating a path there, no matter the promise of such luxury. But then…on Christmas Eve, 1949, it wouldn't have been a dark building in front of her; it would have been lit up and the gardens not overgrown but enticing. There might even have been snow, gently falling.

It'd have been a wonderful place to spend Christmas. Magical.

Even for Alice, at first, whose footsteps she was walking in.

Lights would have illuminated the pathway too, cars driving along it to drop guests off at the entrance, where they'd have been greeted by footmen in smart uniforms – the buttons on their coats twinkling – bowing before ushering them inside. Once in the lobby, they'd be handed ice-cold champagne as a quintet played a melody of songs in the background.

Imagine, Lottie! Just imagine.

It was hard, though. The only thing that lit the path in front of her was the Maglite she'd brought along for the trip. Supposed to have a powerful beam, she wasn't impressed so far.

Imagine the laughter, the excitement! Her *excitement. Alice's!*

Again, she couldn't. The only rhythm was the beating of her heart, growing louder and louder, *thumping* in her ears. Not with excitement, with fear.

A fear that threatened to swamp her.

She'd done nothing like this, gone somewhere so remote at night on her own, to a building that held such promise once but was now derelict. A ghost of itself. That's what the Abingdon was. An inconvenience. A burden. This grand old lady, who when young had been loved and adored but who'd now passed the point of usefulness. Despite signs telling you to keep out, that you'd face prosecution otherwise, there was no one to care for her, not anymore. Fear *and* sadness swamped Lottie, but she had to push past both. And continue. Or it'd be a long way she'd come for nothing.

Today was Christmas Eve *eve*. It shouldn't be so hard to imagine how glorious and bustling this place would have been on the day it threw its doors open to the world again. A *treat* to come here. Yes! That's exactly what it had been. For Alice, something…to make her smile again. To make *them*. She and the person she'd been with. *The one who'd disappeared. Whom Alice was searching for. Her mother?*

They'd lost so much. But at the Abingdon, there was something to gain. The promise of a future that might just get brighter. A gift indeed.

The entrance to the hotel was boarded up.

Having got so close, Lottie took a step back and looked upwards. The building, once pristine, would now be grime-ridden in places, huge chunks of render having cracked and fallen from it. Would room 241 be at the front? Overlooking the sea? Or was the sea just too pertinent a reminder of what they'd only recently endured, and so a room overlooking countryside had been requested, *English* countryside, some of the trees bereft of leaves, perhaps, but hinting at what was to come, somewhere as lush as they were used to. Winter wouldn't last forever; spring would arrive.

An expensive place to stay, but if it reminded you of better days on the horizon, then worth every penny.

She'd have to go around the side of the hotel, towards the back, to find a way in.

Again, she started walking, head down against the wind, which now and then howled in her ear, sometimes drowning out the sound of her heartbeat, sometimes not. She fancied she could hear the roar of the sea also, beating against the cliffs, angry at being abandoned too.

Round the side, the hotel was boarded up still, and Lottie

conflicted about that, frustrated, but also relieved. If she couldn't get in, then she could leave. Because she could feel nothing good, nothing magical here, and who knew what horrors lurked within.

Alice's history was not hers. She, Lottie Beck, should not be going to these lengths to be her. *I am…I am…I am NOT Alice Danes!*

The words exploded in her head. Strange words appearing like a flash of lightning, every bit as jagged, before fading. *I am NOT Alice Danes!*

Emphatic. Determined.

No way in. And nothing was clearer; she was more confused than ever. She thought she'd have more insight here, feel more connected, able to read a building like she could a person, but she was wrong. And now her mind was railing against her, warning her.

It was as she was about to turn, walk the distance back to Crooklow – which was in itself a strange place, featuring only a main street and a pub, the Black Dog, in which she'd wait as she called for another Uber – that she saw it: a way in.

Her heart no longer thumped. It plummeted.

There was no excuse now not to enter. Follow in the footsteps of the ghost hunters rather than Alice.

The way in was through a boarded-up window, but those boards had been ripped off, maybe even recently, and no one had come along since to hammer them back in place. A *huge* window, the glass having been knocked clean out, although she shined her torch round the rim to make sure no shards remained. That was the other thing, if she hurt herself out here… She'd checked her mobile earlier. It had worked well enough in Crooklow, and here there was still a signal, but it was weak. Checking again, she saw it was weaker still, one bar, not two. So if she hurt herself out here, here she would lie until someone found her, that group of ghost hunters, perhaps. *Christmas Eve* ghost hunters.

She climbed in. She'd be quick. Very quick. Hating the silence inside, even the wind not bothering to follow her in, preferring to whip its way round the outside of the Abingdon instead. *Nothing* dared venture in there except idiots like her on the hunt for something. *I am NOT Alice Danes.* Again, the words resounded, and she shook her head to clear them. She wasn't Alice, but she was trying to help her. *Go to room 241. Just go straight there.*

It was a dangerous thing she was doing on many levels. She could bump into the living; she could bump into the dead. The roof could collapse on her head and bury her alive. As her feet crunched over debris, the light from the torch was truly struggling now, virtually useless. Such a foreboding place, the only comfort was in trying to recall what it had been, see beyond modern times into a past era, but she couldn't do it, couldn't push past the darkness, a greater understanding of Alice dawning in that respect, at least, just how difficult it was.

She knew what Christmas was, the jollities that came with it. The excitement it stirred in the pit of your stomach no matter what. *That's* why Christmas was special, because it reminded you of the good times, of what it was like to believe in something, to have hope. And that's why it was also the saddest, why those like Reggie White booked a hotel room in a town he probably didn't even belong to, sat in it alone and cried, because remembrance was a double-edged sword.

She found the staircase, suitably wide and suitably

sweeping, and climbed, the boards creaking ominously beneath her feet, the oak bannister not warm to the touch as oak should be, but cold. Still no imaginings of Christmas, just despair. The *building* was in despair. It dripped with it. And if ghosts lingered, despair was theirs also.

Alice is alive!

Despite what she'd thought before, her ghost would not be here. But what of the person Alice had come with, her mother, perhaps, who'd disappeared? And what of the others, the suicide in room 241? What if he was here, swinging, as Alice's father had swung?

Two hundred and fifty rooms in the hotel, and so she'd have to climb higher, to the top floor. There were elevators, of course, but no longer in use, and damned if she was going to put that to the test, the doors opening but then clamping shut, closing forevermore on her.

Another creak of floorboards. But not beneath her feet this time. Elsewhere. Not just her heart thumping, she could feel sweat break out on her forehead, beads of it.

Who or what was in the Abingdon with her?

She broke into a run. Took the stairs two at a time, higher and higher. So dark upstairs! So cold! A merciless cold that could easily fell you. In a corridor at last, she ran down it to the end, drawn there because that was where room 241 would be. A long, long corridor, the torch useless, completely useless, so only darkness in front. Stretching on and on.

Where are you? Where are you?

Alice? She knew where Alice was. But what about her companion, her mother?

What have you done with her?

Who? What had *who* done with her? Had the doctors

taken her away too?

It was like running through molasses, progress slow and painful, although at other times she felt like she was flying along, her feet barely touching the ground. Just a corridor. That's all it was. And it would come to an end. She'd come screeching to a halt. Outside 241.

It was there. The *1* barely attached, hanging off at an angle.

It was there, when somehow she'd expected it…*not* to be. For it to have vanished, as Alice's mother had vanished. But it was there. Brazen. The door remaining firmly closed.

The scene of the crime.

What crime?

Should she open it? Go inside?

What would she find?

When you've seen, you can't unsee.

She'd feared being trapped in this building before, in the elevator. But in room 241, she was in more danger. There'd be horrors in there. Only that. Horror felt by Alice, by Alice's mother, and the young man who'd hanged himself, who, like Lottie, could sense extremes of despair, and it had fed on his own until, finally, it all got too big.

What he'd done, he'd done on Christmas Eve too.

But this was Christmas Eve eve.

Not the anniversary.

Was that enough to save her?

"I am not Alice Danes," she repeated as she reached out.

Chapter Twenty-Seven

Christmas Eve 2023

"What's that sound? Oh shit, Tony! What is it?"

"Aye, it sounds bad, right enough."

"Just a bit. Oh no! The car's shuddering!"

"It could be a flat."

A flat tyre? Is that what he meant? If so, Lottie was relieved. He'd have a spare in the boot, surely, and could replace it. Then they could be on their way. She glanced at her watch as he diverted the car from their lane into the hard shoulder, some drivers honking the horn at him for having the temerity to do so. It had been such slow going today; a journey of five hours by road had so far taken more than seven. The weather had hampered them at first, the north in the grip of a storm, but, as she'd kept on saying, it was better down south, closer to London. What wasn't, however, was the traffic. There, everyone and his wife seemed to be travelling, trying to reach loved ones. In some places it had been gridlocked. They'd just under forty miles to go, but now with the flat tyre adding to their woes, they could be hours more.

Nearly 6.00 p.m., and whether Alice had had her annual fit by now, shouting, '*Wish, Wish, Wish, Wish,*' Lottie didn't know. It could be she was too weak…would never speak again.

On the hard shoulder, Tony went to inspect the tyres. She watched him through the windows as he bent, then straightened, bent and straightened again. *Shadowy* glimpses because of the darkness, which made her shudder as the car had, remembering too how scared she'd been when she'd reached out towards room 241 and seen another shadow…

She opened the door and called out, "Tony? Tony, is it okay?"

"Stay…where…are." That's what she thought he said, but the sound of the traffic and a wind that wasn't perhaps roaring anymore, but certainly remained a little on the riled side, quickly ate his words. She began to exit, then jumped when Tony suddenly appeared.

"I said stay where you are," he said, having to raise his voice to make himself heard over an ear-deafening racket, the cars contributing to it. "Dangerous…here."

Lottie raised her voice too. "Is it the tyres?"

He nodded and held up his hand to indicate two of them.

"Two?" she gasped in disbelief. "Have you got two spares?"

A shake of the head. "No."

"Then we need to call someone! The AA or RAC!"

"I know. I will. But…" How despairing he looked. "Christmas Eve. Look at…traffic."

"They could take a while?"

"A *long* while."

"Shit!"

Just under forty miles, so no way to walk it or – ironically – call another cab. No way they'd come out here to the side of a busy motorway.

"Get…out…car."

"What?"

"I said…get out…car."

"Are you serious? You just said to stay where I am."

Tony bent down, leant further into the car so he could be heard better. "I know. But it's dangerous to stay in there too. If we get struck…" His eyes darted around the car's interior as he seemed to weigh the alternatives, then he shook his head. "No. I mean it. Get out of the car. We have to stand on the embankment, away from it."

She hesitated given the cold and wind, but only for a few seconds, considering her options and realising she had none. There was no real shelter out there, but it was the lesser of two evils; they'd be sitting ducks otherwise, too vulnerable. She abandoned the car. How could this be happening? What the hell had caused the flats? And to them? *Only* them? As she followed Tony up the embankment, shivering, she couldn't help but wonder what force was preventing them from reaching Silver Birches. Was it the darkness Alice was so entrenched in? Refusing to relinquish control? It had grown too used to her company.

Christmas Eve. But you'd never bloody know it. It was bleak; it was miserable, and as Tony pulled out his mobile phone and punched numbers in it, she felt like crying.

He connected to someone, was speaking to them, shaking his head at one point, and she was sure she heard him say something like "No, no, that can't be the case. We can't stay that long out here!" Again, there was a protest. "I've a young lady with me. She has to be somewhere." But so what? So did a lot of people.

Tony finished speaking to whoever he'd called and walked back towards her. She had to admit it: he didn't look hopeful.

"Bloody useless," he was muttering. "Unbelievable!"

"How long?" Lottie said, repeating herself when Tony inclined his head. "How long?"

"Too long!"

"Well, how long is that?"

No wonder he'd been reluctant to tell her. "Hours. Two or three. Maybe four."

It was like something shrivelled up inside her and died. Hope. No way they could stay out there for so many hours on an embankment by the motorway, for God's sake!

"Someone else…we have to ring someone else to come and get us."

She dug her own phone out of her pocket, shocked when she noticed she'd missed several recent calls, and all from her mother. There was a message too.

Where are you? What's happening? I'm at the home. I thought you'd be here by now.

Her mother was at Silver Birches? Why? Yes, Jenny was friends with both Patsy and Gillian, Lottie's replacement, but she normally didn't go visiting the home, had absolutely no reason to. Unless…

Frantically, Lottie returned her calls, Tony staring at her all the while, perplexed.

The first attempt failed; it kept ringing and ringing, wouldn't connect. Same thing happened the second time, and third, until finally she almost hurled the phone from her.

"It's not connecting," she told Tony.

He shrugged helplessly. "Wi-Fi black spot? Try mine."

He handed his phone over, and she took it. Rang her mother's mobile number, and this time got a voice message:

'Sorry, we can't connect your call at the moment. Please try again later.'

She almost screamed this time. "It's not working! Why?"

Tony took his phone back and examined it. "Don't know. At least…got through…AA."

Hopeless! Absolutely hopeless! Lottie felt like reverting to childhood, to stamping her feet on the ground and yelling out, 'It's not fair! It's just not fair.' She was on the verge of it when she had to remind herself life *wasn't* fair, that others had it worse. *Much* worse.

So what if they had to wait two or three or four hours? It was *only* that: hours. She'd still reach Alice today, but around nine or ten. Why the panic?

And yet the panic continued. Her mother was at Silver Birches, her mother who knew where she'd gone and why. And so she'd only be there for one reason, because ninety-two-year-old Alice *didn't* have days to go, maybe not even hours.

She dashed off a text to her mother:

Keep her alive! Broken down. Won't be long.

Whether or not it made sense, she didn't know, but she sent it and then cursed as *Try again* appeared in red beside it.

"Fucking hell! Fucking, fucking, fucking hell!"

What Tony's reaction was to her cursing, she didn't know, wasn't looking at him, was staring bitterly at the traffic instead, at all the people speeding merrily along, bumper to bumper but still moving. No doubt they'd glance at the two unfortunates on the embankment, thinking how glad they were it wasn't them, on this night of all nights – what rotten luck! They'd feel sorry for them, but once out of sight, they'd be out of mind too.

She turned to Tony. "Try again."

"The AA?"

She nodded. "Beg if you have to."

"I did!"

"Tony—"

"Love…can't make them…faster. No…wand."

"BUT IT'S CHRISTMAS!"

Thank God for a gust of wind that gobbled up the worst of that screech. For that's what it was. A full-on bellow. As petulant as she feared.

Tony just looked at her. Looked as if he agreed, actually, was as bewildered and as upset as she was, and he'd likely be feeling guilty too, as it was his car that had let them down, the not so trusty Ford, so easily bloody sabotaged.

Shit! There were tears in his eyes! And not just because of the wind either.

She reached out. "Tony? Tony, I'm sorry. I didn't mean––"

The images came as thick and fast as snow would. A gentle man. A simple man. A man who tried his best. Who'd found a woman, married, and then that woman had left him. He'd picked himself up, dusted himself down, and tried to carve a life for himself following his divorce, but the pain ran deep. His confidence shattered. This was a man who thought he was of no use to anyone. There were childhood images too. One of his parents drunk – his father? In the other, his mother, whose anger and resentment kept building. Despite this, there was obsession. Not with the child they'd produced but each other. Neglect. That too. Lashings of it. They were parents who neglected their child, neglected each other, and neglected themselves. Yet Tony had survived it, torn himself away, tried *not* to follow their

227

example, wanted a life, a happy one, the woman he married, and children. The simple things. No great plan. What everyone wanted in the end. And yet it had eluded him; it had all gone wrong.

Loneliness. She'd suspected him of that, and she was right. So many were lonely in this world, those who beat a path to Peg's at this time of year and other places like it. Discarded. The merriment of the season cruel, because it was a reminder they'd been discarded. No family. None who wanted him, more fool them. Because what Tony was, above all, was kind, a quality so undervalued. He'd seen someone in distress and put himself out to help them. He'd do that for anybody. The world needed more people like Tony! And it needed to stop treating them like trash too.

So guilty. He'd let her down. Let Alice down. Alice, whose story he'd become invested in. Proved himself a failure yet again.

Not just holding his arm, Lottie stepped closer and hugged him, hard. How surprised he was! Clearly. His own arms remained stiffly by his side.

No one had hugged him in a long, long time. In years.

Slowly, slowly, his arms came up and held her too. He *was* crying; she could hear him sniffing in her ear, trying to control himself, and so she didn't let go, held on longer.

No darkness in him, but hardly any light either. Like Millie, he should be *flooded* with it.

"Thank you, Tony," she said, hoping he could hear her well enough. "You're the kindest man I've ever known, the kind I'd be proud to call dad."

Finally, they stepped away from each other, there on the embankment. He *had* heard her, and it had hit home. He'd been a father, technically, but his wife had lost the baby, by what means Lottie couldn't tell. And she had a dad – a dad who didn't want to know her. But bonds weren't always forged in blood. Would she and Tony keep in touch? After Alice? She'd try to. And she suspected he would as well, their friendship continuing to grow. Another gift.

A Christmas gift.

Christmas.

Christmas Eve.

She had to get to Silver Birches. Tell Alice what she'd discovered. Couldn't wait hours.

She turned from Tony and squinted. Saw it in the distance, a van coming towards them. Red, like the one in the adverts, the Coca-Cola lorry, although nowhere near as big. It had lights strewn across the top of the windshield, though, twinkling away *festively*.

Tony yelled as she darted back down the embankment towards the traffic, but she carried on, ignoring him.

On the hard shoulder, she positioned herself. Jumped up and down, waving her arms.

"Stop! Stop! Stop!" she yelled, not at any other vehicle, just the red van hurtling towards them. Her mother had told her once, if you're out somewhere and you need help, don't just yell out randomly, look at someone, pinpoint them – *you* help me. They'd be far less likely to ignore you then, put their head down and walk off, pretend they didn't see. They'd help, and once someone had, others would too, follow their lead. She'd never had cause to put that theory to the test, thankfully, until now, applying the same principles. *Believing*. Because that was another thing Christmas was all about, believing. *Stop and help us, red van. You're the one that's going to do that.*

The driver spotted her. They made eye contact. A man,

an *older* man, with a shock of white hair and a white beard to match. On seeing him, Lottie smiled, she laughed, she waved some more. He indicated left, slowed, and pulled in just ahead of her, Lottie whipping back round to Tony, Tony staring wide-eyed, then racing down to meet her.

Tony could ring the AA back; they could fetch his car tomorrow, on a far calmer day.

They simply couldn't wait.

As they climbed into the driver's cab, the man laughed too, a real *ho ho ho* straight from the belly. The saviour of the night. Nicholas.

Chapter Twenty-Eight

"Hey! Hey, there! What do you think you're doing?"

That creak she'd heard, thinking it was other floorboards settling, *hoping* it was, wasn't. Someone else was in the building, not someone phantomlike, made of miasma, but as substantial as she was, flesh and blood.

A security guard. Those signs saying *Keep Out* had some substance behind them too, it seemed, the company that had erected them checking out the property, perhaps, from time to time, and it was just her rotten lock it had to be tonight. Or maybe…good luck.

Because she'd been terrified at the prospect of going inside 241, of what she'd find there, emotions so intense she'd also have to do something to expel them. *Hang herself.*

A thought as rotten as this building had become.

"I said what do you think you're doing? Did you not see the signs? You can't read or something? You're. Not. Supposed. To. Be. Here."

He came storming towards her, a young man, she realised, not much older than her, dressed in a black bomber jacket, black jeans, and boots. She should have been scared too at the sight of him, but he actually looked nervous, perhaps more so than she was, although he was desperately trying to conceal it.

"Sorry," she said, eager to appease him. "I'm so sorry. It's just…"

What could she say? How could she explain why she was there? A lone female. He was looking at her as if she were crazy. And she didn't blame him. It was a crazy thing to do. But then a crazy thing had happened just a few feet in front of her; she mustn't lose sight of that. And Alice had suffered because of it. "This room," she blurted out before he could reply. "What is it about this room? Is it haunted? By the man that hanged himself, or someone else too? A woman who'd…disappeared. Just vanished into thin air?"

He didn't tell her, steadfastly refused to, it seemed, his breathing becoming a bit more laboured. He escorted her off the premises, and then, realising how she'd got there, he offered to drive her back to Peg's, almost grabbing at the chance, the wind having picked up on the headland and the drizzle, which she imagined *plagued* the Abingdon, more like full-on rain.

He hardly spoke during the drive either. He was uncomfortable, she could tell, shifting in his seat, swallowing hard, knowing he had to return there tonight, to the Abingdon, because it was his job to patrol the grounds, check them. And he didn't like it. Not one little bit.

No, it wasn't him who told her; it was Peg. Later that night at the bar.

That's where Lottie learned the truth about Alice. At least some of it. Alice, who was not just an old lady, dying in a care home, but an urban legend.

* * *

Nicholas had become interested in Alice's story too.

"So what's the big hurry?" he'd asked once they'd

climbed into the van, Christmas jingles on the radio, which he turned down low. "Why'd you almost run into the traffic like that, like a loon? Someone dying or something?"

He'd meant it as a joke, but as Lottie looked at Tony and Tony gazed back at her, he'd sensed his comment was perhaps a bit close to the knuckle and apologised.

"It's fine," Lottie said, "but you've guessed right. We don't have a lot of time left."

"If I can help in any way—"

"You already are. You stopped," Lottie pointed out.

"So, who is it? A relative?"

Again, Lottie looked at Tony, who nodded at her. *Tell him.*

Delivering a potted version, Lottie intended to gloss over some of the more...*outlandish* details regarding how she'd found out about Alice, but Tony was having none of it.

"Don't do that," he said. "Don't be ashamed of what you can do. Own it."

Like Bobby had insisted, so was he. But what would Nicholas's reaction be?

Such a jolly man, Scottish – from Glasgow, he'd told them – on the road to London, delivering urgent medical supplies. "Some jobs cannae be put off because of a wee thing like Christmas." He looked so intrigued, as much as Tony had when she'd first started telling him about Alice, and so she *would* explain about her ability, how the connection came about, though she wasn't wholly comfortable, still a little embarrassed about it no matter how much recent people in her life had encouraged her. She guessed Jenny's opinion, her *disapproval*, still counted for a lot – her mother, whose presence at Silver Birches remained a mystery to her, but one she'd solve soon. At the point of describing Alice as an urban legend, there was now less than ten miles to go before they reached the care home.

"So, the security guy dropped me back at Peg's, and I went back in really, like, despondent, if I'm honest, intending to go straight to my room. But Peg was there and saw me passing. 'Hey,' she called. 'Come for a nightcap, why don't you?' I went into the bar, the only other person there a man sitting in the window, nursing a drink, just…staring at it. She poured me a vodka and Coke and asked me how my night was."

"Did she ken what you were up to?" asked Nicholas.

"She'd had no idea, thought I was visiting friends. But…I told her. Couldn't help myself. A version of it, anyway. That a friend of mine had stayed at the Abingdon, had had an incident there, and I just wanted to find out what the place was like. Frame it in my mind."

Once again, Lottie settled into the story, losing herself in what had happened.

"Ah," Peg had said, "the Abingdon. What kind of incident?"

"Well…she lost something."

Peg raised an eyebrow and crossed her hands over her ample bosom, which, unlike Patsy's, was entirely natural. "She did, did she? A recurring theme there, if you believe the rumours."

"The rumours?" Lottie sat up straighter on the barstool and leaned in closer to Peg. "What do you mean? What rumours? That it's haunted, you mean?"

Peg sighed heavily. "Aye, that it's haunted. Everyone knows about the Abo in these parts. A splendid hotel it was, once, and set for stardom again. Only it never did reach the dizzy heights of pre-war days. It originally opened in the late eighteen hundreds, shut down post-World War II, then opened again in 1949 to great acclaim."

Lottie nodded. She knew all this.

"Didn't prove as popular as before, though, no matter what luxuries were on offer. The war'd sobered everyone up a bit, as wars tend to do, and although people may have been desperate for something special, most of 'em didn't look to the north to find it. They stuck to London, to the south. The hotel struggled on, for quite a while it did that, but bad luck seemed to blight it. There was a suicide there."

"Yeah, yeah, that's right."

"It took place in the room at the heart of the rumours. Room two forty-one. It was said that those who checked in there never stayed long or asked to move to another room, just couldn't settle. In the late sixties, the hotel was used as a hostel, then it became a conference centre of some kind until, finally, in the early nineties, it closed its doors for good. Been left to rot ever since. Every now and then, you hear it's being transformed into something wild and woolly again, but nowt ever comes of it. S'pose once a place gets a bad reputation…"

Her voice drifted tantalisingly off, and she poured herself another drink – gin, offering Lottie more vodka and Coke, on the house, which Lottie accepted gratefully.

"This urban legend?" she prompted.

"It's probably just that, pet, a legend, a story with no meat on its bones, but if you want to know about it, I can tell you right enough."

"Please." There was a plea in her voice as she said it, the man in the window lifting his head and looking their way too, intrigued by something other than his own loneliness.

The bar in Peg's hotel was like a living room. Certainly,

it was furnished like one. As well as the faded red carpet with its swirling pattern that ran throughout the entire building, there was chintzy wallpaper and a selection of art on the walls, nothing fancy but pleasant enough, seascapes and landscapes, plus a fireplace, in which one of those fake electric fires blazed authentically enough. The atmosphere was cosy and now also expectant.

"The urban legend…aye, this is what happened," Peg began, eyeing both her and the man in the window. "A young lady arrived at the hotel with her ma. They'd travelled from somewhere a long way away – overseas, it was said – then arrived in Sunderland via train and finally motorcar for a stay at the Abingdon. They checked into their room, but soon after, the daughter returned downstairs and reported to reception that her ma was feeling unwell, so a doctor was called. After examining the woman, the doctor stepped out of the room, then came back with a prescription for the woman, telling the daughter she needed to go and fetch it, that he'd arrange a private taxi for her. There were delays on the journey, however, what with it being Christmas an' all, at the pharmacy too, and the daughter was gone far longer than she intended. When she arrived back, that's when the fun and games started."

Lottie took a big swig of her drink. "What fun and games?"

"She hurried straight to her room – room two forty-one – only to find the key she had no longer fit the lock. She tried again and again until, confused, she knocked on the door, banged on it. 'Ma! Ma! Doctor! You in there?' she shouted, until eventually the door was flung wide open, and a stranger stood before her. It was a man, his eyebrows way up on his head, no doubt. 'Where's Ma?' she said, checking the number on the door. Another person joined the man, his wife, wanting to know what all the fuss was about. The girl insisted two forty-one was her room, hers and her ma's, told them how she'd fallen ill and was in there. She rushed past them, wouldn't be swayed against it, but there was no sign of her. No sign of the baggage they'd brought with them either, the clothes they'd hung in the wardrobe. It was gone, all trace of it. Whatever was there belonged solely to the couple."

"So what did she do?" It was the man who asked, not Lottie, calling across.

"She went back down to reception, is what. Asked them what they'd done with her ma whilst she'd been gone, where they'd *moved* her to. 'Your mother?' they said, or something like it. 'No, no, no. You arrived at the hotel alone. Quite alone.' She held the medication up. 'What's this, then? These are for her! I was sent into Sunderland to get it; it was the doctor that sent me. Where is he? He's disappeared too. All our clothes, our belongings. Where's everything gone?' Again, they said she'd arrived alone and, peculiarly, without baggage and that before checking in, she'd had to go out again, *straight* out. 'No name on the medication,' they pointed out. 'They could be for anyone. For you, even?'"

Peg shook her head.

"Oh, the poor lass. Talk about confused, right? She carried on insisting. She must have yelled at them again and again, starting to make quite the fuss, rushing back to room two forty-one, and demanding entrance again, to the rooms beside it too, to *all* the rooms on that floor. 'Where's my ma? I did not arrive alone! I was with her! She was ill! She'd started to get sick, really sick. Room two forty-one was the room we were shown to. It's *our* room. Where is she?' She ran up and down the corridor, scared and bewildered when she'd been so excited about staying in such a fancy hotel. With all this going on, people were starting to stare, to whisper, and so a doctor was indeed called, likely several.

"The 'vanishing hotel room' is what this particular urban legend is called. There are variations of it all across the world, as there are with all legends, although of course with the Abo, it's more a case of the lady vanishes rather than the physical room. And then…then the girl vanishes too. Is never heard of again. And the whispers became rumours, *fearful* rumours. It could happen to you if you booked that room. Aye, you'd vanish an' all like a puff of smoke; you'd disappear into thin air. That boy who committed suicide in that room in the fifties breathed further life into it all. More rumours circulated, that he'd left a note saying he could hear it, the pleading and wailing of the mother asking where the daughter is, and the pleading and wailing of the daughter as she cried for her ma. Saw their faces, even, their mouths wide open and screaming, tearing at their hair, they were so frustrated, pulling it clean away from the roots, and, already troubled, he couldn't bear it.

"Aye, they're daft stories, really, stories that…come out of nowhere. Fanciful. Insensitive. The daughter's supposed to haunt the hotel, runs and up down the corridors, still yelling for her ma: 'Where are you? Where are you?' All she finds is a body swinging on the threshold of the room she says is hers, that of a stranger, her screams getting wilder. A reputation as a haunted hotel suits some, I suppose, thrill seekers of a macabre kind, but it didn't quite attract the type of clientele the hotel were looking for. Mud sticks. *That* story stuck, kept getting bigger until, finally, people stopped coming altogether. The rest, as they say, is history."

Lottie, who'd been listening intently, finally breathed. "Christmas Eve, 1949. That's when it happened, wasn't it? The mother went missing and then the daughter?"

Peg had frowned briefly, such a deep furrow between her eyes. "Aye, aye, that's right, pet, it's a Christmas Eve urban legend. If it is true, I wonder what became of the pair of them."

Regarding the mother, Lottie didn't know, but the daughter...

In the cab of the red van, all three sat quietly for a moment.

"What I still don't get," Tony said after a while, "is why?"

"How d'you mean?" Nicholas asked.

"Why would anyone want them to disappear like that? For what purpose? That's the trouble with urban legends. They sometimes make no sense."

Again, there was a brief silence until Nicholas cleared his throat.

"I'll tell you a possible reason, although you might find it hard to believe too."

"What?" both Tony and Lottie said eagerly.

"The plague."

Chapter Twenty-Nine

"Here we are! It's up that road. I think you can just about get your van along it."

He could, the big red van with the twinkling lights a sight to behold as it squeezed down the road to Silver Birches and parked just ahead of it.

What Nicholas had said about the plague, whilst adding to the outlandishness of the story, also fit. Made sense of it all. Like most kids, Lottie had been taught about the bubonic plague at school, something that had happened in medieval times, carried by fleas on rats and killing thousands upon thousands. It was a horrible death – fever, headache, chills, and tender, painful swellings as your lymph nodes were attacked, plus vomiting and diarrhoea, the whole shebang. What she didn't know, nor Tony, was that there'd been a suspected outbreak of bubonic plague as recently as nineteen hundred and in the heart of Glasgow, of all places, Nicholas's hometown, a kind of lockdown imposed as authorities acted quickly to not just stamp it out but conceal it, fearing mass hysteria. Far from solely medieval, Nicholas also told them the bubonic plague had broken out in California in the 1920s, and been detected too during that era in China, Madagascar, Australia, and India. Alice and her mother had come from afar – that was part of the legend, part of the *true* story too – India, on the HMS *Wish*, as

Lottie suspected. If so, if her mother had started showing any signs of a strange illness, something…exotic, they would have had to act fast at the hotel as well.

"The Abingdon sounds like a pretty swanky hotel," Nicholas surmised, "a bit up itself, you ken? And a lot was riding on the reopening of it. Nothing could be allowed to go wrong. Now, look, imagine…it was Christmas Eve, so many excited guests turning up, so much money had been spent, and there was much, much more to be made. And then word gets out a guest has taken ill? Seriously ill? Right there at the hotel. Guests that have come from abroad… Who wants something like that to bring the mood down, to blight it? Forcing again a dose of reality. The war had only just ended, a terrible time of hardship and tragedy for so many. An injection of something light and bright was needed, in the north especially. The people were desperate for it."

"So…collateral damage was what Alice and her mother were?" Tony mused.

"Aye. They were two people, *just* two people. If the mother was suspected of having contracted something terrible, an exotic disease that was infectious, then find a ruse to separate mother and daughter – send her across town, as you say, for medication. And in her absence, quickly and discreetly remove the mother, swab the room down quickly and yourselves, mind, then send members of staff in there to act like it's *their* room. Brief other staff members too, the authorities, everyone in on the act. Then remove the girl, a *mad* young girl, deluded, who's turned up out of nowhere and started shouting off about someone that didn't exist. Remove her via sedation if you have to, and hope to God she's not infectious. Hose her down, *disinfect* her. If she is, though, and they put her somewhere like an asylum, then those infected are collateral damage too, easily disposed of."

Easily disposed of. The trio mulled that over too.

"If mother and daughter had come from abroad, if they had no roots in this country, not yet, then papers could be easily destroyed. False names applied, even."

What Tony just said made Lottie start. *I am NOT Alice Danes.*

It *was* a false name, forced upon her, hence why she wasn't on the passenger list of the HMS *Wish* either. But whose name? Someone from that first asylum she'd been sent to? Whose room she'd been placed in, someone freshly deceased and therefore a name going begging, or simply a made-up name, just plucked out of nowhere?

"Wonder what happened to the mother," Tony continued with vaguely a whisper.

"Could be she was taken from the Abingdon to a hospital," Nicholas replied, "and there she died in isolation, completely alone. A travesty, I agree. I hope I'm wrong, but––"

"You're not," Lottie breathed. "It's fallen into place. Every bit of the jigsaw. And yet…people know about it. She's an urban legend. Everyone was briefed––"

"Aye, but someone leaked it too, the story. No names, admittedly, but they couldn't resist…a bit of drama, you ken? A bit of…gossip, spreading it like butter. One of the guests, maybe, who'd come out of their room into the corridor to see what was going on. I guess we'll never know, not everything. It was all such a long time ago."

"Not everything, no," Lottie agreed. "But enough. We know enough."

"So," Nicholas continued, "the big question is, what are

you going to do about it?"

"What I wanted to do," Lottie replied, "was let her know that someone knew her story, the full facts, what really happened. That it wouldn't die with her unheard. She was wrongly incarcerated, wasn't mad. Never that."

Nicholas shrugged. "It's something, I suppose. It might help."

"That's what I was *going* to do, but I've changed my mind."

"Oh?" Tony asked, clearly confused, for validation had been the plan all along.

They were outside the cab now on the pavement, and – quite suddenly, quite *startlingly* – snow started falling. Big, fat flakes, each one as unique as it was beautiful.

For a moment, Lottie forgot everything, reaching out a hand so the snow could collect in her palm. "A white Christmas," she whispered. "I've *never* seen a white Christmas."

Nicholas rubbed at his beard. "Strange. No snow forecast for London today."

Lottie knew that. It was only supposed to be in the north, not the south. The forecast for further down the country had simply been for grey skies and a bit of drizzle. But seeing was believing. Snow *was* falling. And finally, *finally*, it felt like Christmas. So very like Christmas. Outside a care home, in Watford, in full swing.

"What is it you're planning?" Dear, sweet Tony, he was still so anxious to know.

Lottie beamed at him, the courage of her convictions growing. "I'm not going to remind her of the past," she told him. "Why would I this close to the end? She's relived it enough, every day of her life since she was eighteen."

Vehemently, she shook her head. "No, that's no gift, making her do that. They took her history from her, cancel culture in action even before it became a 'thing'. She was wiped clean off the face of the earth. No one has a right to do that to another and for the sake of something like money. *Everyone* is valid. *Everyone*'s unique. There's no one that's disposable. And everyone should have a voice, be listened to." She had to take a breath before continuing. "I won't let her take darkness into death with her. Clinging to it, unable to let go. A ghost, full of wrath and sadness. Confused and bewildered still. She's been a ghost for a long, long time, a living, breathing one. I guess they do exist after all. So, in answer to your question, Tony, I'm going to do what so many people wish they could: *rewrite* history. Make it every bit as magical for her as her mother wanted it to be before she took ill, because she deserved it, they both did. Some magic."

"Rewrite it?" As well as Tony, Nicholas also looked bemused. "How?"

"Via what makes *me* unique, of course, my ability. It really is time to embrace it. Come on, don't just stand there. You won't want to miss this. I'm going to make it legendary."

* * *

Jenny must have spotted Lottie coming up the path to the care home from the windows of the dayroom, because she came flying out the doors towards her.

"Lottie! There you are! I've been trying to reach you for ages!" Spotting the two men flanking her, she came to a halt. "Who are they?"

"Mum? Mum, look at me. There's no time to tell you

right now, is there? You're here because of Alice, aren't you? What's happened to her? Is she…?" She closed her eyes as her heart thumped in her chest. "She's not dead, is she? I'm not too late?"

Jenny's eyes were on her daughter again. "She's not dead. You're not too late. She's still breathing, but only just. Oh, Lottie, it won't be long. Her time's nearly here."

Nearly. "Thank God! Oh, thank God! I've got to get in there."

"Lottie, wait. Alice isn't the only reason I'm here."

"Mum, it doesn't—"

"Yes, love, it does. The police are in there too because…because…you see, I *do* listen to you. To what you said about Patsy creaming money off the business, cutting corners all the time, *dangerous* corners. That's why I got my friend the job here after you. She's ex-police. I told her, and she kept an eye out, found a spare key to Patsy's office. She keeps it in a bag of flour, of all things, in the kitchen, an obvious place, according to Gillian, although I'd never have guessed, but then I'm not ex-police. Anyway, she got into Patsy's office on a night shift, went through the books, and they made for very interesting reading. The police are in there now, like I said, questioning her. So, I do listen. And I listened about Alice, told Gillian to contact me if she deteriorated, that I'd tell you, come and sit with her until you arrived. Look, the police are with Patsy in her office, and Gillian's trying to keep the residents calm, but I can sneak you in through the kitchen into Alice's room. Not sure about those two, though."

Lottie turned to look at her companions, saw how their faces fell.

"Mum, smuggle us all in, okay? Alice means something

to them too."

Such confusion on her face, but finally she nodded and beckoned for them to follow.

It wasn't just Lottie, Jenny, Tony, and Nicholas in the room with Alice; Lottie knew that as soon as she entered. This ability of hers…how strange it was…give it attention, and it noticed, became sharper. Once tonight was over, she would have to find ways to deal with it properly, in a more controlled manner, but only so it didn't drown her, so she could continue to use it as a force for good, because now, in another room with yet another number on it – so many numbers on all the rooms Alice had been in over the years – it was packed. All those who Lottie had sensed following her on the night shift were there too, curious as to what would unfold. Even Nicholas sensed something, shivering slightly. As for Tony, he simply kept his eyes on Alice, an urban legend made manifest.

Alice was not her real name. But it was the only name Lottie knew her by, and so she'd use it, crossing over to the window first, the smell of something in the air, something sweet, a diffuser that likely Jenny had brought in, cinnamon and spice. Lottie smiled. A nice touch, thoughtful, something to cover up the smell of death, for now able to dispel it.

"Alice," she said. "Alice, I'm going to open the curtains, okay? It's snowing outside! On Christmas Eve. Like it does in books and in stories and in poems, like we always imagine it will, like we always hope. It's going to be a white, white Christmas."

Alice's eyes remained closed, her breathing somewhat laboured, rattling slightly.

It was snowing heavily, beginning to accumulate on the

ledge. Snow made everything look beautiful, even the nondescript buildings opposite, even a road such as this.

"Oh, look!" Lottie breathed, her eyes widening. "A robin's come to visit! Two of them! Three! I wonder who they are, who's really here?" Matt? Bobby? Alice's mother, torn from her daughter, waiting to be reunited not at the Abingdon but far closer than that?

Finally, Lottie approached Alice, sat on the edge of her bed and took her hand. There was some shouting going on from down the corridor, Patsy no doubt railing against any accusations despite there being evidence in black and white, all those receipts. As she listened, love surged for her mother, who *always* listened despite what Lottie sometimes thought, who had her back and who'd come to understand, in time, that an ability such as hers wasn't something to be frightened of but was an asset, especially when working in a capacity such as this – caring for people. Because she *would* care; that was another promise she made herself. She loved this job and the people who had lived, *truly* lived, even when, like Alice, they hadn't lived at all. They still had a story to tell.

Lottie's hand enclosed Alice's. Life pulsed through her, no matter how faint. She was hanging on, anticipating, this warrior who refused to let go until someone did listen.

A girl from India, who'd left India, travelled to England on the HMS *Wish* to a strange and foreign country, the skies grey when she'd arrived so close to Christmas, the buildings grey too, so drab, the architecture entirely different to that which she'd been used to.

A girl who'd stayed in a hotel there for a few days, downcast, depressed, the memory of how she'd lost her father all too fresh in her mind. And her mother, her rock, had been desperate to cheer her. To offer some hope. When she'd found out about the Abingdon – by accident, quite by accident, having overheard some people talking, what a grand reopening it was set to be – she knew they must go there. It was the Christmas present they needed. She felt unwell, just a little, a slight chill and a cough, but nothing to worry about, nothing at all. They'd go there, and to hell with the cost, then afterwards find somewhere to settle, begin again, just the two of them. Forge another life.

But first…the Abingdon.

On the journey was trepidation but something else too, finally: *excitement.*

It was snowing. Of course it was! The snow not hindering their journey, though, only serving to enhance it. Such beautiful scenery! No longer grey and drab, the air choked with city smog; it was fresh and clean instead, snowflakes glistening as they fell, covering an abundance of hills that swelled and dipped. The man who drove them from the train station to the hotel was excited too about the reopening of the Abingdon, telling them how grand it was going to be, what a treat they were in for. The best time of their lives, surely?

That was a departure from reality, perhaps, but Alice and her mother had indeed taken a cab to the hotel. Alice, however, had been worried, so worried on that journey, her mother's pallor growing more ashen by the hour as beads of sweat had erupted on her forehead, as she'd slumped in her seat, one hand travelling to her chest to rub at the skin there, finding it increasingly hard to breathe. Those were the real memories creeping in, which not only Lottie pushed aside, but Alice too, willingly.

"You arrived at the hotel, Alice, you and your mother,

and it was exactly as the driver had described. A sight to behold! A *beautiful* building, as white as snow itself, the Jewel of the North, sitting proud on the headland, overlooking a tumbling blue sea, somewhere movie stars would stay, royalty, the elite.

"An array of footmen were waiting to greet you. They came and took your hand, took your mother's hand too, helped you from the cab, treated you like royalty yourselves. Once inside, there was champagne, there was music, there were so many people, and all were like you, happy and smiling, raising their drinks in celebration. Behind them was a Christmas tree, adorned with baubles and tinsel. It *towered* over you, an angel at the top whose porcelain face wore such a serene expression."

There was no response from Alice, not yet, but Lottie continued regardless, those at her back, living or otherwise, crowding closer.

"You were shown to your room, and it was sumptuous! Furnishings brand-new and of the highest quality, and a carpet you could sink your toes into. Room two forty-one, on the very top floor, and from it you could see the countryside that surrounded you, a huge expanse of it and creatures too, running wild. Deer? There were! A host of them! One of them stopping as you stared, turning its head to stare right back at you, your gaze holding.

"There'd be dinner that night – only the finest foods served. You were both to dress for it. How beautiful your mother looked! Her hair piled high, a ruby at her throat and, best of all, a smile on her face. *Always* a smile, despite everything. She was an angel too. Wanting only what was best for you, what would make you happy." Only briefly did Lottie look back at her own mother and smile too, saw she had tears in her eyes that she was struggling to conceal. She turned again to Alice. "You looked beautiful as well, so young, so…perfect, your dress red, of course, the colour of the season. As soon as you entered the dining room, you caught his eye, a young man, only a little older than you and handsome. You were seated, the food served on platters, and more champagne poured, a crystal flute brought to your lips as you sipped, a rush of bubbles that made you laugh.

"After dinner, the handsome young man asked you to dance, and you accepted, relished the warmth of his arms as they gently encircled you. Outside, the snow continued to fall. It was a winter wonderland, the night so bright with snow and moonlight! And inside, in the ballroom, your mother was gazing at the two of you, knowing that what she'd done, taken you to the Abingdon for Christmas, was the right thing and that, afterwards, life *would* work, it would be good again. Hope is such a wonderful thing. We must never lose sight of it. Another dance and another, a whisper in your ear as you laid your head against his shoulder: 'Let's dance through our lives together.' Oh, Alice, it couldn't have been a better evening! And no matter the clock would soon strike midnight; Christmas Eve was just the start of it all. That was the way it should have been. The way it is now. Alice? Alice?"

A beautiful story, but was it having an impact? Chasing away the nightmares? Miracles happened. Not often enough, but they did. Matt had deserved one but never got it. Although…Matt was okay now. Death wasn't the end, was a kind of beginning too.

"Alice, it's Christmas Eve, and it doesn't matter what the year is. It's all just beginning, okay? Oh, Alice." She mustn't let tears choke her, must speak clearly and firmly. "You'd lost so much, and then you lost more. Now take it back. Right now, in this moment, be the warrior you are, the *legend* that you are, and take it back. Live the dream. Only that."

A rattle in Alice's throat was harsh this time, and another hand settled on Lottie, her mother's.

"Darling, the duty nurse will be here soon. She'll take over. You've done your best. You've done a *wonderful* thing. I'm proud of you. But it's time to let go. You tried."

Jenny was right. She had, so hard. And like she'd failed Matt, she'd failed Alice.

Magic didn't exist. Not even at Christmas. There was nothing to believe in.

"Love," her mother cajoled.

Tony came closer too. "Well done, pet. Well done. You're a good girl." Jenny was clearly impressed when he said that, was *touched* by it, smiling up at him, almost seeing him anew.

No way to stop the tears, they were blinding her. Such a dark room, the only light from the lamp by Alice's bedside. She'd lived in darkness, and now she would die in it too. And maybe, maybe it *wouldn't* be all right. Maybe Matt wasn't either. It was all just imagination. Wishful thinking. Lies. Her own dark room calling out to her again, begging for her return. Not wanting to let her go either. The penknife she hid under the bed, glinting.

Jenny had her arms around Lottie and was gently turning her.

"That's it," she said, her voice so low, so soothing, "that's it. Come on."

What was the point in resisting? There was nothing more to do except say goodbye.

"Sleep well, Alice. Sleep well." It was a whisper, barely even that, as she turned further. "I wish...I wish I could have... Bye, Alice."

And it was barely a whisper she caught, that stopped her in her tracks.

"Elsa."

Elsa?

Shaking off her mother, Lottie returned to Alice, almost stumbling in her haste.

"What? What did you say?"

"Not...Alice."

"You're Elsa?"

"I...am."

Lottie smiled, just as the door opened and another entered the room. The duty nurse, or Nurse Ratched, as Bobby'd insisted on calling her, with her poker face. She was clearly surprised at what she encountered, a room full of people with a dying 'client', but whatever she said about it was lost on Lottie as Tony or Nicholas, or both, coaxed the nurse back out of the room, Jenny assisting them, to leave them alone, quite alone, Lottie and Elsa.

Not alone... Those at her back remained there, past residents, and there were now those either side of Elsa's bed. A woman she didn't recognise, just the shadow of her, the merest outline, but the love that poured from her was as vast as an ocean. And on the other side was someone she *did* recognise, Bobby, a young Bobby, her hand clutching someone, again just the merest shadow, but oh, they were happy. Happy *and* proud.

Lottie returned her gaze to the woman in the bed. "Your name is Elsa." She remembered seeing an Elsa on the passenger list for the HMS *Wish*. Her finger had hovered briefly over the name, she'd thought for no other reason than she hadn't heard it before and thought it pretty. "Elsa, happy Christmas. *Please* have the best Christmas."

A hand reached out to her this time, and Lottie quickly took it. Was there darkness in the woman still? Did it cling? How could it when such love existed?

There was another by Elsa's bedside, right beside Lottie, a presence felt and a faint voice in her ear. *His* voice. Matt's. *I'm all right. I really am all right. She will be too.*

A sob caught in her throat to hear it.

It was the happiest of Christmases, magical, a smile on Elsa's face as her eyes briefly fluttered open, looked to the left and to the right of her, then at Lottie. The first smile on her face in years, perhaps. Many, many years. Since she was eighteen.

Her eyes were closing, for the final time, but not before Lottie saw in them not just the soul, perfectly intact, no man able to destroy it no matter what he did, but an answer to what she'd said:

It's the best Christmas. More *than I could have wished for.*

A note from the author

As much as I love writing, building a relationship with readers is even more exciting! I occasionally send newsletters with details on new releases, special offers and other bits of news relating to the Psychic Surveys series as well as all my other books. If you'd like to subscribe, sign up here!

www.shanistruthers.com

Printed in the USA
CPSIA information can be obtained
at www.ICGtesting.com
LVHW022318261123
764989LV00035B/985

9 781739 246952